buried

(a twisted cedar mystery)

by

C. J. Carmichael

other twisted cedar mysteries

The root of the modern day library goes back to the United Kingdom and 1847 when Parliament appointed a committee, led by William Ewart, to consider the necessity of establishing, throughout the nation, free libraries, assessable by all.

- per Michael H. Harris in *The History of Libraries in the Western World*

* * *

During the post-Civil War years in the United States, the establishment of public libraries was spearheaded chiefly by women's clubs. They contributed their own collections of books, conducted lengthy fund raising campaigns for buildings, and lobbied within their communities for financial support for libraries.

- per Paula D. Watson, in *Library Quarterly*

* * *

A truly great library contains something in it to offend everyone.

- Jo Godwin

* * *

Libraries...
are the collective memory of the human race.

- Donald C. Davis, Jr.

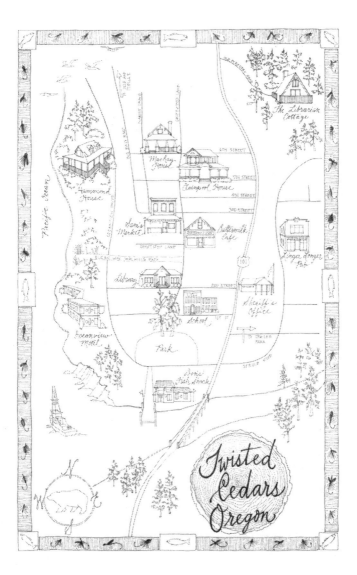

The Librarian Cottage

Hammond House

Pacific Ocean

Mackay House

Quinpool House

6TH STREET
5TH STREET
4TH STREET
3RD STREET

Sam's Market

Buttermilk Cafe

Zinger Zonger Pub

101

Library

Sheriff's Office

Oceanview Mall

School

TRAILER PARK

Park

SPRUCE ROAD

Doris Fish Shack

Twisted Cedars Oregon

N
W   E
S

chapter one

May, 2010

*b**ack in the seventies four women were killed. Librarians....* The odd message arrived in Dougal Lachlan's Inbox on the last Friday in May, channeled through his website into a special folder he used for fan mail. He was slouched into the sofa in his East Village apartment, going through line-edits on his latest true crime manuscript. His cat Borden, having been denied her favorite perch—the one on his lap—was curled up on the cushion beside him.

Normally Dougal pursued his writing with single-minded devotion. But since his mother's death last year, he was often, and easily, diverted.

You don't know me. But you should. I've got a story that will be the best of your career. Back in the seventies four women were killed. Librarians. No one ever solved the cases. But I know what happened. Ever hear of Elva Mae Ayer? She was the first. Check it out then let me know if you want the names of the others. I am here and willing to help.

The message was from a Hotmail account with the name "Librarianmomma."

At thirty-four Dougal had been researching murders and serial killers—and writing about them—for about eighteen years. During that time, his website had attracted a fair amount of crackpot emails. Some messages threatening, others claiming insider information about grisly crimes that were beyond the power of his own vivid imagination. In the beginning of his career, he passed these emails to his local NYPD precinct. Over the years, though, he stopped bothering. At conferences, when he spoke with other authors of mystery, thriller, and true crime—they had similar stories to tell.

Getting letters from wing nuts came with the territory. You just ignored them and carried on doing your job.

Which is what Dougal intended to do this time. He switched screens back to his line-edits, working his way through a cup of instant coffee and twenty more pages. Normally he loved this stage of a project—the penultimate fussing with details and tweaking of words before his manuscript went in for printing.

But this last book hadn't flowed like the others. He hadn't felt his usual passion. The research was tedious, the writing laborious. Maybe Belinda had been right after all. He should have set the project aside for a while. Taken some time to grieve.

He'd broken off with Belinda instead. And kept writing. He didn't think the story had suffered as a result...at least his editor seemed pleased with the final result. He wasn't so sure himself.

The typed lines on the page began to blur and Dougal let his hands drop from the keyboard. Borden blinked, stretched, and then pounced to the hardwood floor, in search of her premium cat food, a special brand formulated for senior cats, which she sometimes deigned to eat.

Dougal needed a break, too. He switched back to email, but there were no new messages.

So he read the one from Librarianmomma again.

It was different from his usual crackpot email. Most of them expounded on the grisly details of the crime, to a nauseating degree. This one was almost clinically detached when referring to the crimes. Also notable was the element of enticement, as evidenced by the invitation to write back, the promise of more details, and the story of his career.

Also, most of his prank mail involved unsolved crimes that had received a lot of press coverage, usually infamous or very recent killings. Whereas Librarianmomma was referring to an obscure murder—or series of murders—that occurred decades ago.

Check it out, the email had said. Maybe he would.

Dougal typed "Elva Mae Ayer" into a search engine. There were no exact name matches.

He should let it drop, but his instinct for story kicked in. He grabbed his phone from the table where it sat next to a pile of his unopened mail. Danny Delucy, a former cop who'd been derailed by disability into opening his own private investigation agency, sounded surprised to hear from him. "I didn't know you were working on a new story."

"Me either. I'm supposed to be finishing up the latest one. But something just distracted me." He relayed the essence of the email and the name of the librarian who'd supposedly been murdered.

Two hours later Danny called back. "Wow—that took some digging." The sound of papers shuffling carried over the line, and then Danny spoke again. "I did find a homicide case from 1972. Victim was Elva Mae Ayer—a forty-year-old librarian. Strangled in the basement of the library where she worked."

So the woman was real. And she *had* been murdered.

Dougal's eyes burned from too little sleep and too much staring at pages on a computer screen. He shut them. What would a librarian in the early 1970's have been like? He knew the era best from old TV re-runs like The Brady Bunch and, his Mom's favorite, the Mary Tyler Moore Show, where the women were portrayed as perky, pretty and morally upstanding.

Whatever the decade, however, a librarian seemed an unlikely target for murder. Dougal pictured a Mary Tyler Moore lookalike in the basement of a library, surrounded by stacks of books, file cabinets, archives. This would be before the computer and internet revolutionized libraries. There would still be cards at the back of every book. Card catalogues and basements filled with aging newsprint.

The librarian would likely be in a knee-length skirt and sweater. She'd be wearing glasses, of course, and as she worked at filing books from a cart he visualized a man with murderous intent sneaking up behind her...

He shook his head. Overactive imagination. Curse of the trade. "Did they find the guy who did it?"

"Nope. This is one cold case. How did you hear about it?"

"Anonymous email."

"After all these years? Bizarre."

"Agreed." And it was the extreme weirdness of the message—and the fact that it was grounded in truth—that piqued his curiosity. That and the fact that he was bored of his edits and had no new project waiting in the wings. Not even a germ of an idea. Ten years ago he'd had a notebook crammed with possible book concepts. Last year, after the funeral he hadn't attended, he'd tossed the notebook.

"Anything else you can tell me?"

"Guess what she was strangled with? A woman's red silk scarf. That's weird, huh?"

A memory assailed Dougal, long-forgotten, but vivid. His mother giving him a kiss before she went out for an evening of dancing, the edges of her soft scarf tickling his cheek. This one multi-colored, not red. Dougal had been four at the time. Thirty years ago...

Dougal coughed to get rid of the sudden lump growing in his throat. He'd been having a lot of flashbacks to his childhood in the past year. Stuff he hadn't thought of in decades. He wished the memories would cease and desist. Hadn't he moved here eighteen years ago to get rid of that baggage?

"So where did this happen?"

Danny paused, presumably to check his notes. "Roseburg, Oregon."

Adrenaline pumped through Dougal's body. His skin literally tingled. "You sure?"

"You heard of the place?"

"I grew up near there." In a small town by the ocean called Twisted Cedars. He and his sister had lived with their mother in a trailer park on the east side of town. He'd hated that town, that trailer, their life. Right after he graduated high school, he'd left, and he hadn't been back since.

Had the email come from someone who knew him? Roseburg was only a few hours from Twisted Cedars.

He thanked Danny, then disconnected. For a while he just sat, letting the information soak in and settle. When his stomach gurgled, he noticed he was sitting in the near-dark. No wonder he was hungry. He'd been sitting here working since he'd dragged himself out of bed this morning.

God how his muscles ached—neck, shoulders, back. He rubbed a hand over his face and realized it had been more than just a day or two since he'd shaved.

He ought to shower and clean himself up. Go out and get a meal. Rub elbows with other members of the human race. But he didn't have the energy for any of it.

Was this depression? Was Belinda right, again? Was that what was the matter with him?

Dougal's empty stomach growled again. His sated cat, perched on the window ledge, looked at him haughtily, as if to say, *Why don't you just eat, already?*

But there were no cans of people food to open in his kitchen. Not unless he lowered his standards to Borden's mushy chicken and liver food. His fridge was bare, too. Remembering a brochure for Thai food, he went to the pile on the table and sorted through the mess of unopened envelopes and fliers.

The fancy envelope, which had been delivered two weeks ago, caught his eye. The paper was thick, expensive, the kind used for invitations to life-changing events. The return address was familiar—it had been his for the first eighteen years of his life. He'd wondered if his sister Jamie had sold the old doublewide after their mother died. Apparently not.

He stood in the hallway holding the wedding invitation for a long time. His sister had loved fairy tales when she was little. *Happily ever after* had been her favorite ending. Despite the hard facts of their existence—deserted by their father, dirt poor, living in a trailer—she'd believed in it. Jamie, like their mother, saw the best in everyone. Until recently, that had included him. He expected his sister's adoration had dimmed somewhat in the past year. After all, what kind of ungrateful son doesn't come home when his mother is diagnosed with cancer and then doesn't even show for her funeral?

Belinda had actually booked them plane tickets. Her last action as his girlfriend. He'd asked her to move out after that, and frankly, her departure had been a relief. With her gone he could finally wallow in his misery, without the additional burden of feeling guilty about it.

The envelope felt heavy in his hand. He should either throw it out, or open the damn thing. He opened it and pulled out a "Save the Date" card with a collage of photographs, several of a romantic couple, another with the same couple but including two kids, a boy and a girl.

Dougal's face burned with anger and shock as he stared at the man posing beside his beautiful, sweet sister. No. Not Kyle.

He checked the printed name inside the card, and there it was, confirmed in black and white, *Kyle Quinpool and Jamie Lachlan would be so happy if...*

Back in high school, Dougal played football with Kyle. In Dougal's mind Kyle was the Great Gatsby of Twisted Cedars. He had it all—wealthy family, golden-haired good-looks, and a great talent as a quarterback as well. After graduation Kyle married the prettiest girl in town, went to work with his dad, fathered twins. But his storybook life took a twist at that point.

Dougal had heard most of the details from his mother. Apparently Kyle's wife, Daisy—also a friend of theirs from high school—changed after the twins were born, suffered some sort of breakdown. A few years later, she and Kyle divorced, and shortly after that Daisy left town. Just like that, abandoning her children as well as her parents and a younger sister.

"Poor thing was so disturbed," Dougal's mother had

said.

But Dougal had wondered if she was just that anxious to get away from Kyle.

Once Kyle had been someone Dougal envied and admired. But now, with the distance of miles and years, Kyle was someone he despised. He was not someone Dougal wanted anywhere near his sister. Let alone married to her.

* * *

After a night filled with dreams and numerous trips to the john—had it been the Thai food he'd ordered in? Or the beers?—Dougal awakened knowing what he had to do.

As a writer, Dougal believed in the power of three. First had been his mother's death. Second had been that curious email. And now, third and finally, was Jamie's impending wedding.

He'd once sworn he would never do it. But he had to return to Twisted Cedars. He had to try and talk his sister out of making this mistake or he'd never forgive himself. And while he was there, he might as well hit Roseburg and check into that homicide. Flying would be the quickest option, but getting around in Oregon wasn't like here in the city. There was no metro. No taxi waiting around every corner, either. He could rent a car, or he could buy one here and make a road trip out of it. That would take longer, but the idea of driving across the country was appealing for some reason.

The biggest problem was Borden. He doubted his eighteen-year-old cat would enjoy a cross-country road trip. In the past, his editor had taken care of Borden when he was traveling. But those were mostly book tours. This was personal.

There was that crippled, old guy next door. Monty something-or-other. He'd moved in about a year ago and been reasonably friendly when they passed in the hall or by the mailbox. Once Borden had snuck out Dougal's door when the old guy was in the hall, and he'd mentioned that he'd like to get a pet himself, if he was younger and healthier.

It was worth a shot, Dougal figured. So he headed down the hall to 5C. He knocked, then listened to the sound of the man's cane hitting the wooden floors as his neighbor made his way to the door. With his long gray hair and scruffy beard he looked like a guy you'd cross a street to avoid.

Dougal held out his hand. "Don't believe we've formally met. I'm Dougal Lachlan."

"Monty Monroe."

Dougal looked beyond him into the living room of the apartment. Monty's place was pretty tidy for an older man living on his own. "I have a big favor to ask." He explained about needing someone to feed his cat and change the litter.

"I'd be glad to. Maybe she could stay here with me while you're gone?"

Dougal smiled. "That would be great. Thanks. Tomorrow morning okay?"

"Sure. Where are you going?"

"Road trip."

Monty looked like he wanted to ask more questions, but Dougal cut him off, promising to drop by early the next morning with Borden and her supplies.

The rest of the day was spent making arrangements and by six o'clock Dougal had purchased a Ford Escape, packed his bags, and let his editor know about his plans.

Early the next morning he took Borden over to 5C.

Monty opened the door quicker this time, as if he'd been waiting by the door.

Dougal handed him the supplies, then wrote down his number, and the vet's. When he unzipped the cat carrier, Borden refused to come out.

"Strange place," Monty said. "Doesn't smell like home. But curiosity will win out eventually."

"If not that, then the need to pee. Where would you like me to set up her litter box?"

"Maybe here?" Monty pointed out a corner in the

hallway. He stood nearby as Dougal filled the plastic box with fresh litter. "You goin' on another of those book tours?"

"Not this time. Driving cross-country to Oregon. Maybe do some research for my next book."

"That's a long drive. Got family out there?"

"I grew up on the coast." Dougal pulled out his wallet and peeled off a couple hundred. "This should see her in food and kitty litter until I get back. With some extra to thank you for your trouble."

"Good-bye, Borden," he called as he retreated to the hall. But Borden wouldn't even look at him. Formal farewells weren't her thing.

"Safe travels," Monty said. "And don't worry. I have everything covered."

* * *

Within the hour, Dougal was on the Interstate, listening to John Hiatt tell him to drive south.

But Dougal was heading west.

The days were long in late May and Dougal took advantage of the extra sunlight hours, pushing through to the edge of Chicago before stopping for the night at a motel just off the highway.

First he had a shower, then feeling bone tired, he turned on the news, which was focused on a recent oil spillage. He watched for fifteen minutes until, thoroughly depressed, he turned off the TV and fell asleep.

The next day he was back on the I-80, listening to a Bob Marley CD Belinda had given him. She said he needed to "chill" and "get happy." She had a point. Hadn't his mother said virtually the same thing? He'd overheard her telling her friend and housecleaning partner, Stella Ward, that he was too serious. Too much like his—

She'd seen him listening. Hadn't said the last word. But he'd filled in the blank. He was like his *father*.

Why couldn't he have taken after his mother and his sister, both of whom had sunny dispositions and kind hearts? Even when his mother was diagnosed with cancer, five years ago, their innate optimism hadn't been quenched.

"You can beat this," Jamie had said, and Mom promised she would. Not that Dougal had been around to witness his mother's slow and painful decline. He'd been too busy churning out his latest bestseller in the Big Apple.

Enough of the reggae beat, thank you. He switched the CD for one of Herbie Hancock's. Another gift from Belinda. "Did you ever consider that the reason you like interviewing other people and writing their stories is so you don't have to deal with your own issues?"

Oh, she was full of insights, Belinda.

On another occasion she'd asked him why he never talked about his family. Poor woman. She'd really believed she could find a kind, sensitive soul beneath his gruff exterior, if she could just get him to open up.

"Not much to tell," he'd answered. But the truth was…there was *too much* to tell.

His mom, Katie, had been a good woman. Kind. He didn't blame anything about his childhood on her. In fact, she'd deserved a better son than him. As an adolescent he'd been embarrassed by her, by the fact that she cleaned houses for a living, and worse, that she had a weakness for spending her Saturday nights at the local bar, dancing and chatting with men who always said they would call but never did.

And then there was dear old Pop. He'd left before Dougal started grade school, when his sister had been only a tiny bump on their mother's small frame. They'd been lucky. Ed Lachlan had beaten his second wife to death and had only recently been released from Oregon State Penitentiary where he'd served his time.

Just like your father…

Some legacy.

chapter two

as she watched her fiancé approach, Jamie Lachlan felt like a school girl again. Silly, excited, maybe even a little nervous. Kyle Quinpool had always made her feel this way, even when she was younger and Kyle had been one of her brother's best friends.

The group of older kids usually hung out on Driftwood Lane, or on the beach. Mostly the guys—Kyle, Dougal and Wade—ignored her. But sometimes Kyle would give her one of his smiles, as if he knew she was going to grow up and knock his socks off one day.

These days she knocked off more than his socks.

"Hey there, handsome. I missed you." He'd been away on business in Coos Bay for a few days. She'd wanted to go with him but, as he reminded her, their wedding was in two weeks and she had lots of packing to do.

He was anxious for her to move out of her trailer and into the house with him and his children. If he'd had his way, she would have done it the day they were engaged. She wasn't an old-fashioned sort of woman, but since the children from his previous marriage were only nine and impressionable, she gently suggested they wait.

Kyle had sulked for a week.

But that had been months ago. And now there wasn't much waiting left to be done.

Kyle took her in his arms and kissed her. "I've missed you too. Ready to go?"

She was. As they passed by the mailbox he asked, "I don't suppose you've heard from Dougal?"

"Nope. I guess you were right. He isn't coming." She tried to sound like it didn't matter.

"Maybe it's better this way. It's not like he's an important part of your life anymore."

She wished she could dispute Kyle, but the facts spoke for themselves. When her mother was alive, they'd been lucky to see Dougal once a year—and only if they traveled to him. Dougal never came to Twisted Cedars.

Since he'd missed their mother's funeral, Jamie had stopped phoning and emailing, as well. And he hadn't reached out once with an explanation for his absence.

Kyle held the door open to his black Audi SUV and she climbed into the passenger seat.

"Pretty dress," he said.

She smiled, knowing it was the woman inside the dress he really liked. When she was younger, she'd despaired of her overly generous butt and boobs, but as a mature woman, she loved her sexy curves.

Kyle clearly did, too. Maybe because his first wife had been willowy and tall? Kyle's first wife had once been beautiful—glamorous even, especially by Twisted Cedar's standards. Unfortunately after the birth of the twins Daisy had developed some sort of post-partum psychosis. It was so bad, she'd been hospitalized for a while. Even when she was released, she couldn't cope with her babies on her own.

So Kyle's parents, Jim and Muriel Quinpool, had moved back into the family home, which fortunately was large enough to accommodate them all. But even with the extra help, Daisy couldn't manage. After two years, the marriage finally broke down, and then, shortly after the divorce was finalized, Daisy had left town.

She'd sent an email explaining that she wanted to start a new life, and she hadn't been heard from since.

Some women might feel slightly jealous of their fiancés ex-wife, but Jamie felt only pity for Daisy. She'd had everything, once. It was tragic the way mental illness had stripped everything away from her.

Kyle drove out of the Evergreen Trailer Park faster than the posted speed limit. There were always kids and pets running around, but Jamie held her tongue, knowing he hated a back-seat driver. She expected him to turn toward town, but he surprised her by heading north on the one-oh-one.

"What's up?"

"I wanted us to have a quiet dinner for a change. How does the Sea House in Port Orford sound?"

"Perfect."

Kyle had proposed to her at the Sea House. It was "their" place. She reached over to touch his cheek. His skin was so smooth he must have shaved again, to prepare for their date. How sweet that he'd wanted to please her.

She felt like she was poised at the top of a roller coaster, about to start the most thrilling ride of her life. Sometimes it scared her, how much she loved him. She couldn't help worrying something would go wrong. She'd been programmed to think that way, she supposed. Her dad had taken off before she was born, then her brother had split as soon as he finished school. The only one she'd ever been able to count on was her mom—and even she, as sweet as she'd been—had been undependable at times.

The point was—Jamie wasn't used to relying on people. She had to get over that.

She settled in to enjoy the drive. The one-oh-one had been carved through the rocks and the forest that made up the Oregon coastline and it wasn't the sort of road one could drive recklessly. Two years ago Patricia and John Hammond—Daisy and her sister Charlotte's parents—had been killed in a horrible head-on collision just before the turn-off to the Rogue River Golf and Country Club.

As they passed the spot, Jamie sent out a private prayer, but said nothing to Kyle about slowing down. Maybe he drove a little faster than she liked, but she had to admit he had complete control over the vehicle.

By the time they arrived at Port Orford, the sun looked like a golden beach ball resting on the far edge of the Pacific and the ocean shimmered with streaks of apricot, lavender and rose. They were seated at a table right by the window so they could enjoy the view. Kyle ordered wine and they chatted about the little things that had occupied them during the day, holding hands across the table. Jamie's diamond caught the last of the brilliant rays from the setting sun and glowed as if with magical powers.

I wish, Jamie thought. *I wish we could always be this happy.* She supposed all brides had the same hopes and expectations at the beginning of a marriage, though not all of them were lucky enough to fall in love with a man like Kyle.

Looking at him now, she had to catch her breath. Not just because of his good looks, his blond hair, bronzed skin and sparkling green eyes. He was also a loving father and a successful businessman. Too good to be true? The best thing was—he was all hers.

Jamie moved her foot until she touched his leg. As she'd hoped he would, Kyle reached down to stroke her bare calf. She felt a pleasurable shiver and was glad she'd worn a dress, and heels, and a dab of perfume.

"I can't wait until we're living together," he said.

"Sleeping together..."

"Waking up together..."

She laughed softly. "Yes. Waking up together." They'd only had that luxury twice, when both Cory and Chester had been invited to sleepovers on the same night.

"We get so little time without my kids."

"Don't worry. I get it. And I love them, too, you know." Kyle didn't want more children, but he might change his mind, eventually. And if he didn't, Jamie could live with that. She already had so much to be grateful for.

"I'm just so glad you all get along. Asking Cory to be a flower girl was a smart move. She's so excited she can hardly sleep at night."

"The dress Stella designed for her is beautiful." Winning Cory over would be easy. His son was another matter. Chester was more guarded than his sister. Cautious.

Jamie knew she had to prove to him that she was in his life to stay.

"Your children are easy to love, Kyle."

"And so are you." He waited as the server came to top up their wineglasses. Once they were alone again, he leaned in closer. "Have you thought about what our life will be like after the wedding?"

"You mean whether we'll move into your house or my trailer?" When Kyle frowned, she was sorry she'd made the joke. "Just kidding. But what's to discuss? We've listed my trailer for sale and I've already started packing."

She would have a couple weeks to settle in to her new home, and then after school let out for the summer and the kids had gone to camp, she and Kyle would honeymoon in San Francisco.

"What about your job?" he asked.

"I'm not following."

"I have a good income. Our expenses are low. You don't have to keep working."

The suggestion shouldn't have come as such as shock. Yet, she hadn't seen it coming, at all. "I've been working for as long as I can remember." As a kid she'd delivered fliers and bagged groceries at Sam's Market. When she was in college she'd delivered pizzas. There had never been a time in her life when she hadn't had a job. "What would I do for money?"

Kyle touched the diamond ring on her fourth finger. "Don't you get it? We're going to be a family. I guarantee money won't be a problem."

"But I like my job." Putting herself through college had been a struggle. So had the early years as a junior with the local CPA firm. Now, finally, she'd been promoted and was earning at a level that made all those sacrifices seem worthwhile.

"Some women find it rewarding to be home with kids. You might, too, if you gave it a try. And if you wanted something part-time, you could always take over the bookkeeping at Quinpool Realty for dad and me."

"But Olivia's been your accountant for years. I'd be doing her out of her job."

"Family comes first. But you don't have to make up your mind now. Just think about it."

The sun had slipped away, leaving a quiet aquamarine glow in its wake.

Jamie thought about what Kyle *wasn't* saying. His kids had been through a lot. Just a year ago their lives had been upset again when Kyle's parents separated. Muriel had gone to live in Portland with her sister, while Jim had moved to the apartment above Quinpool Realty. Now the twins had to go to Nola Thompson's house after school. Nola was a nice enough lady, but she had six children of her own. She didn't really have the time or energy for two more.

"I want to help with Cory and Chester as much as I can. But one day I hope to be a partner at Howard & Mason."

Kyle tapped his wine glass against hers. "Fair enough. Just thought I'd mention it."

* * *

Books were in Charlotte Hammond's blood, part of her heritage, the source of her livelihood, and her principle pleasure in life. When she'd finished high school, there had been no question that she would go on to study library sciences. After graduation it seemed just as natural that she should take over from her mother at the Twisted Cedars Public Library, which had been founded by her great-great grandmother back in post-Civil War days.

For the most part, Charlotte was happy with her fate. She couldn't imagine a job more suited to her interests. And she was never bored. During lulls in activity levels she could always read—as she was doing now, thirty minutes before closing.

Charlotte had just started a new mystery series and devoured two chapters before she finally snapped out of the author's spell. Reluctant to stop reading, she closed the book, and then slipped it into her purse so she could pick it up later at home. She went to the windows that banked the west wall where chairs and tables were arranged next to a display of magazines.

Ian Rankin had evoked Edinburgh so deftly that she almost expected to see the Scottish city when she looked out the glass pane.

But the view along Driftwood Lane was familiar. A row of small businesses and restaurants geared to meet the shopping needs of the thousand-odd residents of the town, led to the town square where two cedar trees, many hundreds of years old, grew with trunk and limbs so intertwined you could hardly tell where one ended and the other began.

Come summer, Twisted Cedar's population would more than triple with tourists. But right now the town was sleepy, small and safe, tucked in between the ocean to the west, and redwood forest and mountains to the east.

Charlotte knew no other home. She'd been adopted by the Hammonds when she was only three-months-old, welcomed into the family to provide a sibling to her sister, Daisy. Twisted Cedars had sheltered her all these years. But since her parents' car accident she was the only Hammond left in town and sometimes she wondered what held her here. It would be different if Daisy came back. But her sister hadn't been heard from since she ran off seven years ago.

Kyle had hired an investigator back then. And after the death of their parents, Charlotte had tried again, as the size of the Hammond's estate was considerable. But both times there had been no luck.

It seemed Daisy didn't want to be found, and had either changed her identity, or was living below the radar of modern life. Daisy's only communication with her old life—if you could call it that—were the regular five-hundred dollar withdrawals she made from the joint account their father had set up for her years ago.

The withdrawals were made from various ATMs in

Sacramento, usually at night, with Daisy wearing a hat and sunglasses that obscured her face from video surveillance. Charlotte had been advised to put a hold on the account, but she couldn't bring herself to do that.

Chances were, Daisy really needed that money. And if she was using it for alcohol, or drugs, well, Charlotte only hoped they brought her peace.

Lots of people in town judged Daisy harshly for falling apart after her children were born, and especially for deserting them. But Charlotte had sat by Daisy's hospital bed enough to know how much her sister had suffered. Postpartum psychosis was a devastating illness—one that medical science knew far too little about.

It was just five minutes to closing now. Abigail, the full time library assistant, had left at four-thirty, and since then the library had been deserted. Charlotte doubted any new customers would be arriving now, so she began powering down the computers and turning out lights, preparing to close for the night.

Her boyfriend, Sheriff Wade MacKay would be by shortly to pick her up. She hoped he wouldn't be late. This was her least favorite time of the day.

There was something spooky about the library when the lights went out, even in the summer. A shiver went up her spine as she imagined a man hiding in the stacks, waiting until she was all alone and vulnerable...

She knew the fear was irrational. Unfortunately, irrational fears were her specialty. Her mother put it down to the period of her life before she'd been adopted.

Of course, Charlotte couldn't remember that far back. All she knew was that she was afraid to go into her own basement at night. Afraid of big cities and afraid of flying, too. Her parents had taken her and Daisy on a trip to Disneyland once that had sent her into a full-blown anxiety attack.

College in Portland had been a challenge, requiring daily phone calls home to her mother. Since then, she hadn't strayed far from Twisted Cedars. The occasional shopping trip to Portland, or attendance at the Oregon Library Association's annual conference, was the most she could manage.

Thinking of the conference reminded her she had to reply to the email from Libby Gardner. Libby was the current president of the OLA's Executive Board, and had been a great friend of Charlotte's mother. She had invited Charlotte to make a presentation at this year's conference. "Revitalizing the Small Town Library," or something to that effect.

Charlotte went to her desk and opened up the message. "I'll think about it, Libby," she typed, then hit "send."

But she wouldn't. She'd wait a week or two, then send her regrets. Out-of-town trips were tough enough without compounding them with public speaking commitments.

A chime sounded from the main door, and Wade Mackay walked in, his large frame and clean-cut good looks a familiar and welcome sight.

He'd first asked her out about a week after Kyle Quinpool and Jamie Lachlan announced their engagement. The timing had not been a coincidence, she suspected. Which made her second choice. But she didn't mind.

She really liked Wade. Sweet and kind and trustworthy—he was a good friend, and if things continued to go well between them, she knew he'd make a dependable husband, too. They hadn't yet made love. So whether sex was going to happen, and whether it would be any good, was still a question mark. But the kisses were nice. That was a positive sign.

One thing was for sure. Her parents would have approved of the match. What better suitor for their fearful daughter than the local Sheriff?

"Ready for our big night out in Twisted Cedars?" Wade teased.

"I suppose I can tear myself away from my books for a few hours."

They kissed—just a light peck, a form of hello—then he took the key from her and locked the door, testing the handle before returning the key. Wade was meticulous about matters of security, which she appreciated. He was chivalrous, too. He took her arm in his, considerately matching his longer stride to hers as they headed for the Linger Longer.

They didn't need to discuss their plans, since every Friday was the same. It was sort of comforting, knowing exactly what the evening ahead would hold.

A pub meal followed by a few beers and a game of pool. He'd walk her home and kiss her again at the front door.

Another woman would probably want more passion, but not Charlotte. Just like adventures and mysteries, Charlotte suspected that romance was safest when contained between book covers.

chapter three

after four long days of driving, Dougal reached Roseburg, Oregon, on Tuesday night. He stopped at a gas station off the Interstate to buy snacks, a six-pack and a copy of the local paper, *The News-Review*. Then he booked into a nearby motel and made himself comfortable.

He was about one hundred and forty miles from Twisted Cedars, but in no hurry to get there. In New York he was a successful author, a man of some means—even though he lived modestly. It was only a persona, but he clung to it, knowing the moment he drove into his hometown he'd once again be the poor boy who'd lived on the wrong side of the tracks.

Son of a wife-beater. And murderer.

Dougal scanned the paper while he drank his first beer, then he powered up his laptop and checked out *The News-Review* on-line. Their archives went back only to 1995. He could call their office tomorrow, or the library. Both would have what he needed.

He fell back on the bed, stared at the ceiling. One week ago, he never would have believed he'd be going back to Oregon. Yet here he was, about to start investigation into an old crime on the basis of one, lousy, anonymous email.

Did this story really have potential, or was he killing time, putting off the moment he would see his sister, and Twisted Cedars, again?

* * *

Over the course of the past year Dougal's body clock had grown out-of-kilter. He'd taken to sleeping later and later, sometimes not rising from bed until almost noon. The three-hour time difference between New York and Oregon, however, had him opening his eyes at nine, unaccountably alert. And bored.

What the hell. Might as well get up.

He sat on the edge of the bed, peering in the direction of the window—whose curtains he'd neglected to close last night. The day was already bright and sunny. He wished it was raining. Then he'd have an excuse to crawl back under the covers.

But then he remembered his mission to check up on Elva Mae. Having something concrete to do gave him a reason to move. He reached for his phone and called the local library.

The receptionist connected him to a helpful woman who agreed to check the archives for Elva Mae Ayer's obituary and any articles related to her murder. She'd call him back. Dougal thanked her, and then went out for his next mission—to find coffee.

He ended up in a diner next to the motel where he ordered an omelet to go with his coffee. When he was done he headed to the local library. At the reference desk he explained what he needed, then went to check his email. Ten minutes later the librarian was back.

"I found what you were looking for." She handed him a stack of old newspapers. "We're working on digitizing our old papers, but we haven't gone back this far yet. If you need to make copies, there's a machine over there." She pointed to an alcove behind him to the right.

God he loved librarians. They were so helpful. He wished the last research assistant he'd hired had been half as cooperative. "Thank you. Should I return these to you when I'm finished?"

She nodded, looking curious. "We don't get many people interested in going back that far in our local history."

He recognized it was a leading question, but just smiled. With each new book he wrote, his public profile gained visibility. But he didn't like being recognized by strangers, and did his best to protect his anonymity.

"Thanks again," he said, already scanning through the first of the papers.

Elva Mae Ayer's death had been big news in Roseburg. Dougal read the articles for facts and names of people he could follow up with. He noted the name of the Detective who'd been quoted in the articles, and also the name of the library staff member who had found the body.

The obit provided Elva Mae's next of kin, which turned out to be her sister, Edwina Shaw and brother-in-law Harry. Apparently Elva Mae never married or had children and her parents had pre-deceased her.

According to several editorials, the people of Roseburg assumed some deviant, transient committed the crime. The lack of motive was a sticking point.

As months passed, there were fewer and fewer articles and editorials about the murder.

The last one surmised, "I guess we'll never know what happened to Elva Mae on that fateful spring day in 1972..."

Once he'd made his copies, and returned the papers to the librarian, Dougal went on-line to find addresses and phone numbers. The detective who'd worked on the case agreed to meet him for lunch, but had little to offer other than corroborating the fact that the victim had been strangled by a red, silk scarf.

"Every cop has one case that stays with them after they retire," the detective confided. "For me, this homicide was that case. I've often wondered what would have happened if she'd been murdered twenty years later, when we had DNA, computerized databases, and other tools to work with. When you think about it, back in the seventies, crime investigations were pretty primitive."

The library staff member who'd found the body—a janitor—was no longer living. But Dougal did manage to track down Elva Mae's sister. Over the phone Edwina sounded confused, but eventually agreed that he could drop over that afternoon.

Her tiny bungalow was located just off the Oakland

Shady Highway. Edwina was sitting on the front porch when he arrived. The woman was in her seventies, he guessed, dressed oddly in an ill-fitting dress, socks and sandals too big for her feet.

"Is your husband home?"

"He's out golfing." She eyed him cautiously, perhaps hopefully. "No one's mentioned my sister's name to me in over thirty years."

"A long time," he agreed.

She got out of her chair and took a step closer to him. Squinting at him, she said, "My neighbor, Brenda, gives me books to read. I recognize you from the back cover. You write about real life crimes."

He nodded, surprised that she'd recognized him. Maybe she wasn't as confused as he'd thought.

"Are you going to write a book about my sister?"

He hesitated. "Maybe."

"So you've figured out who killed her?"

He hated to disappoint her and sure didn't want to raise her hopes. "No. Probably too much time has passed to find the truth now. But I'm checking into it."

That was good enough for Edwina, apparently. "We can talk in the back. In the shade."

She led him along concrete blocks to a modest yard, with a patchy lawn dominated by one large tree. Two dusty aluminum chairs were placed on either side of an equally dusty glass-top table. Edwina grabbed a grungy cloth from one of the chairs and brushed off most of the dirt.

They sat opposite one another. Now that he was in the shade, Dougal removed his sunglasses. Edwina had a pronounced tremor, like the late Katherine Hepburn's. Unlike the famous star, Edwina was neither beautiful, nor elegant. She was short, skinny and didn't look especially clean. She folded her hands in her lap and cast an anxious glance in his direction.

"What do you want me to tell you?"

Guilt niggled at him then. He could hear the hope in

her voice, see it in her eyes. She had no idea he was just killing time here, putting off the moment when he would have to face Twisted Cedars and Jamie. He ought to apologize for wasting the woman's time, get up and leave.

"Tell me everything you remember about what happened."

"Where do I start?"

"Do you have any idea why anyone would have wanted your sister dead?"

Expression grim, Edwina shook her head. "My sister was a nice, decent woman."

"Did she have a boyfriend?"

"Oh, no," Edwina said, as if that would have been so terrible. "She loved her books. Elva Mae lived a quiet life."

"Were the two of you close?"

"Not so much when we were little. But our mother had a stroke and died when I was sixteen. Elva Mae was living on her own by then, but she moved back in with me and Dad to take care of us. Dad died a year later, and then it was just Elva Mae and me, until I married Harry and we bought our own house." She glanced anxiously at the home in question, then back at him. "Even after I was married, my sister and I visited or spoke on the phone every day."

"And did your sister and your husband get along?"

Edwina gave him another of her anxious looks. "Mostly."

Dougal guessed that meant they hadn't. Which might have made Harry a potential suspect, except that earlier the detective had told him that both Edwina and Harry had been at work when the murder occurred. A fact corroborated by several witnesses.

After almost an hour of questions about her sister's life, a life which seemed to contain not a hint of conflict or scandal, Edwina seemed tired. "I need to lie down," she said.

"Of course." Dougal stood as she got up.

She headed for the back door, but on her way, she

stopped, turned and said, "I hope you find out what happened to Elva Mae. I'd like to know the truth before I die."

Her words gave him another stab of guilt as he made his way back to his car, careful not to trip on the tree roots that blighted the sparse lawn. The odds of him discovering anything that would bring Edwina the peace of mind she craved were very slight. He was about to slide into the driver's seat, when he noticed a neighbor gentleman watching from the porch next door.

He made eye contact with the man, whom he guessed to be in his late sixties, dressed in gray pants and a wrinkled blue shirt, open at the neck.

The old guy got up. Left his porch and came down to the sidewalk. "You visiting with Edwina?"

"I was."

"That's a first. Edwina doesn't get many visitors."

"Why is that?"

He hesitated. "She hasn't been right in the head for a long time. It's sad that she's ended up alone like this. My wife and I take her food now and then."

"What about her husband?"

The man hesitated again. Maybe he was wondering if he should say more to a stranger. Dougal gave him his name and a brief explanation for his interest. The man raised his eyebrows, as if impressed to find himself speaking to a "real" author.

"They've been divorced a long time. Happened a few years after her sister was murdered."

Fall-out, Dougal thought. Every tragedy left misery in its wake.

* * *

Between his second and third beer that night, Dougal managed to arrange a breakfast meeting with Edwina's ex-husband, Harry, for Thursday.

Harry didn't sound pleased about talking with him. But once more Dougal found his familiar name and New York

Times Bestseller reputation, got him the interview. Now that they were face-to-face, Harry spoke fast, as if to get the meeting over as quickly as possible.

"I don't have any idea who killed Elva Mae, but he might as well have strangled Edwina, too. She went off her rocker after her sister was murdered. Stopped eating for a while, refused to talk, wouldn't leave the house. I tried to be supportive. But a year went by with little improvement. There's only so much a guy can take. Finally I told her she had to start seeing a shrink or I was going to leave. I guess you can figure out what she decided."

"That must have been hard for both of you."

"Actually, I don't think she even noticed when I moved out. I go by her place once a month, drop off groceries, take care of the yard and the exterior of the house. My second wife is a decent sort. She understands my obligation. But I haven't had a real conversation with Edwina since the day her sister died."

First Edwina. Then Harry. Both of them victims, too, in a way. Dougal understood all too well, how far the stain from a murder could spread.

Back at his car, he assessed the slim folder of notes he'd taken so far. Pathetic. He'd figured out nothing.

He couldn't put this off anymore.

Time to put Roseburg behind him. Time to go home.

* * *

The route to Twisted Cedars followed brutal, hairpin mountain roads that paralleled the Rogue River. A distance that would have taken an hour to drive on a normal highway, chewed up almost double that amount of time. Finally Dougal arrived at the edge of the continent, facing the Pacific Ocean and the one-oh-one highway. He turned left.

Only sixty miles separated him now from his destination. So many years had passed since he'd been in this part of the world, he felt like another person. But his memories were stubbornly intact and he had a different one for every mile of this familiar stretch of the Oregon coastline.

Most of them involved his old friends, Wade, Kyle, and Daisy. Kyle had owned a convertible back then, a 1988 red Mazda RX7, and the four of them had clocked a lot of miles looking for thrills, heading out to parties, or just aimlessly cruising.

Though he'd played football with Wade and Kyle, and hung out with them on weekends, Dougal had always been aware he was a misfit. The others were all from wealthy families...at least wealthy compared to his mother.

Wade's father was the Sheriff of Curry County, Kyle's dad owned the local real estate agency, and Daisy's father was a bank manager, the town mayor and the richest of all. No one talked about the fact that Dougal's mother cleaned all of their houses. Certainly none of them ever came to visit him at the trailer where he lived with his mom and sister. He would have died of embarrassment if they'd tried.

Dougal recalled his mother asking him to introduce her to his friends after a football game once. He'd been so embarrassed of her then. Now his jaw clenched with shame for himself. What a jerk he'd been.

One hand on the steering wheel, the other resting on the gear shift, Dougal focused on the scenery—the ocean churning at his right, the dark forest looming to his left. He lowered his windows so he could smell the pine and salt in the air.

The miles flipped by, like pages of a familiar book, disappearing much too quickly. His hair, whipped by the early summer wind and air-borne salt, began to feel thicker, wilder.

He passed a beach that had been the location for one of their wilder parties. Kyle had been dating Daisy Hammond already, by far the prettiest girl in town, but he'd hooked up that night with the girlfriend of the quarterback of the rival football team they'd played against that afternoon.

"Cover for me, Dougal," Kyle had said, as he and the girl slipped into the tall grass beyond the bonfire.

Dougal winced at the memory, at his own weak desire for Kyle's approval, at his guilt for not telling Daisy what had happened.

Maybe Kyle had changed over the years, become a stand-up guy. But Dougal doubted it.

And Jamie, his too-sweet, too-good sister, was planning to marry him.

chapter four

late Thursday afternoon, Charlotte finally had time to file the DVDs that had been returned the previous day. Ten years ago she would have had a huge stack, now there were just a couple. Most people watched their movies on Netflix nowadays or downloaded them from the Internet.

Included with the DVDs was the movie she'd watched after dinner last night. One scene had stuck with her all day. The hero of the story—a young teacher suffering from cancer, about to marry a woman he'd been dating for a long time—shares a joint with a hippy who claims to have been happily married for seventeen years to his childhood sweetheart.

"How did you know she was the one?" the teacher asked.

"If you have to ask, she isn't."

Charlotte couldn't stop thinking about that. Was it true? Did the best romances and marriages come wrapped in that sort of certainty?

She couldn't imagine ever feeling so—swept away. She certainly hadn't in her relationships to date. Not that she'd had many. There'd been Ned Pullman in high school, Craig Turner in college...and now Wade.

They'd made love for the first time on Friday. She'd been surprised, at first, when Wade asked if he could come inside. But sex with Wade had felt natural and, well, satisfying. Nothing like the awkward fumblings with Ned, or the hurried, sweaty sessions with Craig. No, Wade had been sure of himself, sweet and tender.

Lying in his arms afterward though, Charlotte had entertained a very uncharitable thought. It was like they'd gone for a test drive in a prospective new car, to make sure everything was working before they put down a deposit.

Charlotte checked her watch. It was quiet this afternoon. The morning had been busier, but Abigail had been in then, and the work had been easily managed. She wondered if she should speak to the board about reducing hours. It would be one way to manage the budget shortfall.

And just as she'd had that thought, a man came in from the street, a man with dark hair and eyes, familiar and excitingly different—all at the same time.

Her heart skipped two beats when she recognized him. Oh, my God, it was Dougal Lachlan.

She couldn't believe he was here, in real life, looking exactly like the author photo printed in the back of all his books. Rebelliously attractive, intelligent, weary, disillusioned. These were the adjectives that came to Charlotte's mind. His thick, curly hair, so like his sister's, was windswept. He removed his sunglasses and studied her with his dark mocha-colored eyes.

"Are you Daisy's little sister?"

She was surprised and a little flattered that he was able to place her so easily. If she hadn't known what he looked like from his author photos, she never would have connected this man to the scowling teenager she remembered hanging out with her sister's group of friends.

Dougal had been part of the gang, but also apart from it. Never really one to fit in with any crowd, she guessed.

"Yes. I'm Charlotte."

"All grown up now." His gaze swept over her gray skirt, loose-fitting blouse. "You don't look much like your sister."

The muscles along her shoulders and neck tightened. He knew she'd been adopted. Or once he had. Maybe he'd forgotten. "No, I don't."

"How is Daisy doing? Where is she living now?"

"I'm not sure how she's doing." Charlotte didn't try to conceal her frustration. "I believe she's living somewhere in

Sacramento, but she's not good at keeping in touch."

"I guess she and I have that in common."

"Well," Charlotte said awkwardly, supposing he was making reference to the fact that he hadn't come home for his mother's funeral. Which was a shocking thing. After all, he couldn't claim a shortage of funds. Still, it wasn't her place to judge. "Jamie must be happy you're here for her wedding."

"She doesn't know yet. I've been on the road for a week and just arrived ten minutes ago."

That surprised her. "And your first stop is the public library?"

His eyes narrowed and he regarded her silently for several seconds before saying, "I was hoping I could use the Wi-Fi. I have some emails to send that are too long to type out on my phone."

"We do have wireless coverage," she assured him, trying to sound business-like to make up for the personal, inappropriate, comment. She wrote down the code he would need to access the system, and then invited him to sit at one of the tables by the windows.

She returned to her desk, flipping through papers, wishing she had something pressing to occupy her time. Libby Gardener had sent another email. A more insistent email this time. Since her parents' accident, Libby had taken a disconcerting, motherly interest in Charlotte. The day of the funeral she'd cornered her in the kitchen. "You have so much potential, dear. You should really broaden your horizons."

Charlotte had tried to assure her mother's old friend that she was happy with her life—just the way it was. But Libby refused to listen.

She glanced back at Dougal Lachlan, who'd taken out his laptop and was concentrating on the screen, his expression broodingly attractive. She found it difficult to resist staring at him.

At that moment he looked up, catching her gaze. "How

are Chester and Cory?"

Her breath caught in her throat. How did he know...? But of course, his mother and sister would have kept him abreast of the Twisted Cedar news. "They've been surprisingly resilient."

"Does Daisy ever see them?"

It pained her to admit it, but Charlotte shook her head. "No. And they've had more upheaval. Muriel and Jim divorced and Muriel moved to Portland. So they've lost their grandmother, as well."

"And now their dad is re-marrying. How do they feel about Jamie as a stepmother?"

She wondered the same thing. "I'm not sure. I don't see them as much as I'd like."

She didn't explain the reason, didn't think it was right. The simple truth was Kyle made it difficult for her to visit her niece and nephew. She suspected he blamed her for her sister's mental illness and subsequent disappearance. As if she hadn't been just as deserted by Daisy as the rest of them.

"I'm surprised Jamie didn't tell you all of this herself," Charlotte added.

"We haven't spoken much, lately. It's been a busy year for me."

"Yes. You have another book coming out this January, don't you? Congratulations on all your success. We always have a long waiting list for your books. You have a lot of fans here in Twisted Cedars."

And she was one. His probing, true-crime stories were impossible to put down once you'd started. But they were also undeniably creepy—as much an exploration of the soul of a murderer as tales of investigation.

She'd wondered what drew him to such brutal subject matter. But now, seeing him after all these years, she could sense the undercurrents of darkness in him—his wary eyes, tightly controlled conversation, even the cautious way he watched her, as if he couldn't let down his guard even in front of a mild-mannered librarian.

***

Dougal found it hard to believe this plain-looking, serious-minded woman was actually Daisy Hammond's sister. He'd recognized her. Knew she was. But still, you'd think she'd have moved past the ugly duckling stage by now.

Which was superficial of him, he supposed, but Daisy had been exceptionally beautiful, blonde and vivacious. Then he remembered that Charlotte had been adopted.

The story had come out one night when he and his friends had been drinking on the beach. Daisy always talked more when she'd had a few drinks. She'd told them all how, after she was born, her mother had to have surgery and couldn't conceive a second time. Her parents had been so worried about her being an only child they'd chosen to adopt.

"They should have asked me, first," Daisy had grumbled. "I *liked* being an only child. Even if I didn't, who would ever want Charlotte? She's the most ugly, boring kid around. She was scared at *Disneyland* for God's sake."

Dougal didn't know if Daisy really meant what she said. She did sometimes come out with shocking statements, just to get attention.

But he'd felt sorry for Charlotte back then. He hoped her sister had never voiced any of these opinions to her in person.

Dougal turned his attention back to his laptop. His connection was now working, so he opened his email.

Right away he saw it. Another message from Librarianmomma.

He took a deep breath, then clicked.

And this message followed up where the other left off.

The next year Mari Beamish was murdered. There was a pattern, but don't feel bad if you don't see it yet. The cops never did make the connection. Those were different times, before computers and all the advances in forensics. Now you get to be the hero who pieces it all together. You can thank me later.

Dougal's heartbeat pounded loud in his ears. He took a

deep breath. Jesus. He sank back in his chair. The first murder had been real. He had no doubt that this one would be, too.

He typed the new name, Mari Beamish, into a search engine, but came up with nothing that seemed relevant. These murders had happened so long ago, the Internet was pretty much useless to him. He noticed Charlotte still watching him, though she pretended to focus on some papers on her desk. "What's the main newspaper in Pendleton?"

She didn't even have to think. "That would be the *East Oregonian*."

"Is it possible to get a copy of some articles and an obituary that would have been printed in 1973?"

She looked at him thoughtfully. "We don't keep copies of the *East Oregonian*, but I could send a request to the main library in Pendleton. I imagine they could fax me the relevant information in a day or two. What, specifically, are you looking for?"

He decided to take a leap. "Charlotte, have you ever heard about a serial murderer who targeted librarians?"

"Are you serious?" She looked appalled.

"I'm talking about a long time ago. In the seventies."

She relaxed visibly when he mentioned the date. "You and I weren't even born then."

"No."

Her brow furrowed as she thought about it. "My Aunt Shirley was Twisted Cedar's librarian in the early seventies. I wonder if she and my parents ever knew about these deaths."

"As far as I can tell no one connected the dots between the murders back then."

"Is that what you're trying to do now? Connect the dots?"

"So much time has passed, I'm not sure I can."

"How many dots?"

"Four. I think."

Her eyes widened. "No. Really?"

He was tempted to take advantage of her obvious interest, show her the emails and get her input. As a kid she'd been earnest, always trying too hard to please. But she'd also been smart, and incapable of telling a lie. His instincts told him he could trust her.

"About a week ago I received an anonymous email giving me the name of a librarian murdered in Roseburg in 1972. I've checked it out. It really happened. Just now I was sent a second name, another librarian, this one from Pendleton, murdered in 1973, I think."

Charlotte shivered. "How creepy. And weird."

"I know. Why would someone bother telling me about a series of murders that occurred almost forty years ago?"

"Maybe he—or she—was protecting someone. And maybe, that person died and now he wants to clear his conscience."

Dougal nodded. "The emails could be from someone who worked in the library system and saw something suspicious, but was afraid to come forward until now."

"What's the email address of the sender?" Charlotte asked.

"It's a Hotmail account with the name *Librarianmomma*—which kind of supports the theory that this person is a woman who worked at the library."

"What if this person isn't a witness?" A note of fear had crept into her voice. "What if she's the killer?"

"Yes. That's possible, too."

"Dougal, I think you should show these emails to the police."

"Do you really think they'd put any resources into a crime that was committed decades ago—all on the basis of a couple lousy emails?"

"You're saying you don't think they would?"

"I guarantee you, they wouldn't. Crime writers are magnets for bizarre email and letters. I usually delete them unread."

"Only in this case, you didn't. So there must be something different about this one. I mean these *two*."

She had him there. "True." He explained about the lack of gory details, and the fact that the murdered woman had been obscure. "Usually the psychos want to confess to a really high profile crime. What they're really after is notoriety."

She thought about that for a moment. "So what are you going to do?"

He was enjoying this, Dougal realized. The back-and-forth with Charlotte Hammond. She made him think, questioned his assumptions. He eyed her assessingly. When he forgot about comparing her to Daisy, she was actually quite attractive.

Before he could tell her his plan—which he hadn't figured out yet—the door opened and a man wearing a sheriff's uniform entered. A big guy was Dougal's first thought. A second later he recognized Wade MacKay. So his high school buddy had followed his old man into a career of law enforcement. Dougal wasn't surprised. He stood and offered his hand.

"Hello, Wade."

"Hey, man, you're back." Wade's gaze was open, surprised, yet friendly. "I wondered if you might come to town for Jamie's wedding."

"Jamie and *Kyle*. What's up with that?"

Wade shrugged. "Guess you'll have to ask your sister."

"I'd rather she was marrying anyone—even *you*—than that sleazy bastard."

Wade looked embarrassed. "Actually, I'm dating Charlotte."

"Oh." Dougal glanced at the librarian who had started to blush. Now wasn't that cute. He turned to Wade. "So you're the sheriff, now? Impressive."

"And you're a big shot author. Living in New York City."

Dougal nodded, cleared his throat. There didn't seem

to be anything to say after that.

Wade glanced at Charlotte before saying, "We're going to grab a bite at the Linger Longer. Want to come along?"

"Maybe I'll meet up with you later. I need to book into a motel, first."

"You're not staying with Jamie?"

He packed up his laptop, avoiding Wade's gaze. "Oh, I figure the trailer will be a little cramped."

Not to mention the fact that he still hadn't called to let her know he was here.

* * *

Dougal left the library and stood for a moment on Driftwood Lane, getting his bearings. Across the road was the town square and the cedars for which the town had been named. At least a hundred years ago they'd been saplings growing too close to one another. Somehow they'd become entwined, and almost as if they'd been grafted together, had taken the appearance of one tree. Most every tourist who passed through town ended up taking a photo with that tree. But to Dougal it had always seemed grotesque. Something to avoid.

He'd parked his car on the other side of the street from the library, but rather than jay walk, he decided to stroll the length of the block to the intersection and check out the local businesses. Most had been here since he was a kid. The only changes in the pharmacy and the hardware stores were the colors they were painted and the merchandise displayed in their windows. Buttermilk Café was new, but it looked a little precious for his taste.

A few stores farther, he came to Quinpool Realty. About a dozen local listings were posted in the window. As he paused to read them over, a man exited the office. He had the sloped shoulders, sunken chest, and distended belly of an older man. It took a few seconds to realize this was Kyle's father, Jim Quinpool.

Jim recognized him at the same moment. "Dougal Lachlan? Is that you?"

As a kid, Dougal had been in awe of Kyle's father. He was the only person in town who owned a Mercedes Benz, and Dougal remembered the total envy he'd felt when Kyle had been dropped off at school, or football practice, by his father.

Now the older man looked worn-down by life. His grip when he shook Dougal's hand was firm, but Dougal could tell it took an effort.

"How are you?"

"Don't ask. Muriel and I are divorced. She's living in Portland now." His blue eyes appeared foggy as he stared into Dougal's eyes. "You'd know this if you kept in touch with your sister."

Dougal said nothing to that.

"You're back for the wedding, I assume. Last I spoke to Jamie and Kyle, they weren't expecting you."

"My trip was a last minute decision."

"Is that right?" Jim's eyes narrowed. "I guess you can do what you want now that you're rich and famous. My Kyle's done good, too." He puffed his chest a little. "Pretty much runs the business now. Let's me keep an office so I have something to do with my time."

"I always expected Kyle would do well."

Rather than seem pleased, Jim gave him a suspicious look, then straightened his shoulders and nodded. "Well, better get myself home. Guess I'll be seeing you at the rehearsal dinner on Friday."

Dougal doubted it, but nodded anyway. He was sure Kyle and his father had ass-loads of money. His worries for his sister didn't include financial ones.

Dougal drove the four blocks to the Ocean View Motel, which was pretty much as he remembered it. The ocean was all he could hear when he stepped out of his car. He'd been ensconced in Manhattan for so many years he'd grown unaccustomed to the sound of the sea. Now the crashing waves, the almighty noise of them, the power and the salty spray, lifted his spirits a little as he crossed the parking lot.

A gray-haired man was tearing rotten planks from the short set of stairs that led inside. Dougal recognized him right away. Amos Ward, local handyman, a jack-of-all-trades. He and his wife Stella had been like family when Dougal was growing up. Amos had also once been Dougal's dad's best friend. But that had been before, as Stella put it, "Edward showed his true colors."

Amos clasped Dougal's hand warmly, asked how life was treating him. After a brief catch-up, he went back to work, applying his weight to the crowbar and prying away another piece of the disintegrating pine. "Come over to the house some night. I know Stella would love to see you."

"I'll do that." Dougal went around the corner and found a secondary door propped open with a cement block. Inside, a curly-haired blonde smiled from behind the desk. She was a year younger than him—he remembered her from school.

"Dougal Lachlan! Is that really you?" She bubbled on for a while about how long it had been since they'd seen one another. She caught him up on the major events of her life, including marriage to a guy he vaguely remembered from the football team.

"Me and Lance bought this motel last year. We've hired Amos to help us fix it up a little. Sorry for the mess."

Holly. Her name came to him mid-way through her stream of sentences.

"You must be here for your sister's wedding. How many nights will you be staying?"

"I'm not sure."

"That's okay. I'll take an imprint of your credit card and we'll settle up whenever you're ready to leave. License plate number?"

She filled out the paperwork efficiently, and then passed him a key.

"It's the nicest room. Amos just finished renovating the bathroom."

"Thanks." The brass key had the room number engraved on it. Not good for security reasons, but handy for the guest with a bad memory.

Holly looked at him expectantly, probably waiting for him to provide some details about *his* life. He just gave her a smile and a nod, then stepped outside. Checking the number on his key, again, he realized he'd been given the unit farthest from the office, which suited him just fine.

As he neared his room, a house down the beach caught his eye. The two-story home with a wrap-around porch had been white fourteen years ago. Now it was a bluish gray. It belonged to the Hammonds and he realized that Charlotte probably lived there alone now.

He wondered if she found it lonely. But then, she had Wade to keep her company. He had to give her credit for her taste in men. Unlike Kyle, Wade had rock-solid values. He was the sort of man who could sleep well at night. Hell, Kyle probably slept well, too, mainly because he was too much of a hound dog to worry about any harm he might have caused others.

Dougal guessed he was the only insomniac of the group.

* * *

After dropping off his belongings in his room, Dougal took stock and realized he was hungry. He still hadn't contacted his sister, but figured the encounter would go better if he had some food in his stomach. He was sure Jamie was going to berate him for not showing up for their mother's funeral. And while he knew he deserved it, he wasn't sure if he could handle seeing Jamie's disappointment and hurt face-to-face.

He'd have a few beers with his meal. *Then* he'd call Jamie.

It was a short walk to the Linger Longer, and Dougal grew hungrier with each step. But the moment he stepped in the door, heard the blaring nineties rock music, and saw the couple on the dance floor, he realized he should have ordered pizza to his room. His sister and her fiancé were here. His chest tightened at the glow on Jamie's face. God, she looked happy.

They made a striking, if mismatched couple. Kyle, blond, tall and lean was a total contrast to his petite, curvy, dark-complexioned sister.

Jamie had grown her hair long since he'd last seen her, on the trip to Hawaii that he'd organized as a treat to their mother shortly after her diagnosis. The longer hair emphasized her resemblance to their mom.

And hit him hard.

It was so hard to believe she was really gone.

And now he finally understood why he'd put off this trip for so long. Because until he'd actually come here, he'd been able to pretend, in some weird way, that his mother hadn't really died.

But she had.

And Dougal, the ever-disappointing son, hadn't paid his last respects.

But then, he hadn't been very respectful when she was living either. He remembered how ashamed he'd been when he'd seen her get all dolled up before heading out to the bar. Why couldn't she be respectable and boring like his friends' mothers? Why did she have to go out drinking and dancing, often not returning to the trailer until after dawn on Sunday morning?

"I work hard, Dougal," his mother would tell him. "I think I deserve a little fun on the weekend."

A little fun. Is that what you call sleeping around with all the men in town, Mom? He'd never actually said those words to her, but he was sure she had read the message in his eyes all too clearly.

Now he hated himself for being so bloody judgmental. His mother had been right. She'd deserved whatever fun she could find.

The music changed. The new song was soft and romantic. From the corner of his eye, he saw Kyle pull his sister in way too close.

He had to get out of here, before they saw him.

But just as he pivoted to leave, a young server stepped between him and the exit. She wore tight black jeans and an even tighter T-shirt with "Linger Longer" printed suggestively on her chest. She'd probably been in third grade when he'd left town.

So eyes off the merchandise buddy.

"Would you like a drink?"

"No, thanks. I'm not staying." He'd almost made it to the door, almost executed a clean escape, when a voice came to him above the barroom din.

"What the hell? Dougal, is that you?"

He turned slowly, realizing that if he'd wanted to plan the worst possible reunion with his sister, this was it.

He attempted a smile. "Hey there, Sis. Surprised?"

She just looked at him with a familiar, wounded expression. "Damn it, Dougal. You can't do this, you know. Just show up out of the blue…"

Tears began to form in her eyes, which was a bad sign. Some women grew soft and sentimental when they cried. Not his sister.

"Why didn't you call? Tell us you were coming? And why in blazes were you creeping out the door…as if you didn't want me to see you?"

He was damned now. Utterly damned. He didn't know what to say.

The music was still playing, but other than that, the bar had gone completely quiet. Everyone was watching the Lachlan family reunion, including, he suddenly noticed, Charlotte and Wade.

Since anything he said would only make the situation worse, Dougal left.

chapter five

Jamie couldn't believe her brother had come to town without telling her. And that he'd turned his back on her at the bar. She'd been too hurt to run after him and Kyle had agreed it would be better to just let him go.

Presumably Dougal was here for her wedding...so why sneak into town without so much as an email or a phone call?

Jamie pushed off with her feet against the wooden porch floor, sending the two-seater swing flying. The wind was cold tonight, but she didn't care. She couldn't feel the chilly air, only the hurt, and yes—the anger.

Damn it, what was Dougal's problem? He had such a chip on his shoulder and she had no idea what had put it there. Yes, they'd had a hard life when they were kids. Their mother had struggled, both with money and with men. But she had loved them, and done her best. She'd certainly deserved, at the minimum, to have her son show up for her funeral.

But Dougal—who was always quick to offer to fly them to New York for a visit, not seeming to understand, or care, how out of place they felt in that huge city—couldn't lower himself to return to Twisted Cedars to see his mom put to rest.

"Honey?" Kyle came out the front door holding two mugs of coffee. "You okay?"

His thoughtfulness touched her. "Not really," she said.

Kyle sank onto the seat next to her.

"I wonder where he's staying."

"Probably at the Ocean View," Kyle guessed.

Jamie took a sip of her coffee. "I hope he behaves

himself at our wedding."

"I'm still kind of surprised he showed up. You know I'm not his favorite person."

"I don't get that. You used to be such close friends."

"I guess."

"So what happened? Did you guys have a falling out?"

"No. Not really."

Kyle sounded uncomfortable. There was something he wasn't telling her. "What is it?"

"Look, I don't want to say anything against your brother. At one time we were friends. But as the years went by, he stopped acting like one. He resented my family's money. He resented the football scholarships I was offered. And he especially resented the fact that Daisy preferred me over him."

She wished she could believe her brother was a better man than that, but what Kyle said was ringing true. "I never knew my brother liked Daisy."

"He'd hardly tell his little sister, would he?"

Poor Dougal. But unrequited love was no excuse for his behavior. Or for resenting Kyle, just because he had the things that Dougal wanted.

"Well, you may not be high on my brother's list anymore, but you're *my* favorite person." She leaned toward the man she intended to marry, felt his arm settle heavily around her shoulders.

"You're sure about that?"

He had to be teasing. One thing Kyle did not lack was self-confidence. Anyway, he'd have to be a fool not to realize the appeal he had to the opposite sex.

"One hundred percent sure." She kissed the corner of his mouth, teasing him until he set down his coffee and gave her his full attention. The kiss, deep, warm, and thrilling, soon had her blood moving briskly through her body.

"Baby...how about climbing into bed with me?" Kyle's voice was husky and low.

"I'd love to—" She shivered as his hands slid down her

back, then to her hips. Her body wanted to respond, ached to let him hold her even tighter. "But you know I can't."

She had set a rule at the beginning of their relationship. His children were too young, and she did not feel comfortable spending the night at his house.

"Jamie..." He groaned. "You're killing me."

"Just one more week. Then I'll be in your bed every night."

It was a blissful prospect. Maybe she'd grown up as trailer trash, but, like the princess in all those stories she'd loved as a child, she'd found her prince.

* * *

Wade and Charlotte left the Linger Longer after their third game of pool. Charlotte felt unusually tense. Wade hadn't made any comment on the scene between Jamie and Dougal, but she knew it was on his mind, too.

"An interesting night." Wade leaned over the threshold of her front door to turn on the interior hall light.

"Poor Jamie. Why do you suppose her brother didn't call and let her know he was coming? And don't you think it's strange he dropped in at the library instead of going to see her, first?"

"You have to know Dougal. He seems careless, almost cruel sometimes with the things he does. The truth is, he tortures himself more than anyone else."

Yes, Charlotte thought, thinking of Dougal's eyes, how haunted they seemed. That fit. "Why is he like that? You can't blame his upbringing. Look at Jamie. The woman is always smiling."

Wade sighed. "Like everything in life...it's complicated." He kissed her. "You were quite the shark tonight. Next week, you'd better watch out. I plan on winning my twenty dollars back."

She had to smile, not daring to say, *Not if Jamie is in the bar, you won't.* The woman was bad for his concentration. "You go ahead and try, Wade."

He kissed her again, deeper, sweeter, then pulled away.

"I've got to go to court tomorrow."

She nodded, understanding he would want a good night sleep. Yet tonight she had such a restless yearning, she almost invited him in, anyway.

But he said "Goodnight" before she could get out the words. Knowing he would wait until he heard the deadbolt slide into position, she twisted the knob, even though she had every intention of going out again once he was gone.

She often went for a walk along the beach before bed. Oddly, it was the one place she always felt safe, though she knew Wade would try to talk her out of the habit if he knew about it. She'd grown up in this house and their proximity to the beach made it almost seem like 'hers' too. When she was a little girl she'd spent a lot of time with her dad out there. He'd craved the peace and solitude as much as she had.

Her mother was a different story. Though loving and kind, she seemed to feel they weren't making a connection unless they were talking.

And often, what they talked about was Daisy. It had bothered her mother so much that her daughters weren't close. When Daisy refused to play with Charlotte or made cutting remarks to her little sister, Virginia Hammond would assure Charlotte that her sister loved her. She was just at a 'difficult age.'

Unfortunately Daisy had stayed at that difficult stage for a long time. But Charlotte couldn't help wondering, if she had stayed in Twisted Cedars, would they eventually have become close? She liked to believe so. Hopefully, one day, Daisy would come back and they'd have a chance at the sort of relationship their mother had wanted for them.

Charlotte pulled aside the curtain and watched as Wade backed out of the driveway. Once his tail lights had receded up the hill toward the town, she grabbed a light jacket and headed for the sandy path that led to the beach.

The tide was out leaving a broad expanse of rocky beach for her late night stroll. The half-moon in a clear sky provided plenty of light for her to pick her way around the larger rocks and pieces of driftwood.

To her left she could see the hall light shining from inside her house. Next to that, separated by a grove of trees, then a fence, was the motel. Only a few of the units had lights on at this late hour, including the one closest to her property. She wondered if one of those lights was Dougal's. He didn't strike her as the sort of person who went to bed early.

She wondered how he'd felt after the scene in the Linger Longer. He'd looked so miserable when he'd left, like a dog that had been kicked in the head. But really, it was his own fault. Dropping out of his sister's life the way he had, then appearing without so much as a warning phone call.

What could he have been thinking?

Wade had described Dougal as a tortured soul. The description was a good one. Yet, she'd felt an odd connection with him today at the library. She'd felt complimented that he'd trusted her with the content of those emails.

She wondered if he would be back. First thing tomorrow morning she'd put through that request to the *East Oregonian*, just in case he was.

It was kind of fun, helping an author—a New York Times Bestselling Author no less—with his research. And what a story—four librarians murdered back in the 70's. Had her Aunt Shirley been aware of the crimes?

If so, had she been afraid?

Did people who were contemplating suicide worry about their safety? Because that was how her aunt had died. She'd taken her own life. It had been in 1975, so only a few years after the two murders Dougal had told her about.

Charlotte felt a sudden chill at the possibility her aunt's death could be connected to the cases Dougal was investigating. No. The timing had to be coincidence.

A hunk of gnarled driftwood distracted her. She picked up the piece, brushed away the sand. Turning it this way, then the other, she thought she saw potential. This would look nice in the flower beds lining the driveway. Yes, she would keep this one.

She straightened, the piece of wood still in her hand, then froze. A moment ago she'd been alone. But now, about fifty yards ahead of her, she could see a man's silhouette.

She felt a shock of adrenaline, combined with a vague sense of fear. At this time of night she rarely encountered anyone on the beach. Local teenagers tended to congregate on the beaches to the north. And most tourists were fast asleep by now.

But here was someone, moving in her direction. He was tall and broad shouldered, and after a quick glance back at the motel, she realized he could be only one person.

At just the moment that her fear left her, Dougal spotted her, too. He stopped, hands hanging lightly by his sides. For a long moment they stood that way, neither one of them giving any overt sign of acknowledgement.

Charlotte was reminded of Wuthering Heights, of the unforgettable Heathcliff. So much anger and so much pain, it fairly radiated off the man. Guessing that Dougal—like her—had come out here to be alone, she turned back, hurrying across the sand to the relative comfort of her home.

chapter six

dougal had expected to have the beach to himself, but when he saw Charlotte Hammond, he wasn't surprised. He'd already figured she might be a woman who enjoyed her solitude. When she turned away from him, he did the same.

He walked for another hour in the opposite direction, and by the time he let himself into his room he was exhausted. It had been a long day. The drive from Roseburg. The second email from Librarianmomma. The confrontation at the Linger Longer, which he'd left without getting any dinner.

Despite his fatigue, he couldn't fall sleep for a very long time. And when he did, he dreamed of the woman in the second email, Mari Beamish. In his dream, he was there, as it happened. He saw the slip of silk slide around her neck, felt it tighten… heard her gasp.

Right before she lost consciousness, she managed to look over her shoulder, toward her attacker, and he was shocked to see Charlotte Hammond's features, tight with fear and panic. Her wide gray eyes looked accusingly...at him. Because he was the attacker, the one with the scarf, the man who had murdered both women.

* * *

No!

Dougal jerked up from the lumpy motel-room pillow. He could tell by the quantity of light in his room that he'd slept late.

He refused to think about the nightmare that had awoken him. Refused to speculate on what it might mean. He had to see his sister as soon as possible and try to right what had gone so terribly wrong.

Jamie would already be at work at Howard & Mason. It had surprised him that his dreamy sister had gone for a career as a CPA. Her success there proved she had a strong logical side to her personality. He hoped to appeal to that today when he tried to talk her out of the wedding.

He got up, brushed his teeth, and showered, but no amount of water could make his head stop pounding, or clear away the grit he could feel behind his eyes. As he dressed, he sipped at coffee he'd made in the machine provided in his unit, using the contents of a foil pouch that promised him a smooth Colombian roast, but fell short in the delivery.

It was quarter to ten when he finally grabbed his laptop case and left the motel. The sky was clear blue again today, but a mist hung over the shore. But God, the air tasted good. Thick and salty. He crossed the highway, passed by the Ranger Station, then turned onto Driftwood Lane without seeing a soul. He'd pass the time before Jamie's lunch break by doing a little research.

Charlotte was sitting at the front desk of the library when he walked in. He inhaled the comforting aroma of old books. Felt the muscles in his shoulders and neck relax.

"Hi, Dougal. I've just received a long fax from the Pendleton Library. They've sent a copy of Mari Beamish's obituary for you and the main articles that were published about her murder."

Right down to business. No mention of seeing him on the beach last night. Nor about the scene at the Linger Longer yesterday. He appreciated her discretion.

"Thank you."

She wore another gray skirt and matching sweater, both cut so conservatively, she could have time-travelled from the fifties. Did she downplay her looks on purpose?

He found a table in the back corner and settled in to read. A few people came and went. Besides Charlotte, there was another woman working at the library. Older, almost retirement age, he would guess. Not very friendly.

At eleven o'clock, Charlotte asked him how things were going.

"It's been interesting. The facts, and the lack of success with the investigation, are disturbingly similar to Elva Mae's homicide. But I was wondering if I could take a look at the archives for the *Curry County Reporter*? While I'm here I might as well dig into those—see if they mention anything about the murders."

"Current issues are on microfiche, but if you want to go back to the seventies, we'll need to reference originals." Charlotte caught the eye of the older woman, who was re-shelving books in a quiet, methodical manner.

"Abigail, I'm going to show Dougal the archives in the basement. Keep an eye on things, okay?"

"Of course."

Dougal followed Charlotte downstairs into the windowless basement. The space was well lit, painted a gleaming cream color and filled with rows of shelving units.

"Smells like paint."

"Amos just finished building us some extra shelving units. We figured we might as well have the place painted at the same time." She peered at the labels on one of the bookcases. "Just around this corner."

As he followed, he was suddenly reminded of his dream. The basement setting had been similar to this one, only darker. With sudden insight, it occurred to him that both Elva Mae and Mari could have been attacked from the rear while looking for reference materials, just as Charlotte was doing right now.

Dougal clenched his hands, relaxed, and then balled them again. What had the murderer been thinking as he lured the helpless women to their deaths? Had he been excited? Angry? Calm and collected?

"Here they are." Charlotte indicated a shelving unit filled with back issues of the local paper. "Everything you need should be in this box."

She wouldn't sound so cheerful if she knew what he'd

just been thinking. Dougal forced a smile. He scared himself sometimes with his crazy thoughts. "Great." As he grabbed the cardboard container, he noticed another set of boxes on the adjacent shelving unit. "*Oregon Library Association*," he read. "What's in there?"

"Quarterly publications from our state library association. My Aunt was the president of the board for a number of years. Our collection of newsletters dates back to that time."

"Hm. Mind if I take a look through these, as well?"

"Help yourself. But none of this reference material can leave the premises."

He nodded, grabbed a second box and followed Charlotte up the stairs. On the way he asked, "So how long have you and Wade been seeing each other?"

She hesitated. "About six months."

"Is it serious?"

She seemed surprised he would ask that. He was surprised, too.

"I-I'm not sure."

He set the boxes on the table by his laptop. It was just past twelve. "Okay if I leave these here for an hour or so? I think it's time I had a little talk with my sister."

chapter seven

Jamie stared at the Excel spreadsheet on her computer screen. Two years ago she'd graduated to her own office at Howard & Mason and she loved it. She always worked best when it was quiet, but this morning, even with her door closed, she couldn't concentrate. Damn that brother of hers. She'd never been able to understand him. Mom said Dougal took after their father, as if that explained everything. Maybe it did, but Jamie wouldn't know since she'd never met her dad. According to her Mom, he had left before she was born, before he even knew his wife was pregnant again. Even though everyone was always telling her she was better off without him, she couldn't help wondering if things would have worked out differently if he'd known about her. Maybe he would have tried harder to reform. Somehow won her mother back, and been a better man.

It would have made a big difference to have had a father. Not just for her, but especially for Dougal.

She sighed. She needed to focus on her work, not stew about her personal life, but it was difficult. Besides worrying about Dougal—and trying to figure out why he was such an idiot—there was the wedding. Her mother had brought home discarded magazines from the homes she cleaned, and Jamie had mooned over the occasional Bride issues that came her way. She loved the pretty dresses, the flowers, the lovely place settings. Of course what really mattered was becoming Kyle's wife. But planning this wedding had been a thrill.

Tonight was the final fitting at Stella's for her bridal gown and Cory's flower girl dress. Then on Saturday, Stella and a few friends were taking her out on the town. Jamie grabbed her to-do list and added 'phone florist' to order a boutonniere for her brother. She also needed to let the caterer know they'd need an extra place setting for the dinner. Annoying to have to make these last minute adjustments. But even though she was currently pissed off with her brother, she was glad he'd be available to walk her down the aisle.

Jamie tried again to concentrate on the trial balance in front of her. Instead, her mind drifted, this time to Kyle's suggestion she quit her job. It had been sweet of him to make the offer, but she loved her work. Not only that, she was used to earning her own money and couldn't imagine being dependent on someone else in that way.

At noon, Jamie took the lunch she'd packed that morning, and decided to eat outside to enjoy the beautiful day. As she left her office, she waved at Bonny who was busy talking on the phone at the reception desk. Heading for the beach, she crossed the highway, then passed the Tourist Information Office. Several vehicles were parked in the lot today and she noted the different license plates as she walked by: Missouri, British Columbia, Washington.

Inside the bureau a map of the world was mounted on the wall—visitors were encouraged to stick pins on their home states or countries. Jamie loved the idea that her small town could draw visitors from all over the world, from as far away as the Middle East, and Australia. But she had little urge to travel. This was her place, and she'd always known it.

Jamie left the path, shoes now sinking into the dunes. The weather was perfect—she hoped it would hold until next weekend. So often spring and even summer days on the coast of Oregon were windy, cool and damp, but she still wouldn't consider living anywhere else.

She stepped over a clump of bull kelp to reach a large chunk of driftwood, molded by water and time into the perfect perch for sitting and enjoying the view. Once settled she scanned the ocean, on the look-out for gray whales, even though it was too early in the season. A cormorant swooped past her, heading for the sea stacks that rose majestically through the water to her left.

"Jamie?"

Dougal's voice. Her spine stiffened. She didn't turn around, just waited for him to get closer. A few seconds later, her brother joined her on the log, stretching out his long legs and planting his heels in the sand.

He put a hand on her shoulder.

"I'm sorry."

She let the apology sit between them for a while. It sounded good. And sincere. Finally, she sighed.

"I wish to hell I could understand you, Dougal."

"I think you're lucky you can't."

Dougal always said the most cryptic things. She knew better than to ask him what he meant. He never explained himself. Still, she found herself returning to the one thing she could never quite forgive him for.

"I can't believe you're here now when you wouldn't come for Mom's funeral."

She glanced at him, saw his jaw grow firm.

"I wanted to remember her the way she was in Maui."

That had been Dougal's reaction to the news that their mother was dying. He'd sent the two of them tickets to Hawaii, where he'd joined them for a week in a luxury condo in Kaanapoli. It had been a lovely escape from reality, but in the end, it was Jamie who had returned to Twisted Cedars to look after their mother in the final stages of her disease, Jamie who had dealt with the doctor's appointments and the respite center, Jamie who had arranged the funeral and settled the estate.

"Maybe I would have liked to remember her that way, too."

Dougal lowered his head. "I—You're right. It wasn't fair. I guess I owe you an apology for that, too."

It was never satisfying giving her brother a hard time. No one could be harder on him, than he was on himself. Jamie let out a long breath and gave him a closer look. He'd aged in the two years since she'd seen him last, and he was thinner, too. She knew his lifestyle was crap. He never ate properly or got enough sleep. Chances were he was drinking too much, as well.

"You look like shit."

That elicited a smile. "Gee, thanks, Sis."

"I guess I should thank you for at least showing up for my wedding. Though a little warning would have been nice."

"About your wedding..."

Her back tensed again at the tone of his voice. She studied his face. Seeing his miserable expression, her heart grew heavy.

"Are you sure you're doing the right thing? Marrying Kyle?"

She stared at him, dumbfounded. "Seriously?"

He didn't flinch from her gaze. "Damn it, Dougal. My wedding is in one week. Of course I'm sure. Why would you even ask me something like that?"

"I know you don't want to hear this. But Kyle is not the great guy he seems to be."

"You have a lot of nerve." Her half-eaten sandwich fell to the ground as she scrambled to her feet. Glaring down at her brother, she wondered when he would ever be there for her. Supportive. Helpful. Caring.

The way a real brother ought to be.

"And I thought you were here to walk me down the aisle."

He blinked. "I'm telling you, Kyle is not a man you can trust."

"You haven't seen him in fourteen years and you think you know him better than I do?" Kyle was right. Her brother was insanely jealous. How else to explain this strange attack?

"He doesn't treat women well, Jamie. He used to cheat on Daisy all the time when we were in high school."

He was going way too far, now. "Don't talk to me about Daisy. She is long gone from here. And you can't possibly paint Kyle as the bad guy in that. Kyle was a *saint* with Daisy. She went totally crazy after the twins were born. Kyle did everything he could to help her. He cared for the kids, did all the cooking, took Daisy to a bunch of doctors and followed all of their advice. And in the end, what did she do? She left him. And her kids, too. Do you know that she never calls or writes? Her *own kids*, Dougal. She hasn't seen Chester or Cory since they were toddlers."

"Maybe there's more to that story than you know."

"Give me a break. You haven't lived here. I have. Kyle is a terrific father and I love him."

Her brother let his hands drop. He looked defeated, suddenly.

She had an urge to tell him not to worry, she was going to be fine. But she was still too angry with him for that. Just two days ago she had been happy. Blissfully, joyfully, innocently happy. And now, even though nothing had changed, nothing real anyway, she knew she wasn't ever going to get back that feeling.

* * *

Charlotte sat at her desk while eating her chicken salad sandwich. She never went out for lunch, because they didn't have enough staff. Twisted Cedars Library had been running on a shoe-string budget ever since its inception. Sometimes she dreamed about what she could do for the community if she only had more resources.

But whenever she went to the board with her ideas, they were never able to see past the bottom line.

Charlotte was partway through her sandwich, when thirteen-year-old Laila Gill came in with a backpack full of books. Laila never dropped her books into the return chute out on the street. She always delivered them personally to Charlotte, thanked her politely, and then asked for more.

Laila was probably the library's best customer. The girl reminded Charlotte of herself as a young teenager. Books had been her lifeline then, as she suspected they were for Laila.

Charlotte put her hand on a stack she'd been collecting since Laila's last visit. "I managed to find the next three in the series. Want to look at them?"

"I'll just take them all." Laila pulled out her library card, which, despite being laminated, was tattered at the corners.

Charlotte was helping Laila pile the books into her pack, when Dougal returned from his break. She wondered how his conversation with his sister had gone. Not well, judging by Dougal's scowl.

Charlotte slipped the hardcover of *Smokescreen* into Laila's pack. "See you soon, honey. Say hi to your mom for me."

The words were for Laila, but her eyes were on Dougal. He brought a certain energy to the library. It was exciting having a real, published author doing his research here. Was it crazy of her to hope he might decide to move back home and do all his writing from Twisted Cedars? An author could live anywhere, after all. And she would find it so interesting to help him with his research.

He gave her a nod before returning to the table where he'd left copies of the local paper and the library quarterlies.

An hour later, she couldn't resist asking him how things were going.

"Well," he said. "Can I ask you a question?"

"Sure." She slipped into the chair next to his.

"Tell me more about your Aunt Shirley."

This was the last subject she'd expected him to bring up. "What do you mean? About her involvement with the library?"

"Everything. Her work life. Her personal life." His dark eyes were intense as he leaned closer. "Let's start with this— was she married?"

"No. She lived with my parents for a while, and then moved to a little cottage off the Old Forestry Road. Maybe you've seen it. Wade calls it the Librarian Cottage. He checks on it from time to time. It's about five miles from town. My father didn't like her being so isolated, but she said it suited her."

"I do remember that place. We used to party there sometimes."

"So Daisy had a key? I always wondered if she had. I noticed one was missing when I was settling my parents' affairs."

"Yeah. She and Kyle used to go there a lot, as well. Just the two of them."

"Oh."

"So that's where your aunt lived? On her own?"

"Yes. Until she...died."

"Do you know the circumstances of her death?"

Last night her mind had gone to just this subject. She thought back to a family gathering when she was pre-school age. Her sister had invited her into her bedroom—a rare occurrence—then told her she was old enough to know the family secret.

"What is it?" Charlotte had been beside herself with curiosity.

"Aunt Shirley killed herself. But we aren't supposed to tell anyone."

Not until she was much older, an adult, had Charlotte confirmed the facts with her mother. Not that her mother had been able to explain much. Apparently the suicide had come as a complete shock to the family.

Charlotte couldn't help but feel defensive. "Why all these questions about my aunt?"

"Shirley Hammond was listed as a board member and president in the OLA Quarterly from 1972 until 1976. Suddenly in 1977 there was no mention of her. Most former board members get a special write up if they retire or pass away. Which made me wonder if there was something— unusual—about the way your aunt died."

"If you're thinking my aunt was strangled like those other cases you're investigating, I can assure you that was not the case."

Dougal looked at her steadily for a long time. Then he

asked another question she wasn't expecting. "What happened to your aunt's cottage? Did your family sell it?"

"No. We still own it." Since her parents' death, Charlotte managed all of the family's assets, but she never thought of them as hers. Her parents had been quite wealthy and if—when—her sister returned, Charlotte would be all too happy to relinquish Daisy's share of the inheritance. In the meantime, it was her responsibility to pay the property taxes for the cabin. Occasionally she drove by to reassure herself the building was still standing, but she never went inside.

Too spooky.

"Do you rent it out?"

"We never have. Who would want it?" The little A-frame was small, not worth much, tucked so deep into the forest that it could hardly be seen from the road.

Dougal leaned his elbows on her desk. "Would you *consider* renting it out?"

"I suppose. But it's very isolated."

"Which makes it perfect for me. I've been thinking about staying in Twisted Cedars to continue my research."

It was what she'd hoped for earlier, but suddenly she wasn't so sure. Dougal wasn't just probing into a long forgotten mystery. He was digging into *her* family history, which was not comfortable territory, at all. "I'm not sure the cottage is even habitable."

"I'm not fussy. And it would be better than staying at the motel."

He had other options. Like the home where he'd grown up. After the wedding, Jamie would be moving in with Kyle and the trailer would be vacant.

"I could show you the cottage after work. If you still want the place after you see it, I'd have to get the electricity turned back on. There's a well and septic tank—not sure what shape they'll be in after all these years."

"I can get all that sorted out."

She frowned, trying to imagine what the place would

look like inside after being vacant for so long. "We'll also need to book a cleaner."

"Is Stella Ward still working?"

"Yes. You remember her?"

He paused a second then said, "She and my mother were partners."

"Of course." Charlotte had forgotten Dougal's mother had cleaned houses for a living. In fact, Kate Lachlan had cleaned for her parents, for decades.

"How about we grab a bite after you've closed the library, then head out to the cottage to take a look around?"

It was a casual suggestion, and Dougal knew she was seeing Wade. But Charlotte still felt a little excited, and a little guilty, as she accepted.

chapter eight

When Dougal and Jamie were kids, they spent a lot of time at Stella and Ward Amos's house. Stella had been his mom's partner and best friend, and the Amos's were like family. Now, standing by their front door, Dougal was struck by how small the three-bedroom bungalow seemed. He knocked, and heard a shuffling sound from inside. After what seemed like a long time, Stella opened the door.

She looked older, grayer, and she peered at him with first suspicion, and then dread.

"Ed?"

Hearing his father's name hit Dougal like a slap. Involuntarily he took a step backward, but Stella was already correcting herself.

"Oh for heaven's sake, you must think I'm losing my mind. Of course your father must be in his sixties by now. You've just grown to look so much like him. Come in Dougal, come in. It's so nice to see you."

"Hi, Stella. How are you?" He hated that he sounded stiff and polite, like a stranger. But her reference to his father had really unnerved him.

"I'm just great, Dougal. Though my arthritis is slowing me down, I can't deny. And how about you? I see your books every time I go shopping in the city. Bestsellers now, aren't they?"

She'd been leading him to the kitchen as they talked, every now and then throwing him curious looks.

"I've had some good luck with my writing," he allowed.

She chuckled. "Your humility is *not* something you inherited from your father. Tell me, are you hungry? I was just about to make an egg and some toast."

"You go ahead. I'm eating later." As Stella puttered around the kitchen, Dougal checked out the view to the backyard.

"You still have the tree house."

She smiled, opened the fridge, pulled out two beers and handed him one. "Amos keeps saying he's going to tear it down, but he never does."

Amos had often played with them out in that yard. He'd been the one to show Dougal how to throw a football, properly. How to fish and ride a bike. Dougal remembered his mom telling them that Stella and Amos had been unable to have children of their own. It was too bad. They would have made great parents.

"I suppose you're in town for Jamie's wedding?"

He avoided the question by countering it. "What do you think of Kyle?"

"I clean his house every second week, but I don't see that much of him. I come when he's at work and the kids are at school. I have a key."

"Mom used to clean for Mr. and Mrs. Quinpool when I was a kid. She didn't care for them much. *Not like the Hammonds*, she used to tell me. *Now those people have class.*" He straddled a chair and folded his arms on the table. "I don't think she'd be happy about Jamie marrying Kyle."

"A lot of people around here would say he's a great catch. Myself, I share your reservations. But, like your mother, Jamie has a stubborn streak. If she thinks she loves Kyle, then that's it."

"You're smarter than I am, Stella. I've been in town about twenty-four hours and already I've managed to have two fights with my sister."

"You better patch things up. She's your only family now."

He looked down at the table. "Did Mom suffer a lot?"

"The doctors did as much as they could for her pain. And she was never alone. Jamie and I kept a twenty-four hour watch for the last few days."

He should have been there. Stella didn't say it, but of course she was thinking it.

"I still have trouble believing she's gone, sometimes. Your mother was so vibrant. I have to say, I miss her terribly."

Dougal's gaze was still on the table. "Thank you for being there for her."

"She was my friend even longer than she was your mother," Stella pointed out.

Dougal glanced around the kitchen. "We had a lot of great meals here when we were kids."

"I used to enjoy cooking back then. Now I don't bother, much. Amos eats mostly at the pub, anyway." She turned her back to him, added an egg to the frying pan.

Was something wrong between the two of them? "I saw Amos at the Ocean View. He was fixing the front steps."

She shrugged. "He keeps busy enough. But what's new with you? Any chance you'll be having your own wedding one day soon?"

"Me? No way."

"You sound pretty sure about that." She turned from the stove to look at him. "The right partner could be a real blessing, son. Trust me, when you get to be my age, being alone isn't that much fun."

Again he wondered about her and Amos. "I'm just not the marrying kind."

"I hope you're not saying that because of your father. You may look like him. Doesn't mean you aren't your own man."

He nodded, discounting her words, even as he pretended to agree. Stella could say things like that because she didn't know what it was like to be him. The darkness and the demons he lived with. The nightmares and weird twisted places his imagination always led him. He might channel those things into stories now...but maybe the day would come when they would spill out into real life. He didn't want to have a wife or children if that happened.

"Do you ever hear from your father?"

Dougal grew cautious. "I used to get the occasional letter or email when he was in prison."

"He's out now, isn't he?" She made it sound like a casual question. But he could tell she was as tense as he was.

"Last March. He sent a letter through my publisher. Wanted to see me. I tore it up."

"You don't want to talk to him?"

"Don't see the point."

"Right." She removed the bread from the toaster and buttered it. "He still doesn't know about Jamie, does he?"

"Not from me he doesn't."

"That's good."

"Do you think he would hurt Jamie if he knew about her?"

"Not physically, no. I'm more worried that your sister, with her soft heart and all, would try to bring him into the family fold, and end up being disappointed. That man just was never meant to be a father." She turned her focus back to Dougal. "How long are you in town for? Just the wedding?"

"Longer. I'm considering renting a cottage from Charlotte Hammond. She's helping me with some research for my next book."

Stella frowned. "Are you talking about the Librarian Cottage?"

"You know the place?"

"If it's the one I'm thinking of. About five miles east of town, on the Old Forestry Road?"

He nodded.

"Dougal, that house hasn't been lived in for decades. It's got to be a big mess."

"Charlotte already warned me. Which reminds me, I wanted to ask if you had time to clean it for me. I'd pay extra since it's been unused for so long."

Stella hesitated. "My knees are acting up pretty bad these days and just my regular jobs are all I can handle. But when your mom got too sick to work, I advertised for a new partner. Her name is Liz Brooks. Maybe she can help you."

Stella pulled Liz's business card from a drawer. "Here's her number."

"Thanks." He glanced at the card, then pocketed it. "Do you remember much about Shirley Hammond? She used to live at that cottage in the seventies."

Stella placed the cooked egg on her plate, along with two slices of toast, then sat down. She didn't touch the food though. Just sighed. "Shirley was our librarian back in the sixties and seventies. She was a lovely woman. But very quiet."

"I understand she died young. But how?"

Stella's face paled. "She hung herself in the basement of the library. Everyone was shocked, of course. Saying what a waste, and things like that. She never left a note for her family."

Charlotte's defensive reaction to his questions about Shirley made sense now. Strange how suicide still seemed to carry a stigma. But he was surprised by the lack of a note. "Kind of ironic that a women who valued the written word didn't leave any of her own behind."

"I never thought of it that way, but that's a good point. Why are you asking about Shirley, anyway?"

"Just curious. That's all."

She picked up her fork. "Sure you don't want any?"

"Thanks, but I'm eating later. You go ahead."

"I feel a little rude eating in front of a guest, but your sister and Cory are coming for a dress fitting in about fifteen minutes. And I haven't eaten for hours."

He recalled Stella had worked part time as a seamstress. "So you're making Jamie's wedding dress?"

"Made, not making. The wedding is in just one week, you know."

He knew, unfortunately. "I should go. Let you eat in

peace."

He definitely didn't want to be here when Jamie arrived.

* * *

After work, Jamie went home to grab a quick bite before the dress fitting. It only took five minutes in the cozy trailer to put together a grilled cheese sandwich. While she was excited about making a new life with Kyle and his children, she was sad about leaving this place. If her mom was still alive, it wouldn't be so hard. But this trailer was so steeped in memories, it was going to be difficult to say goodbye.

When she finished her sandwich, Jamie headed to Kyle's to pick up Cory. The little girl was waiting for her on the porch—she'd lined up four plastic lawn chairs and was hopping from the porch swing to each of the chairs without touching the floor. Jamie had played games like that as a child, too. *The porch is an ocean, teeming with sharks. You have to jump from one island to the other without falling or the sharks will eat you.*

Jamie imagined a pretty set of wicker furniture replacing the plastic chairs one day. And two big urns of flowers flanking the door. Geraniums. Her mom had always loved geraniums.

"Hey, you," she called out to the little girl. "Ready to pick up our dresses?" They'd already gone through several sets of measurements and fittings—hopefully everything would be perfect today.

"I'm ready, Jamie!" Cory hopped from a chair to the top rung of the stairs, grasping the banister, then throwing one leg over and gliding to the lawn.

"Whoa, careful girl. You don't want to be walking down the aisle in crutches."

Cory looked appalled at that possibility. Jamie was pretty sure that the little girl was looking forward to the wedding just as much as she and Kyle were.

"I'll be careful," she promised solemnly.

"It's okay." Jamie smiled, and held out her hand. "Is

your dad—"

Before she could finish, Kyle appeared at the door, dish towel in hand. Jamie felt the usual rush of love at the sight of him. He took such good care of his children. She wished Dougal could see him now, as he smiled and waved them off. He'd realize how crazy his warning had been.

Stella Ward's house was just six blocks from Kyle's. Jamie drove the familiar streets slowly. The weather was warm and lots of residents were sitting on their porches, or watering their gardens. She waved to everyone she recognized.

Beside her, Cory was quiet, sitting on her hands, her blue eyes huge in her pale face. When Jamie glanced at her, she discovered the young girl staring at her anxiously.

"Is something wrong, Cory?"

"No. Everything's perfect."

Jamie didn't believe that. Kyle's children were often on edge around her and she had no idea why.

She turned onto Stella's block, then frowned at the sight of Dougal leaving Stella's house. He didn't notice her car as she pulled to a stop by an eight-foot tall cedar hedge. He just glanced at his watch, got in his SUV and took off in the opposite direction, toward Driftwood Lane.

She wondered what he'd been doing here until she realized, of course he would visit Stella—she was the closest he had to family in Twisted Cedars now.

Except for her.

And she hadn't exactly made him feel welcome, had she?

Suddenly the throbbing heat of her self-righteous anger dissipated, leaving her hollow inside. Dougal seemed so alone. So unhappy. She was reminded of how depressed she'd been in the first months after Mom died. She still missed her mother, sometimes with a physical force that could snatch away her breath. But having let go of the worst of her grieving meant she could recognize it when she saw it in others.

"Who is that man?" Cory asked.

"He's my brother. I guess he didn't see me."

"Is he coming to the wedding, after all?"

Cory must have heard her father predict that he wouldn't. "I'm not sure," She made herself smile. "But speaking of the wedding, shouldn't we go inside and try on our dresses?"

That was all the encouragement Cory needed. Quickly she unsnapped her seatbelt and jumped out of the car, running so she could be the first to knock on the door.

It turned out that the dresses fit perfectly. While Cory was in the bedroom, changing back into her regular clothes, Stella said quietly. "You just missed your brother. He popped in to say hello."

"I saw him leaving."

"Did you two make peace?"

So Dougal had told Stella they had argued. "I was still in my car. He didn't notice me. He seemed preoccupied."

"Dougal always did spend too much time living inside his head. I guess that's what makes him such a good writer."

"Have you read his books?"

Stella nodded. "Haven't you?" As she zipped a fabric bag over Cory's dress, Jamie did the same with her gown.

"Yes. But if he wasn't my brother, I wouldn't. They're pretty dark."

"He says he's working on a new one. He's planning on renting the Hammond cottage on the Old Forestry Road and writing it here."

"Really?" Maybe he hadn't come to town for her wedding, after all. Maybe it had been about his book all along. She wondered what grisly serial murderer he was writing about this time. "Why would he want to rent the Hammond cottage? It's five miles from town and he could have the trailer for free."

"Knowing Dougal, I'd say he prefers the isolation."

Or maybe he still hadn't gotten over the humiliation of growing up in a trailer park. Jamie frowned, her annoyance at her brother mounting again. "I guess he must be rich now. He can afford to stay wherever he wants."

"Hm," Stella said noncommittally as she put away her measuring tape. Her sewing room, like the rest of her home, was meticulously clean and organized. "Has he talked to you about his new book? He had some questions about Shirley Hammond, the old town librarian. I was wondering if she had anything to do with the reasons he's planning to stay."

"All we've talked about so far is my wedding—which he disapproves of, by the way."

"He probably feels it's his role to protect you. Especially now that your mother's gone."

"Yeah. Maybe." But protect her from what? He couldn't seriously think Kyle would hurt her. She didn't want to think ill of her brother, but it was almost as if he'd come back just to stir up trouble.

chapter nine

now that she was in the midst of it, Charlotte wondered why she'd felt guilty about having dinner with Dougal. He'd barely spoken to her since they'd met at Doris's Fish Shack on the wharf. And since their meals had been served, he hadn't looked up from his plate.

She flaked off a piece of her trout. The food was delicious and fresh, as usual. Too bad she couldn't enjoy it.

She'd canceled her usual Friday plans with Wade for this. She'd called him earlier, and as she'd expected, he hadn't been upset. "Having a busy day?" she'd asked.

"Oh, you know, the usual excitement. Just finished approving a new pump grinder for the jail sewer system."

"Who knew a sheriff's job was so glamorous?"

He'd chuckled. "How about you? Anything earth-shattering happen at the library?"

She'd had to take a deep breath. "Not quite earth-shattering, but interesting. I've been helping Dougal Lachlan with the research for his new book."

"Really?"

"He's planning to write it here, in Twisted Cedars, so he's looking for a place to rent. He's asked to see the Librarian Cottage. In fact, he wants me to show it to him tonight. Would you mind?"

"Not at all. Do you want to grab a bite, first?"

"Actually Dougal suggested stopping at the Fish Shack on our way out of town..."

Wade had been silent a moment, digesting all that. "Hope he doesn't go running when he sees how dilapidated the old place is."

"I'll let you know how it goes," she'd promised, ringing

off, and feeling marginally less guilty about spending her evening with another man.

Now all she felt was a growing sense of resentment.

"We might as well have eaten separately if you were planning to be silent for the entire meal."

Dougal finally looked at her. "Sorry. I'm not used to having company when I eat."

She didn't know if she could believe that. He lived in New York City, after all. "You must go out to restaurants with your friends."

"You're presuming I have any."

"You don't?"

He sighed. "I'm a solitary sort. When I go out, it's usually to a bar. Noisy places bars. Not much conversation required."

"Required for what?"

His eyebrows went up. He looked amused. "A little action."

Of course. Though she could feel her cheeks warming, she forced herself to keep meeting his gaze. "Don't you have to talk to these women in the morning?"

"Not if I can help it."

Her cheeks burned hotter. She wondered what it would be like to meet someone like Dougal in a bar, to go home with him and have sex with him. One thing she was pretty sure about—the sex would not be comfortable and sweet, the way it was with Wade.

"Isn't it awkward, having sex with someone you've only just met?" She didn't know where she was finding the nerve to have this conversation. But at least she was no longer feeling bored and neglected.

"That's what the alcohol is for." Dougal touched her hand. "You're pretty innocent for a woman your age, aren't you?"

"Not so innocent. It's just—things like that don't happen to me at the Linger Longer."

"Maybe if you lingered just a little longer, they would."

His words weren't meant to be flirtatious...or were they? The heat she'd felt in her face turned into a different kind of hot, and she found herself imagining Dougal touching more than her hand. Maybe her knee, under the table.

She forced another bite of the trout into her mouth. But oddly, now that she'd finally engaged Dougal in a conversation, she was no longer interested in food.

* * *

After dinner they got into Dougal's car and Charlotte gave instructions to the cottage. He asked her questions about the place, while keeping his eyes on the road. Had she considered how much rent she was going to charge? What about utilities? And a damage deposit?

Charlotte replied, giving little thought to her answers. She felt...flustered. A little embarrassed at having initiated such an intimate conversation earlier. And a little aroused, too. Why should dark, moody Dougal Lachlan have this effect on her?

The man was such a puzzle.

After practically flirting with her in the restaurant, he was now distant again, frowning as they entered deeper into the forest. Thanks to the long summer days, it wasn't yet dark, and she was glad of that as she kept on the lookout for the forestry road. The sign was small and easy to miss.

"The turn is up ahead."

He slowed, not bothering with the turn signal since they hadn't passed a single car since they'd left town.

It was another two miles down the forestry road before they reached the cottage. The cedar A-frame was tucked into the woods, and as soon as she stepped from the car, Charlotte felt a chill.

"You have the key?" Dougal asked.

She passed it to him. He seemed happier now that they were here, almost excited as he fitted the old brass key into the lock and opened the door. She tried to follow but he firmly held her back.

"Let me go first. Just in case."

"In case of what?"

"Who knows what critters might have taken refuge in here over the years."

She cringed, then nodded and let him go.

After a few moments, he gave the all clear. He'd turned on the switch for the main light and she was relieved when it went on, since she'd only called to have services renewed that afternoon. The inside of the place wasn't nearly as dirty as she'd expected. The furniture had been covered with old sheets which held a layer of grime, and sure there were some cobwebs in the corners, but all-in-all it wasn't bad.

Dougal took a few steps forward toward the kitchen, setting dust motes dancing in the air. "It's just like I remember it."

"It's pretty dark in here. Even with the lights on."

"The windows need cleaning."

She sneezed. "And it's awfully small."

"You should see my apartment."

The chances of her ever being in New York City, let alone being invited to his apartment, were next to zero. Yet Charlotte, who hated travel, couldn't help wondering what his home would be like.

Sophisticated, she imagined. Leather furniture in the living area and granite countertops in the kitchen. Not shabby and make-shift like this cottage. The main floor plan was open with a pine table dividing the space between the kitchen and sitting area. A stone fireplace dominated the wall to the right, and in the far corner a set of stairs led to the loft.

Dougal opened a door behind the kitchen, revealing a turquoise-colored toilet, sink and tub.

Charlotte sneezed again. "Did you ask Stella if she would clean it for you?"

"Her new partner, Liz Brooks, said she could squeeze the cabin into her schedule tomorrow."

"So you still want to rent it?"

"It's not in bad shape, if you look beyond the dirt."

She opened a closet door and found several coats, pairs of boots and a large umbrella. "I didn't realize my aunt's things would still be here."

Dougal checked some of the kitchen cupboards. "Yup. Dishes, and everything. This is great." He opened the fridge. "This has been cleaned out, thankfully."

"Sure are lots of books." The case in the living room was stuffed. There were also stacks on the coffee table and windowsills.

"Is your house like this?" Dougal asked, picking up a book on growing your own vegetables that looked well-thumbed through.

"Aunt Shirley wasn't *that* old. And yes, I suppose my house has lots of books, too. But they're mostly in shelving units."

"I kind of like the look. Makes the place feel like home."

Her eyes were drawn to a tall cabinet beside the fireplace. On one shelf, a clock, stopped at twelve minutes after four. How long had it ticked on, marking out hours and days after the death of her aunt, before finally giving up?

Below the clock was a collection of Dresden figurines, and on the next shelf down were four snow globes from various cities in Oregon. The tacky souvenirs seemed at odds with the other contents of the cabinet and Charlotte wondered why her aunt had bothered to keep them.

She moved from the living room to the bathroom, where she found the cabinets full of forty-year-old drug store products. She'd never known her aunt, but she felt oddly touched to see the blue bottle of Noxzema crème. The container was almost empty, and yet it was a cruel reminder that something as inconsequential as beauty lotion could outlive a human being.

Leaving the bathroom, she followed Dougal up the stairs to the bedroom. "You say you like the 'lived-in' feeling, but just the same, I'll bring over some boxes and get rid of the clothing and personal items, at least."

"I don't want to put you to any effort. You're doing me a favor, after all, letting me rent this place."

"Our family should have cleared Aunt Shirley's stuff out years ago." She and Dougal removed the cloth covering the double bed and found a violet-patterned quilt with matching pillow shams. It looked so prim and proper. Hard to believe her sister and Kyle had made out here when they were younger. Daisy had taken pains to make the room look tidy, afterward.

Charlotte ran a finger over a book on the nightstand. *And Then There Were None* by Agatha Christie. A bookmark was positioned about half-way through the novel.

"She didn't finish her book. I've always thought that as long as there were books left to read, life would always be worth living."

"I guess in your Aunt Shirley's case books weren't enough."

She tensed. "Who told you?"

"Stella."

She let out a long breath. "I don't know why I didn't, when you asked. Habit, I guess."

Dougal moved to the bureau where he picked up a picture frame and cleared away the grime with his sleeve. She came up beside him to see the photo. Her mother, Shirley, and another woman stood together in what looked like a library.

"Do you know these people?"

"That's my Mom in the light-colored suit. My aunt is wearing the flowered dress with the red scarf. I'm not sure about the third woman." She took a closer look. "Maybe Libby Gardner. The three of them used to go to Library Conventions together. Maybe this was taken at one of them." She reached for the frame. "I'll take it with me. I don't have many pictures of my aunt."

Dougal stared at the photo for a few more seconds before passing it over.

chapter ten

back at Kyle's, Jamie helped Cory hang her dress in her closet. There was plenty of room, as most of the little girl's clothes were in a scramble on the floor.

"Are these clean or dirty?" she asked, picking up a T-shirt and giving it a once-over.

"Clean. My hamper is over there." Cory pointed to a plastic laundry basket, full to the brim. "Mrs. Stella washes them when she comes to clean the house. I'm supposed to put them away, but sometimes I just..." she sighed, and shot Jamie a guilty look. "Chester's room is even messier," she defended herself, but seemed to regret admitting it. "We'll probably get neater as we get older. Our birthday is in October."

"Relax, honey. This is not a big deal." Jamie put the T-shirt into a drawer and smiled. "Let's find your dad. Maybe we can have a snack before your bedtime."

When they'd walked in ten minutes ago, Kyle had been on the phone in the room he used for an office. Through the glass panes of the French door, she saw him hold up a finger indicating he needed a few more minutes to resolve whatever problem was making him frown so intently.

Chester had been sitting at the computer in the kitchen and had barely acknowledged their arrival. While his sister was always eager to spend time with Jamie, and even more anxious to please, her twin brother was exactly the opposite—aloof to the point of rudeness.

Jamie didn't push, trusting that with time, and patient kindness on her part, she would eventually win him over.

Cory followed her to the kitchen—a large room with good bones but outdated cabinets and appliances. One day, a complete renovation would be in order, but for now the luxury of all this space—compared to the cramped trailer—was enough for Jamie. She put her hands on her hips and turned to the children.

"So, what should we have for a snack? What does your dad usually make for you?"

"Um..." Cory looked blankly at her brother.

"I'm not hungry." Chester didn't even look up from the computer game he was playing.

Jamie opened the pantry door, marveling at all the cabinet space. "What about popcorn?"

"Yes! I can help." Cory took a bag out of the package, placed it in the microwave, and punched in the appropriate number of minutes with the confidence of one who had done this many times.

Jamie opened the fridge, looking for something to drink. Looking past the beer, she saw milk and juice. She offered both to the kids, but only Cory answered.

"Apple juice, please."

Jamie thought Chester might relent and join them once the delicious aroma of popcorn and butter filled the kitchen, but he kept his back to them as she and Cory poured the paper bag contents into a big bowl. Cory sat beside her at the kitchen table, and they were just dipping their fingers in for their first taste when Kyle finally appeared.

"Sorry, honey. That was my mom." He gave her a light kiss, then headed to the fridge, where he popped open a Bud. "Want one?"

She shook her head, no. "When is she arriving?" Kyle had already warned her that his mother wouldn't stay long. His parents' divorce had been a brutal one, and Twisted Cedars wasn't big enough to hold both Jim and Muriel Quinpool for long.

Jamie had no idea what had caused such a massive rift between a couple that had been married—apparently quite happily—for almost forty years. She'd heard some gossip, all pure speculation as far as she could tell, that Jim had done something shady in his business dealings and Muriel didn't approve. The few times the topic had come up with Kyle, he'd been quick to change the subject. She supposed that even for adults, the divorce of parents was a painful event.

And the divorce had been difficult for him in more practical ways as well. Muriel and Jim had been living with Kyle and the kids since Daisy left with Muriel taking care of the twins while Kyle and Jim worked. She'd also prepared the meals and done the laundry. With her abrupt departure, Jim had moved back to their old house and Kyle had found himself a single parent.

"Mom doesn't think she can attend the rehearsal dinner on Friday."

Even Chester looked up at that announcement. "Why not?"

When his father didn't answer, Jamie asked, "But she will be here for the wedding, right?"

Kyle took a swig, wiped his mouth with the back of his hand, and nodded. "She offered to stay with the kids that night if we wanted to book into a hotel or something."

"That would be wonderful." Jamie was fine with postponing their honeymoon until the kids were both in summer camp, but it would be nice to have privacy on their wedding night.

"What do you think, kids? Would you like to have grandma to yourself for a night?"

After a brief hesitation, Chester said, "Sure."

"Grandpa wouldn't come, too, would he?"

Kyle seemed annoyed by Cory's question. "No. They're divorced." He turned to Jamie, with a rueful smile that brought out the dimple in his left cheek. "I've explained it to her so many times. She just doesn't seem to get that divorce is forever."

Now wasn't that a slogan for a greeting card, Jamie thought cynically.

"Average divorce rates are going down in America," Chester announced, his eyes still on the computer graphics in front of him. "But the rates for older couples—and second marriages—are higher."

Ouch. What was with that dig about second marriages? Jamie glanced at Kyle but he didn't seem perturbed by Chester's dire statistics.

* * *

"Sorry about Chester." Kyle had his arm around Jamie's back. They were on the porch swing, having tucked the twins into their respective beds. "He's always spouting statistics these days. Too much time spent on the Internet, I guess."

"Do you think he's right? About the divorce rate being higher for second marriages?"

"This is *your* first marriage." Kyle touched the tip of her nose, his grin endearing. "Besides, I think what we've got going for us is worth betting on."

Jamie reached her left hand up and grasped his palm tightly. "No cold feet?"

"God, no. You?"

She shook her head. Smiled. "I can't wait to be your wife. Only eight more sleeps."

That was what Cory had said to her, when Jamie had pulled the light duvet up to her chin. Cory's hair, even more fair than her brother's, was in neat braids and her blue eyes had looked so large as she whispered, *eight more sleeps.*

Jamie didn't think she'd been a part of Cory's life for long enough for her to truly be so attached to her. More likely, she simply craved a mother replacement. She'd lost her own when she was so very young. Then her grandmother had moved away. That was a lot of loss for one so young.

At least Kyle's children had a father they could count on. Until her mother had passed away, Jamie had never really missed having a dad. Now, she found herself thinking about him often. Thinking and wondering.

Unfortunately, there was no one to ask for more information. Her mother had always discouraged questions.

All she'd said was that they were better off without him.

Perhaps they were. But it still felt wrong to Jamie, to live her whole life, and never meet the man who was responsible for her being here in the first place.

chapter eleven

Saturday morning Dougal tossed his luggage into his trunk, then went to settle the bill with the manager. Holly gave him a cheeky smile. "You leaving town before the wedding?"

"No. I'm not leaving." Not that the wedding had anything to do with it. He'd phoned Monty last night to see if keeping Borden for a few extra weeks would be a problem. The older guy had assured him they were getting along well and he should stay as long as he needed. "I'm moving into the Librarian Cottage."

"The one on Forestry Road?" Holly looked at Dougal like he was crazy. "That place must be run down to the ground by now."

"Charlotte Hammond and I checked it out last night. It's not that bad. It'll be a good place for me to work. Nice and quiet." The place was more than not bad, in his opinion. It was damn perfect. He'd known the second he stepped inside that he wanted to live there.

Seeing that picture of Shirley wearing the red scarf had cinched matters. He couldn't believe it was a coincidence. Both of the librarians who had been murdered back in the seventies had been strangled by a red silk scarf. The women had to be linked in some way, beyond their jobs as librarians.

"Hope you're not afraid of ghosts. Last person to live there was Shirley Hammond." Holly leaned across the counter, lowered her voice to a whisper. "You know she hung herself?"

In an equally quiet voice he responded, "I heard about that."

"I know it happened a long time ago. But I always

thought it was quite a mystery."

Dougal checked the total on the Visa receipt before signing. "It's always difficult to understand why someone chooses to take their own life."

"That's not what I mean. I guess she had her reasons. But why'd she hang herself at the library? Seemed like her isolated cottage would have been a better location."

* * *

Dougal had arranged to meet Liz Brooks at the cottage at ten o'clock. That left him forty-five minutes to grab some breakfast. Rather than head for one of the cafés on Driftwood Lane, he drove to the trailer park on the eastern edge of town. He stopped his car out front of the doublewide where he'd grown up.

He stared at the door, remembering all the times he'd seen his mother standing there—calling out for him and Jamie to come in for dinner. He could also picture her at the mailbox, hand on one hip, frowning at the bills. And watering the geraniums she always planted in the front window box. Red blooms flowered there now. Jamie must have kept up the tradition.

For some reason Jamie never minded growing up dirt poor the way they had. She'd laughed off taunts about living in a trailer and wearing cast-off clothing. He had always admired, and slightly envied, his sister's sunny attitude. He'd tried his best to adopt it.

But he'd hated feeling different—inferior. It wasn't just that they were poor. But his father was bad. *Evil*. Dougal had been sixteen when his father had gone to jail for killing his second wife. He'd seen the looks in the eyes of his teachers and the parents of the other kids at school. He'd known what they were thinking.

The apple doesn't fall far from the tree.

He couldn't wait to finish with school so he could leave this place.

But the trailer, itself, wasn't as awful as he remembered. Terra cotta flowerpots flanked the door. The mailbox had been painted and new curtains hung in the windows. The aluminum siding was clean, too. Maybe Jamie had spruced the place up hoping to get a higher asking price.

Quinpool Realty had posted a "For Sale" sign on the lot. Dougal had an odd impulse to knock it down.

Much as he had hated this place, it was weird to think it would soon belong to a stranger.

He'd seen enough and was about to drive off, when his sister appeared at the door. She put her hands on her hips in a posture that reminded him achingly of their mother.

"Are you going to come in, or what?"

He hesitated, then forced himself out of the car.

Though Jamie had resented his departure from Twisted Cedars, his mother had never complained about the choices he made. If she had a mean side to her, Dougal had never seen it. As a teenager, he hadn't been easy on her. He'd been a minor delinquent, sullen and uncooperative. Not a nice person to be around.

Yet, she'd always treated him kindly.

"He'll come around," he'd heard her tell Stella on the phone, after he'd been expelled from school for drinking beer at a school dance.

He wondered how much longer it would take.

"Jamie, what happened after Mom's funeral? Is she...buried somewhere?"

The skin between Jamie's eyes pinched with pain. "Dougal. No. We rented a boat and sprinkled her ashes on the Rogue River. It was what she asked for."

"Right." He remembered Jamie telling him this, in that long ago phone call when she'd let him know their mother had succumbed to the cancer.

"Have you changed your mind about Kyle and me, Doug? Is that what you came to tell me?"

He could see how much she wanted him to say yes. To give her his blessing. Coming here had been a mistake. If only she hadn't been home.

"I don't know what to say. He's a cheat, Jamie. He used

to copy my papers at school." Always his. Never Wade's. Wade wouldn't have stood for it. But Dougal had been so damn anxious to be liked by the coolest guy in the school.

She frowned. Shook her head. "That's kid stuff. I don't get why you're so hard on him."

"This thing works both ways. I bet he tried to talk you out of inviting me to the wedding, didn't he?"

Her silence was his answer.

"So I think it's better for everyone if I don't go."

His sister stuck out her jaw, a sure sign she was fighting tears. "You didn't come here for me at all, did you? I hear you've rented the Librarian Cottage and you're working on a new book."

"That part's true. But—" He stopped. Jamie wanted his blessing, and if he couldn't give her that, she wasn't interested in anything else he had to say. "Good luck, Jamie. I hope I'm wrong about Kyle. I really do."

* * *

Driving up to Shirley Hammond's old cottage, Dougal felt the same sense of anticipation as starting a new book. For some strange reason, this place spoke to him. Strange, when up to now he'd done all his writing in the city. But as soon as he'd seen this place last night with Charlotte, he'd felt a sense of coming home.

The irony did not escape him. He'd spent his adult years running from his past, and now the Oregon forest was claiming him back.

The silence, the majestic height of the trees, the tang of the sap and the cushion of pine needles under his feet. This was where he belonged.

And the old Hammond cottage was perfect. Built from cedar, the A-frame was simple, functional and more beautiful than the most opulent of Park Avenue penthouses—to his taste anyway.

Even as he dug the brass key from his jeans pocket, he heard another car approaching from the lane. A woman, who had to be Liz Brooks, drove up in a battered green

Jeep. She sat for a minute, studying him, then the house. Then she squared her shoulders and jumped from the driver's seat, her sneakered feet landing with a soft scuff on the dirt driveway.

"Hey there. You must be Dougal."

Liz was about five-foot-four, skinny in a pair of jeans that seemed to hang from her hip bones. Her T-shirt was so faded he couldn't read the logo, and she had a huge quantity of brown, curly hair pulled back in a ponytail.

Her eyes narrowed in a calculating way.

"Better not be any dead animals in there. Stella tells me this place has been vacant for a mighty long time."

"No dead animals. We checked last night." He held out his hand, introduced himself.

Liz's palms were calloused and her hand slid out from his a second after he'd touched it.

"Are you from Twisted?" he asked. She seemed only a little younger than Jamie, but he didn't find her familiar at all.

"No. I moved here a few years ago. Saw the job listed on the Internet."

That struck him as odd. There were dozens of towns like Twisted Cedars along the coast of Oregon. And surely cleaning jobs weren't that hard to come by.

She narrowed her eyes again. It seemed to be a habit of hers, and he wished she wouldn't do it. It made her seem far more perceptive than she probably was.

"You don't look much like your mother," she finally pronounced.

"So I've been told."

She stared at him a second longer. In her odd, slanted gray eyes he saw mistrust—as if his lack of resemblance to Katie was a strike against him.

Then, abruptly, she seemed to lose all interest in him.

"My gear is in the car."

"I'll help."

"No. I've got it."

Fine. He headed into the cottage, leaving the door open behind him. Last night he hadn't noticed how stale it smelled in here, but this morning the air was thick enough to choke on. No wonder Charlotte had been sneezing. He opened all the windows on the main level, and then made his way upstairs.

He wished Charlotte hadn't removed the picture of her aunt from the bureau. That red scarf. He wondered if he would find it among Shirley's clothing.

He went through the bureau drawers, in search. Mingled in with the underwear drawer—staid, no-nonsense briefs and well-constructed bras—he found a couple of silk scarves, but none of them were red.

"You want me to clean those out for you?"

He hadn't heard Liz climb up the stairs and he started at the sound of her voice. Worried she'd think checking out women's underwear gave him a perverse thrill, he slammed the drawer closed.

"That's okay. Charlotte said she would come by later to box this stuff up."

She kept looking at him, as if to ask, *Then what were you looking for, anyway?*

He would have been hard pressed to give her an answer.

chapter twelve

Kyle's mother arrived in Twisted Cedars at five o'clock in the afternoon on Friday. Jamie was French-braiding Cory's hair. She was almost done, weaving the strands the way she remembered her mother once doing for her. Cory held a mirror in both hands, watching the progress with an expression bordering on awe.

"Do you like it?"

Cory nodded.

Then suddenly Jamie saw Muriel Quinpool's face in the mirror. Cory spotted her grandmother at the same time.

"Grandma!" She jumped from her chair and ran to the woman, hugging her around the waist. Muriel looked teary-eyed by the reception. She patted Cory on the back, while her gaze met Jamie's.

"Muriel! What a surprise...hello, how are you?" She went to give her mother-in-law-to-be a kiss. She hadn't expected her to arrive tonight since Kyle had said she definitely wasn't attending the rehearsal dinner.

Muriel clasped her granddaughter's face between her hands. "How are you, sweetie? Excited about the wedding?"

"I'm going to be the flower girl! I have a long pink dress and shiny shoes and I'm going to the hair dresser tomorrow."

"Then why was Jamie braiding your hair?"

"For the rehearsal dinner," Jamie explained.

"It's tonight? I thought Kyle said Thursday." Muriel sank onto a kitchen chair, looking concerned.

Jamie hadn't seen Kyle's mother since she'd moved to Portland. Muriel had aged noticeably in that time and she had a nervous tic in her eye that was very distracting.

"Now you can come with us, grandma! I'll go tell Chester." Cory shot out of the room, leaving an uncomfortable quiet in her wake.

Jamie sat in the chair opposite Muriel's. Her mother-in-law-to-be was rubbing one wrist in a compulsive manner.

"I can't go. It isn't possible," she murmured. "The wedding is going to be difficult enough." She lifted her gaze to Jamie. "Where is Kyle?"

"He's helping Chester get dressed."

"Chester's been dressing himself for years."

Jamie grinned. "His father doesn't want him wearing sweatpants and a T-shirt tonight."

Jamie had taken the day off from work. She'd been too excited to work, anyway. The day had sped by as she worked through a checklist of items, including picking up the kids after school and bringing them home to get ready for the rehearsal dinner.

Cory had been thrilled at the excuse to wear another pretty dress, but Chester wasn't impressed with the shirt and trousers he'd found pressed and waiting on his bed.

"But I have to wear that stupid suit tomorrow. Can't I be comfortable tonight?"

Jamie might have given in to him on this one—only close friends and family were invited and the clambake was being held at the beach—but Kyle was standing firm.

"Are you sure you won't come with us?" she pressed Muriel. "I know the kids and Kyle would love for you to be there."

"I'll stay at home. Maybe I can make myself useful." With that, Muriel moved to the sink and began running the hot water.

Though the place wasn't yet her responsibility, Jamie felt embarrassed. The kitchen was frankly a disaster—remnants of breakfast and lunch were still cluttered on the counters. Jamie had planned on a quick clean-up once she'd finished with Cory's hair.

"Sorry the place is such a mess."

"No problem. I like to be useful." She sighed. "I've missed all this."

Then why had she moved so far away, Jamie wondered? "Are you settling in okay in Portland?"

"I'm fine. I have my sister."

But she missed having her grandchildren around. That much was obvious. And again Jamie had to wonder why she had felt compelled to put so many miles between them.

* * *

The rehearsal dinner didn't last long—only a few hours. Jamie wanted an early night and she was glad of it the next morning—*her wedding day!*—when she woke at dawn, with the birds. She stared at the low ceiling of the trailer above her. *This is the last time.*

From now on, she'd be waking up in Kyle's house, in his bed, with him lying beside her. She turned her head to one side and tried to imagine him cuddled up beside her.

She smiled.

So much to do today. She was glad she'd awakened early. Quickly she showered, ate breakfast, and then organized her trousseau. She and Cory would be dressing at Stella's home. Stella had a beautiful old claw-foot tub and Jamie was looking forward to a nice, long soak before getting dressed.

But she had a lot to accomplish before then.

Phone calls, last minute arrangements, a trip to the salon.

On the way to Twisted Locks, she stopped at Kyle's house to pick up Cory, who had an appointment booked for the same time. Muriel was outside watering the shrubs when she arrived.

"Hey, Muriel. Isn't it a wonderful day!"

The older woman straightened, frowned up at the sky. "So far, so good."

"I booked an extra appointment if you'd like to come with us to get your hair done?"

"Oh no. I couldn't."

Jamie frowned and was about to try to persuade her when Cory came bounding down the porch stairs. Kyle followed, with a garment bag in one hand and a duffel bag in the other.

Jamie had no time for silly superstitions like avoiding her groom on their wedding day. She ran up to kiss him.

"Hey, beautiful. I have something for you." He set Cory's bags in the trunk of her car, then took her hands and led her around the back of the house. Cory stayed behind with her grandmother, grinning, obviously in on the plan.

In the backyard, shielded behind a cedar hedge, Kyle kissed her again, then took a blue box from his back pocket. Holding her breath, she opened it…and let out a gasp when she saw the diamond necklace.

"It's stunning."

He placed it around her neck, fastened the clasp. "You'll wear it today?"

She had planned to wear an old necklace of her mother's. It was vintage and lovely, but not nearly as valuable as this. "Of course, I will."

"I love you, Jamie."

"I love you, too."

* * *

At ten minutes past four, Jamie was in the Church vestibule with Cory, missing her mother and trying not to cry.

Not until this moment had she realized she'd been counting on Dougal to pull through in the end. A tap sounded on the door and Stella Ward walked in, dressed in her best floral dress. "Are you ready?"

Jamie nodded. In the absence of her brother, she'd asked Stella to walk her down the aisle. "Dougal still hasn't shown up?"

"Afraid not, honey." Stella used a cotton handkerchief to dab away Jamie's tears. "Your mother was my best friend.

I know you must be thinking of her today. Wishing she could be here. But since she can't—I'm very honored you asked me to take her place."

Jamie nodded, so grateful to the other woman but still unable to speak. Stella crouched to Cory's level. "Sweetie, you look beautiful. Are you ready?"

Cory nodded, her eyes huge. Today the little girl shone. Her hair had been curled, styled and decorated with tiny daisies. The dress Stella had made for her was pink satin perfection.

"Okay. Smile big ladies. This is show time."

* * *

Wade figured he was the only one in the room looking at Kyle, and not Jamie, as the bride walked down the aisle. Seemed like most of his life he'd been trying to fight his attraction to Jamie Lachlan. First because she was too young, not to mention the sister of one of his best friends. After that there had been years when he'd lived away from Twisted Cedars. He'd only just returned to make his run for the Sheriff's job, when Jamie had suddenly started dating Kyle.

If he'd ever had an opportunity with her, he'd missed it.

And it wasn't right for him to regret that. Not when he had Charlotte Hammond by his side. She was one of several who had let out a sigh when they caught their first glance of Jamie. Wade didn't doubt she was making a beautiful bride.

But for him it was safer to focus on the groom. And so far, Kyle was spending more time scanning the room than looking at Jamie.

Wade didn't care what he was looking for. The point was, in this moment, Jamie deserved to be the only thing Kyle was thinking about. The trouble with Kyle, however, was that most of the time he was thinking of only himself.

Wade shifted his weight, then glanced at Jim Quinpool. The groom's father looked more worried than happy. And Muriel, his ex-wife, appeared downright anxious. He'd heard the two of them could no longer abide being in the same room. Apparently that was true. Standing between them was their grandson, Chester. One thing was for sure. He wasn't as happy about this wedding as his sister. Cory's face glowed as she joined her father at the front of the church.

And then, Jamie was there, too.

All Wade could see was her back, and then, when she turned to face Kyle, her profile. God, she was lovely. Quickly, he averted his gaze toward Charlotte, who gave him her usual calm, sweet smile. He smiled back, patted his jacket pocket, and told himself to relax.

* * *

The evening was almost over. Charlotte felt that Jamie and Kyle would consider their wedding a success. The reception had progressed smoothly. Hardly anyone had noticed when Muriel Quinpool slipped out of the receiving line. She'd surprised Charlotte by seeking her out.

"How are you doing, dear?"

Slightly puzzled, Charlotte had said, "I'm fine, thank-you. How are you enjoying living in Portland?"

Muriel hadn't answered. She'd taken hold of Charlotte's arm, gripping it tightly. Her face looked sad. Troubled. She took a breath, seemed about to say something, then shook her head.

A moment later, she slipped out of the Rogue River Country Club, without saying good-bye to anyone, without so much as a single backward glance.

Her ex-husband was the only other person who had noticed her departure as far as Charlotte could tell. Jim's jaw had tightened. For a moment Charlotte thought he would follow his ex-wife. But he'd turned resolutely from the door and headed to the bar, instead.

Now he was drunk, sitting quietly at the table that had been reserved for him and other assorted Quinpool relatives.

Charlotte was thankful that she and Wade, despite her official Quinpool family status, had been seated with friends they knew well. For them the evening had passed pleasantly and just moments ago, when the band began playing a slower, more romantic set, Wade had asked her to dance.

Now, as Jamie made her way to the microphone—presumably to toss the bouquet—he guided her to the far end of the room, where a patio door was open to the outside terrace. Thanks to a cool wind, they had the place to themselves.

Wade wrapped his arms around her waist. "Are you cold?"

"No," she lied, because she suspected that Wade needed a little distance from the wedding proceedings. On the whole, he had held up well, she thought. If she hadn't known how he felt about Jamie, she never would have guessed based on his behavior tonight.

"I wanted a minute alone with you," he said.

"Oh?" She glanced up, studied his eyes. He looked very serious. Very intent.

"You deserve better than me." As he spoke, he let go of her with one hand and pulled something from the pocket he'd been guarding all night.

And then she knew.

Her heart began to pound. She felt the same dizzy fear that accompanied her usual panic attacks. No, she told herself. Not now. She took a deep breath and held it while she counted slowly to five.

Wade took hold of her left hand, slipped down on one knee. "Will you marry me?"

Oh my God. It was the most perfect marriage proposal. And just at that moment, a full moon broke out from the clouds, as if part of the script.

"Wade."

He was standing again, showing her the ring, and it was beautiful. The diamond, at least a carat, twinkled enticingly from its velvet nest, but it had nothing on the man who held it. Wade was the best man Charlotte had ever known. He was solid, dependable, not afraid to do the right thing. If she married him, he would be her pillar and, for a woman who was afraid of almost everything in the world, that was an incredible enticement.

chapter thirteen

the day of his sister's wedding, Dougal was restless, unable to focus on anything, knowing his sister was making the worst mistake of her life. He had no appetite for dinner. Instead, he tried to settle down with one of Shirley Hammond's books, and failed.

He glanced at the clock, which was working again. The ceremony would have been over hours ago. Now they were probably dancing and making speeches.

He should be there.

Dougal went to the kitchen table, hoping to distract himself.

This was his new makeshift office. He'd put away the place mats and salt and pepper shakers, making room for his lap top and printer. His notes were strewn here, too. A study in disorganization.

Like his thoughts.

He laid out the printed copies of the emails he had received so far.

You don't know me. But you should. I've got a story that will be the best of your career. Back in the seventies four women were killed. Librarians. No one ever solved the cases. But I know what happened. Ever hear of Elva Mae Ayer? She was the first. Check it out then let me know if you want the names of the others. I am here and willing to help.

Then the second: *The next year Mari Beamish was murdered. There was a pattern, but don't feel bad if you don't see it yet. The cops never did make the connection. Those were different times, before computers and all the advances in forensics. Now you get to be the hero who pieces it all together. You can thank me later.*

It had been a week since the last message. He wondered when the next one would come. According to that first message, there had been two other women killed and he had no way to identify them. He supposed he could search death records—but from where? So far the murders had taken place in small cities in Oregon. But the pattern—if there indeed was one—was still very unclear.

He wished Charlotte was here to talk to about this.

But he hadn't seen her since his official moving day. Liz had done a great job of cleaning up the place, though he'd been relieved when she'd finally left. He'd caught her looking at him in the oddest way several times and it had made him uneasy. But he couldn't fault the job she'd done.

Even Charlotte had approved. "The place even smells clean," she'd said.

She'd arrived in a sporty '97 BMW—not the car he'd pictured her driving, not by a long shot—wearing faded jeans that molded to curves librarians weren't supposed to have.

He'd helped her box up her aunt's clothing and personal items.

"Want me to clear out the bookshelves, too?" she'd asked.

"Not unless you want the books." He'd already checked the titles: a complete collection of Sherlock Holmes mysteries as well as over twenty Agatha Christies—some featuring Poirot, some Miss Marples and even a couple with Tommy and Tuppence.

"Your aunt liked her mysteries."

"It runs in the family," Charlotte had replied, her voice muffled since she was in the closet. She'd emerged with her arms full of coats, which she stuffed into one of the boxes. "What do you like to read? True crime?"

"Not so much. Thrillers, horror...Stephen King is probably my favorite author."

"Have you ever considered writing fiction?"

"That's what I started out to do." But then he'd met an attractive woman at a bar one night. She turned out to be a New York prosecuting attorney who'd just finished working on a horrific case involving a serial rapist. They'd talked for hours, and at the end of the evening, he'd realized he'd found a story that needed to be told.

"Maybe you'll get back to fiction one day," Charlotte had said.

Dougal looked down at the messages, again, wondering if she was right. Maybe he should just throw these away, and start a new project. Fiction this time.

Hadn't he had enough of reality to last him a lifetime?

But there had to be some reason these messages were being sent now...and to him. He knew he ought to be appalled at being the pen pal of someone who was either the killer, or guilty of withholding evidence for so many years. But the truth was, every time he'd received one of the messages, he'd felt a sick shiver of excitement.

* * *

Dougal was too ramped up to sleep, or even to write. He needed to blow off some energy. Because it was too dark to walk in the woods, he decided to drive to town. He parked his car at the wharf. Doris's Fish Shack was locked up for the night. Several local boats were tied at the dock.

For some reason he found himself thinking of his mother. He knew he hadn't fully accepted the fact that he would never hear her voice again, see her smile, feel her small arms wrap around him in a hug. The holiday in Hawaii had been the best he could do for her. But it had left him with memories that felt out of kilter. The last place he saw her should have been in the trailer, or the hospice where she had died.

Not sipping Mai Tai's at the Hula Grill at Whaler's Wharf.

Dougal removed his shoes and ambled out to the sand, heading north, his thoughts swirling, his heart aching. So much had gone wrong in life for his mother. Most of her problems stemmed from her weakness for picking the wrong men. And now his sister had married Kyle. He'd known he couldn't talk her out of it. Why had he bothered to try? He'd only succeeded in creating a rift that might never be mended.

Was it possible she was right about Kyle? That the guy had changed? He so wanted to believe it was possible.

But people didn't change in Dougal's experience. Selfish bastards didn't turn into thoughtful husbands.

Nor did violent murderers become respectable citizens.

A single light from the Ocean View Motel was visible in front of him. He wondered if pretty Holly Williams was working the desk this late. Beyond that he spotted Charlotte Hammond's porch light. He supposed she would have gone to his sister's wedding. Possibly she was still there.

But a few minutes later, when he saw someone walking toward him, he realized if Charlotte had gone to the wedding, she was home now, out on the beach, moving silently in his direction.

Last time he'd given her space. But tonight he kept going. Charlotte Hammond intrigued him. So bookish, proper, and reserved...the perfect small-town librarian. But there was untapped depth in her cool, gray eyes. And these midnight strolls of hers spoke of a restless longing he understood all too well.

She was wearing a dress that fell to her knees. The wind blew the silky fabric tightly to the left side of her body, molding into the curve of her hip and the length of her thigh.

The outfits she wore to work were pure camouflage. He remembered how sexy she had looked in her jeans. While checking out a few titles in her aunt's collection, she'd slipped on a pair of glasses that had sat on her nose in a most adorable fashion. He'd never thought glasses could be cute. But on Charlotte, they were.

"Dougal." Charlotte was the first to speak, and clearly she'd recognized him, too. "Are you all right?"

It struck him as very sweet that she asked him that. And as soon as he'd had a minute to consider the question, he realized he wasn't.

So he didn't answer.

"How was the wedding?"

"It went over very well. Your sister looked happy."

"And Kyle? How did he look?"

She said nothing, at first. Then, "Very pleased."

"I'll just bet." He shoved his hands into his jean pockets and stared out at the sea. Talking about things that never change... He turned back to Charlotte. Something glinted on her face. Tears. "What's wrong?"

Now it was her turn to look out at the ocean. He moved closer to her, close enough to smell the perfume she'd put on for the wedding. She'd taken some effort to look nice. Her hair was curled and she was wearing make-up. Or *had* been wearing make-up. Now black smudges were under both of her eyes.

Normally he avoided situations involving overwrought emotions, but it felt natural to put an arm around her shoulder. She pressed her body into his, and that felt natural, too.

He found himself using his thumb to swipe at the black streaks. Her cheeks really were wet. He pulled her face to his chest. She sighed and relaxed for a moment. He put an arm around her waist. Brushed his hand over her hair.

One second he was feeling protective and concerned. The next moment, aroused. When she looked up at him with her streaky, sad face the most natural thing of all was to kiss her.

Charlotte reacted instantly, as if this had been her intention all along, though he doubted that was the case. God, the librarian could kiss. She clung to him and together they were sinking, him to the earth, and her onto him.

His fingers wove through her hair as he kissed her lips, her cheeks, her eyes. He kissed everywhere, and then he turned to her body, hands sliding under her silky dress, to discover skin that was just as satin-soft.

Clothes half-on, they made love, pausing only to use the protection Dougal carried out of habit. He was shocked at how quickly the pleasure built, drowning out every bit of common sense in his brain. Charlotte was above him, hands planted on his chest, her hair wild in the wind, her expression lost to the needs of her body.

She collapsed on him when it was over. He wrapped his arms tightly around her to shield her from the cold, and then gently rolled until she was beside him. Gradually their breathing slowed, but neither said a word and he relished the extended silence. Only the surf was speaking, and it was enough.

He could have stayed there, with her, all night long. But this was Oregon, and even in June, it was cold.

He pulled back a little so he could see her face. "Let me walk you home."

She nodded, suddenly shivering as she stood, pulling her dress back into position. He picked up her underwear, passed them to her. Zipped his jeans.

In the moment, everything had seemed perfect and right. But now, as so often happened after love-making, it was different. Now he didn't know why he had given in to his desire so quickly and easily. She wasn't the sort of woman he usually picked for his one-nighters. And yet, he wasn't interested in starting a relationship, either. He didn't know whether to apologize or what.

"Are you okay?" he asked.

"I'm fine. Now." She smiled.

"But you were crying, earlier."

She hesitated, then she said, "Wade asked me to marry him."

That was a shock. "Considering what just happened here, I hope you said no."

She gave a short laugh. "I did."

More questions begged to be asked. Why had she said no? Did she think she might change her mind? But she didn't seem to want to talk any more. They made their way up the path that led to her house. She'd left the back light burning, the door unlocked. Before slipping inside, she paused, and he used that opportunity to kiss her good-bye.

chapter fourteen

Kyle had a friend with a vacation home thirty miles south on the one-oh-one. That was where they spent their wedding night. The house was on a private cove, with an ocean view and all the amenities including an outdoor hot tub. Kyle had arranged for the delivery of a dozen roses and a bottle of Dom Perignon White Gold champagne.

It was one in the morning by the time they arrived. Jamie kicked off her heels and headed straight for the wall of windows overlooking the ocean. It was too dark to see much, but even with the windows closed, she could hear the roar of the tide coming in.

Kyle opened the champagne, brought her a glass. "Mrs. Quinpool?"

The bubbles slid down her throat, effervescent with hope. She leaned on Kyle, they kissed.

"Upstairs?"

She nodded.

They made love on the king-sized bed—windows open to the salty air, the thundering ocean. They had made love before, but with his children and their work schedules, opportunities to be truly alone had been rare.

She loved having him all to herself. And waking up with him by her side the next morning was almost the best part. She'd rarely seen him with stubble. She touched the coarse hairs on his chin, his upper lip, his chin, again. His eyes opened.

"I need a shower."

She laughed, put her arms around him. "Not yet, you don't."

Sadly, they only had a few more hours to themselves

before they had to head back to Twisted Cedars. Muriel wanted to be on the road before dark. Jamie had invited her to stay a few extra days, but the prospect had seemed to make her nervous.

So she and Kyle would just have to make the most of the little time they had.

* * *

Waking at dawn, Charlotte felt disoriented. Had last night really happened?

It must have, or else she would be in her bed. But she wasn't. She was sitting in her father's favorite chair, dressed in a robe, a bottle of scotch and a glass on the table beside her. Her head ached. Her stomach was queasy.

She got up slowly, made her way to the bathroom, passing by the soggy pile of silk that had been the dress she'd worn to the wedding. She filled the tub with hot water. Her brain and her body both felt a little numb. Last night one man had asked her to marry him and another had made love to her.

All the excitement of her entire life packed into about four hours. It was more than one small town librarian could be expected to handle.

Could she have imagined it?

But no. The smell and feel of sex on her body was quite unmistakable.

Charlotte tossed her robe into the hamper then sank into the bath. As her muscles relaxed, her thoughts whirled.

She had said no to Wade—would he be disappointed or relieved? Would they still date? Or just be friends? They had discussed none of this, though if he knew what had happened between her and Dougal, then she kind of thought the answer would be no on all counts.

As for Dougal...how on earth had it happened? One minute she'd been walking on the beach, having a good cry, just letting it all out. The next he was there. Reaching out his hand and touching her. She couldn't even say with certainty that he had made the first move. It was like they'd both had the impulse to kiss at the same time.

And the biggest shocker of all...

Despite the cold, the grit of the sand, the unforgiving hardness of the beach, that impromptu sex was the best she'd ever had.

* * *

Dougal woke shortly after nine. Instantly reached for his cell phone, which he'd placed next to the vintage alarm clock that had come with the place and still worked fine.

He had to phone information to get Charlotte's home number. Fortunately she was listed.

"How are you?" he asked, his voice sounding rougher than he intended. Maybe he should have had a cup of coffee first.

"I'm fine. But rather busy right now."

Code for, *what happened last night doesn't change anything between us.* Dougal spoke the language, was more than ready to be let off the hook.

Still, he thought about her quite a bit that day.

chapter fifteen

On Monday Dougal headed for the library right after breakfast. Charlotte was at her desk when he walked in, and he had to smile, seeing her in her sweater and pearls. Miss Prim and Proper, but now he knew she had a wild side, too. He was tempted to walk up to her and kiss her. It would be interesting to see her reaction. *But no, be honest with yourself here. You really just want to kiss her.*

Which wasn't a smart idea. Whatever the reason Charlotte had turned down Wade's proposal, the two of them belonged together. Wade was a solid, dependable, loyal man. He'd make the sort of husband a woman like Charlotte deserved.

Once Charlotte had time to think it through, she'd realize her mistake and patch things up with him.

So he should be a gentleman and pretend their sex on the beach had never happened.

"Morning Charlotte."

She nodded, seemingly preoccupied by the book in her hands. It was Ian McEwan's *Atonement*. She didn't seem to be reading it. Just examining it like a puzzling artifact.

"Good book. Have you read it?"

"Years ago."

He raised his eyebrows.

"I found it in the return chute this morning." She frowned, then flipped to the title page, which she showed him. Someone had hand-written in a faltering, flowery script: *Charlotte I'm sorry.*

"Sorry for what? Returning the book late?"

"But it isn't a library book. It's not coded and it doesn't have a protective cover."

"It didn't come from me, if that's what you're wondering. The other night shouldn't have happened. But I'm not sorry it did."

She wouldn't meet his eyes.

"You, on the other hand, probably have a different opinion."

A young mother with two children entered the library then and Dougal left Charlotte in peace, settling at his usual table where he quickly set out his laptop and notes. Out of habit, he checked his email first.

Nothing new from Librarianmomma.

He knew it was wrong—possibly sick—to feel disappointed. But he did.

He turned his attention to his notes on the second murder. Based on the information in the faxed articles from the *East Oregonian*, Mari Beamish had a husband and a four-year-old daughter. This was where he'd start. First he needed a phone number.

He tried various computer searches, looking first for anyone with the surname of Beamish, who still lived in Pendleton. He was jotting down numbers and addresses when a hand touched his shoulder.

"Finding what you're looking for?"

The mom and her kids had left, so they were alone again.

"I got what I came for." He set down his pen and looked her directly in the eyes. "And then some."

Cheap shot. Just went to show what a bugger he was. Charlotte blushed. God—it amazed him how easily she did that.

"About Satur—" she began.

"No explanations necessary. I figure you and Wade just need a little time to work things out. If you're worried I might make trouble—don't."

She crossed her arms over her chest and leaned against the next work station. "How reassuring."

"Right. One more thing. I'm heading to Pendleton

tomorrow. Just for a few days to follow up on Mari Beamish. I'll drop my rent checks in your mail box before I leave. You forgot to take them with you last time you were over."

She raised her chin a little. "You do that, Dougal."

Suddenly it was difficult to breathe in here. Maybe too much library dust. He gathered his notes and gave her a final nod.

* * *

Leaving on a road trip was more difficult this time. Suitcase in the trunk, laptop case in the passenger seat, he went back to the cottage to lock up.

He didn't want to go.

Like Goldilocks, he'd stumbled across a house in the woods that felt just right. He'd never had this feeling before...a sense of belonging. Suddenly he could understand the concept of putting down roots, of preferring to stay in rather than go out on the weekends.

But Mari Beamish was calling to him. For some reason her life had been taken—and he needed to know how.

And why.

And most of all...who.

* * *

Driving from Twisted Cedars to Pendleton was one of those, "you can't get there from here" situations. The towns were on diagonally opposite corners of the state, and thanks to the mountains and dense forests, the route was indirect and the roads challenging. Dougal opted to cross over the Coastal Range at Reedsport, white knuckling the death-wish hairpin turns until he finally emerged on the Interstate and headed north. Nine hours, and over five-hundred miles later, he finally arrived.

He'd left the ocean far behind, along with the rainforests and mountains. Here the sky seemed bigger, the clouds tumultuous and low, the land undulating in gentle waves. He drove past ranches, wheat fields and blueberry farms until he came to what was billed as the largest city in

Eastern Oregon, but still had a population less than twenty-thousand.

After a long day behind the wheel, he needed some rest. It was almost seven now. He'd planned to start at the library, except it wouldn't be open until ten o'clock the next morning. He stopped for gas, first. It felt good to stretch out his legs and clear his head with the cool evening air. He grabbed food, next, from a hamburger joint, then went in search of a motel.

He didn't sleep well. The room smelled funny and the pillows were too big and hard. The fact that he was still pissed at himself for having sex with Charlotte Hammond didn't help. Picking up women in bars was one thing. They knew the game and what to expect.

Charlotte was something else...way too much sugar and spice and everything nice. Damn, but she'd surprised him, though. There'd been nothing shy or inexperienced about the way she made love. Not that he'd expected her to be a virgin or anything. But the way she dressed, those prim glasses of hers...

Dougal groaned as he rolled to his other side. If he wasn't going to sleep, he might as well watch television. He found a re-run of *Dexter*.

Perfect. Fifteen minutes later he was lulled to sleep by the escapades of a serial killer.

* * *

The Pendleton Library was in a beautiful, modern building, with extremely helpful staff. At ten minutes after the opening hour on Tuesday morning, Dougal was already reading copies of an article in the *East Oregonian* that hadn't made the first cut Charlotte had rounded up for him. Plus he had an amazingly good cup of coffee on the desk beside him.

Mari Beamish's murder was front page news back in 1973. At first details were sketchy, but over the course of several weeks, a fairly complete description emerged.

She'd been killed shortly after library closing hours,

strangled in a storage area of this very library—pre-renovations, Dougal assumed. The red scarf wasn't mentioned in the initial reports of the killing, but it came out later that this was indeed what had been used to strangle her. The scarf did not belong to the victim—her husband claimed to have never seen it before.

No motive for the killing was ever found. She hadn't been robbed—was still wearing her wedding rings and her wallet was intact. Nor had she been raped. She was, however, discovered to have been two months pregnant at the time of her death.

Dougal closed his eyes. This time fallout included a life that never came to be.

After thanking the librarian for her help, he left to find the address of Mari's daughter he'd looked up on Monday at the Twisted Cedars Library. Sue Graham nee Beamish lived in a large two-story home on a generous, wooded lot backing the Wild Horse River. He'd called earlier to set up a meeting for one-thirty. As it was only twenty past now, he waited in his car, until her Subaru Outback pulled into the drive.

Sue looked about his age—athletic body, dark hair. She wore workout clothing and sneakers and her hair was in a ponytail. She pulled a gym bag, as well as her purse, out of the vehicle.

Leaving his car unlocked—in this neighborhood it did not feel like a risk—he approached her slowly. "Hey there."

"Hi." She pushed her sunglasses up on her head. "Dougal Lachlan?"

He nodded.

"I've read some of your books. My husband's got them all."

"Well, I'd be happy to sign them, if you think he'd like that."

"Oh, he would. Come on in. I've just dropped the kids back to school after lunch so we have lots of time." She kicked aside a tiny pair of sneakers to make room for him in the foyer. The house was pleasant, furnished for comfort and cheerfulness. The floors were dark maple—"Don't bother taking your shoes off," Sue told him—and the hall led to a sunny kitchen at the back of the house. Sue cleared off a place at the island, offered him a choice of drinks as she worked.

"Iced tea sounds great."

She brought out several copies of his books next, and once that was taken care of, sat on a stool two down from his.

"I was very surprised when you called asking questions about my mother. May I ask how you heard about her?"

"I came across the crime in the process of some research I'm doing." The answer wasn't totally honest, but he wasn't about to admit to the anonymous emails.

"For a new book?"

"I think so. Yes."

"So my mother wasn't the only one? Other women were murdered?"

"It seems so. The red scarf...that's an important clue."

"I remember reading about that. My Dad never talked about what happened and I was only three at the time. But when I was ten I became intensely curious about my mother's death. I went to the library, pretending I was researching for a school project on our town's history. I found all the old articles about what happened to my mother and I devoured them."

"Did knowing what happened help?"

"Maybe help isn't the right word. The knowledge was simply necessary. Growing up without a mother, well, it wasn't easy. And then, finding out I'd lost a sibling. My father never told me Mom was pregnant when she died."

"I'm sorry."

She nodded. "I remember feeling as if I had a hollow spot in my chest. To be honest, I still have that feeling at times. Like when my own children were born—especially the first, Megan."

There was something very likeable about this woman. And she was so open. Dougal couldn't imagine telling a stranger how he'd felt about growing up without a father. But then, he wasn't a complete stranger to this woman. Again, it surprised him how having your name on the spine of a book made people think they could trust you.

He took a long swallow of tea, focused his thoughts. "Over the years, no one's ever come up with an explanation for what happened to your mother?"

Her eyes were sad as she shook her head.

"And your father...did he remarry?"

"Yes. He met Glenda about a year after my mother passed away. She's a nice lady and treated me very well, but later, when she and my father had two more children—another girl, then a boy—I sensed the difference in the way she cared for me, and the way she absolutely adored them."

"The evil stepmother?"

"Not hardly. She's a kind person and she's turned out to be a lovely grandmother, too. It's just—I feel so robbed. My mother was a librarian for God's sake, living in a nice town like Pendleton. It's always felt so random to me that she was stolen from us in such a violent way. Random and meaningless."

"I don't know if I can make some sense of it, Sue. But that's what I'm trying to do."

"Well, good. I wish I could give you more to go on."

He finished the iced tea. "Thanks for taking the time to talk to me. Maybe I should speak to your dad while I'm in town."

Her open face fell at the suggestion. "I suppose you could ask. But he doesn't like remembering. What happened to Mom—that's done and finished in his mind."

chapter sixteen

good news, honey." Kyle was home. He came into the kitchen, set his briefcase on the counter, and went to the fridge for a beer. "Want one?"

"Sure." Jamie had been home from work for an hour. Dinner was almost ready. She was surprised at how quickly she and Kyle had settled into traditional roles since their marriage. He'd been such a hands-on dad, she'd assumed they would do things like grocery shop and cook together.

But recently he'd had a lot of calls in the afternoon, which meant he worked at least an hour later than her every day. So she was the one to pick up the kids and start dinner.

"What's the good news?"

"We got an offer for your trailer today." He told her the price as he passed her the Bud he'd just opened. "What do you say? Pretty good, huh? To tell you the truth, it's almost two thousand more than I expected." He tapped his beer bottle against hers. "Congratulations, honey."

"Thanks." She wished she could feel as happy as he clearly did. Selling was the right thing. It didn't make sense to cling to the past.

"Do I need to go to the office to sign the papers?"

"I brought the contract home with me. We'll take care of it after the kids are in bed." He put his arm around her. "Smells good in here. I'm not sure if it's the food, or you."

"I'm cooking spaghetti, if that helps you decide." She kissed him back, placing her free hand on his strong shoulder.

Later, at the dinner table, Cory told them about a class field trip coming up to visit the local Fire Station and Sheriff's Office.

"You can come along if you want." Cory's eyes were on Jamie, hopeful. "Some parents do."

"Jamie isn't our parent." Chester looked annoyed.

"Yes, she is," Kyle corrected his son. "She's your step-mother. But she also has to work, so I don't think she can volunteer for your field trip, Cory."

Jamie had been planning to say the same thing. Seeing Cory's disappointment, though, she found herself changing her mind. "I could take the afternoon off. We're not that busy right now."

"Really?"

Cory glowed and Kyle mouthed "thank you," at her and she felt even better about her decision, knowing she'd pleased him, too.

Later, after the kids had cleared the table, and she and Kyle were finishing the clean-up, he raised the subject again.

"I'm really glad you decided to volunteer for the field trip. That's the sort of thing their friends' mothers do all the time."

"Sometimes fathers must volunteer, too?"

He didn't answer, just changed the subject.

"I have to go out-of-town tomorrow, a quick one-night trip."

"Coos Bay again?" She tried not to sound disappointed, but between his ramped up work schedule and her extra chores with the bigger house and children, it seemed like they spent even less time together now that they were married.

"Yup. But I'll be back for the weekend, if you need help moving out of the trailer."

His cell phone rang then, and he excused himself, taking the call in the room he used for his office. Jamie glanced around the kitchen, at the dirty dishes and counters. There were still lunches for tomorrow to be made, kids baths to organize and a load of laundry to fold.

So, this was what happily ever after looked like from the other side.

* * *

Charlotte logged in to her on-line banking and there it was—another withdrawal, made just that day. She stared at the entry on her computer screen. This was her only tenuous link to her sister. If only the numbers had the power to tell her all she longed to know.

The account was a joint one, set up by their father shortly after Daisy was married. "A woman should always have her own money," their father had insisted. "This is here for you girls, if you ever need it." For as long as he lived, their father had deposited five hundred dollars every month into that account and Charlotte had continued to do the same after his death, using income from the estate.

And almost every month, Daisy withdrew the money using various ATMs in Sacramento and the surrounding area.

In this day and age, it seemed incredible to Charlotte that no one could find her sister. But the investigator she'd hired after her parents' deaths had explained that if a person doesn't drive a car, use credit cards, or pay taxes, they can be very difficult to find.

The more likely explanation, however, was that Daisy had bought falsified ID and created a new persona for herself. Maybe that had been the only way she could go on after the failure of her marriage and the terrible mental collapse she'd had after the birth of the twins.

The phone rang and Charlotte picked up without checking the number, assuming it was Wade. They needed to talk. And facing what had happened wouldn't get easier by putting it off.

But it wasn't Wade.

"Charlotte—so good to hear your voice. Have you given further thought to speaking at our conference?"

Drat. Libby Gardener had her cornered now.

"I'm still not sure..."

"I hate to push, Charlotte, but I really think you should do this. You're an intelligent woman, with so much to offer.

In fact, now that your parents are gone, you might consider leaving Twisted Cedars all together. I have a position at our main library here in Portland that would be perfect for you."

Whoa. Charlotte sank back in her chair. "I appreciate the offer, but I enjoy my life here. A small town library may seem boring, but it isn't always." What could she say to impress the older woman? "Lately I've been helping a local New York Times bestselling author do research for his next book."

"You must be talking about Dougal Lachlan."

"Yes, I—How did you guess?"

"Twisted Cedars doesn't have that many famous authors." Libby gave a short laugh. "What's he working on now?"

Charlotte wasn't sure how much she was free to say. But Libby would have been working in the Oregon Library system when the crimes occurred and it was possible she had heard rumors.

"Do you remember hearing anything about a serial killer who stalked librarians back in the seventies?"

There was a long pause. Then—"Are you serious?"

"So far we know of two librarians who were killed. One in '72, the other in '73..."

Libby listened as Charlotte explained more about the crimes, then she inserted gently. "I can see this man has you fascinated with his theory."

Before Charlotte could reply, the older woman continued.

"Honestly, I think you're wasting your time helping Lachlan with this book of his. Please think about my job offer. I'll email the particulars of the position, and I promise you a salary increase will be part of the package. In the meantime, I'll just pencil your name into our conference program. Think about a title for your presentation, dear. Something snappy that will attract the attention of the younger crowd."

Charlotte hung up the phone feeling both manipulated

and slightly embarrassed. Her attempt to impress Libby had clearly failed.

The truth was, she did, occasionally find her job a little under-stimulating. But she simply couldn't imagine moving to Portland. Just the idea of speaking at the spring conference made her sick to her stomach.

Why was Libby so determined to "expand her borders?" Was this something her mother had asked her to do? Even if she had, Libby's perseverance seemed excessive. Maybe she should have told her she was getting married. *That* would have shut her up.

And now she was thinking about Wade, again.

Maybe *he* was waiting for *her* to call? She took a deep breath, then dialed his cell.

"Charlotte."

"Hi Wade."

There was a long silence. She should have thought ahead. Prepared the right thing to say. "I was wondering if we could talk?"

"Sure. This Friday?"

She sighed with relief at his friendly, open tone. "Great. How about I cook dinner at my place?"

What they needed to discuss could not be talked about over the pool table at the Linger Longer.

chapter seventeen

Paperwork. Wade sighed. The dirge of the profession. This week had been especially bad, thanks to a boatload of careless tourists who'd wanted to go fishing on the Rogue on Wednesday, but had ended up swimming, instead. Thanks to excellent efforts by his search and rescue team there had been no fatalities but there easily could've been.

"Hey, boss. Got a few minutes to talk to a guy named Dougal Lachlan?" His administrative assistant, Marnie Phillips, was at the door. She'd freshened her makeup since he last saw her at the front desk. Probably chomping on the bit to get started on her Friday night.

Wade had expected that eventually Dougal would make the time to see him, but, to be honest, he could have picked a better time. He'd hoped to plow through this admin stuff so he could start the weekend with a clean conscience.

Wade sighed and pushed aside his paperwork. "Yeah, I'll talk to him."

Unlike Marnie, he wasn't looking forward to this particular Friday night. Not now since things had gone sideways with Charlotte.

Wade pushed himself out of his chair, but before he could make his way to the hall to greet his old friend, Dougal was striding into his office, then shaking his hand.

"Good to see you, Wade. Thanks for making the time."

Wade just nodded. This couldn't be a personal call or Dougal would have suggested meeting at the bar. Besides, Dougal had an intense, focused expression that told Wade he was looking for information. Wade sat down and braced himself, not sure what to expect next.

"I just got back from Pendleton. Hell of a long drive."

"What were you doing there?"

"To tell you the truth, I'm not sure. Maybe doing research for a new book. Or maybe wasting my time."

"That's pretty vague."

"I just don't know enough about the situation yet." Dougal dropped into the interview chair, placed his hands on Wade's desk and leaned forward. "I'm looking into something that happened a long time ago. And I'm thinking Shirley Hammond might fit into the story."

Wade's protective instincts went on alert. "You mean Charlotte's aunt?"

"I need to know the details of how she died. People thought it was suicide right?"

"It *was* suicide. My dad was a deputy back then. He's the one who took the call. Shook him up badly."

"How do you know this? We weren't even born when Shirley died."

"Dad always liked hashing over his old cases. Shirley's death troubled him a lot. He couldn't understand why a nice woman with brains and a good family would kill herself. Especially in such a violent way."

"I have to agree with him there. It seems pretty strange. Especially since she didn't leave a note. Plus, why the hanging? That's not a choice many suicidal women make. And even more weird, why do it at the library when she lived alone in a forest filled with trees that would have served her purpose."

"Those are all valid questions. But it's been a long time. Why dig it up now?"

Dougal paused for a second. Took a deep breath. "There were other librarians murdered around that time. In 1972 a librarian named Elva Mae Ayer was strangled with a red silk scarf in Roseburg. Another librarian, Mari Beamish, was killed the same way in Pendleton in '73."

Wade jotted down the names, the dates. Writing helped him to think. "Shirley Hammond wasn't strangled. So where's the connection?"

"Maybe her suicide was motivated by guilt."

That took a few seconds to sink in. "You're suggesting Shirley might have had something to do with those deaths? That's crazy, man."

Dougal leaned back in his chair, as if considering what Wade had just said. He tented his hands under his chin and eyed Wade speculatively. "You just said suicide didn't make sense. But it would if Shirley had been involved in those murders."

"Christ. If you're planning to write a book with that theory, it better be fiction."

"I realize I haven't got much to go on. Not yet, anyway. But I was wondering if you would check the police report for me. Might be some fact or detail that would help me know if I'm on the right trail."

"Those records are over thirty years old." God, Wade didn't even know where they were stored. He rubbed a hand over his tired eyes.

"I know it won't be easy. But I sure would appreciate the help."

Wade wanted to say no. To tell Dougal to drop the whole thing. But he'd obviously put some time into this and Dougal could be pretty bull-headed. Maybe it would be best to give him the information he wanted so he could see for himself that his theory was a pile of crap. "I'll try. Don't expect instant results."

"Thanks."

Wade waited for Dougal to say something else. Maybe suggest they grab a beer, or something. But Dougal just got up from the chair and headed for the door.

Dougal had never been the most talkative guy around. But this was downright anti-social. "That's it? You ask for my help, then leave?"

Dougal turned around. "Didn't want to waste more of your time than was necessary."

"Maybe it's your time you're not willing to waste. Me, I can always find an hour to have a beer with an old friend."

"It's been a lot of years. We don't have much in common anymore. And I'm not one for reminiscing about the past."

"Nah, I guess a big shot *New York Times* bestselling author has better things to do with his time."

"You called me that before," Dougal reminded him. "But I'm no big shot. Never thought of myself that way, never will. Hell, I grew up on the wrong side of the tracks, remember?"

What was he talking about? The fact that he'd lived in a trailer?

"As if that mattered in a town like this."

"Oh, it mattered plenty. I never noticed you guys coming around my place after school."

Was he serious? "If we did or we didn't, I don't see that it mattered. We hung out together, played football, had good times."

Dougal smiled. "I like the way you see the world, Wade."

"That's the way it was."

"Maybe we should grab a beer. When do you get off for the day?"

"Soon. But I can't do it tonight." He felt bad, putting him off, when he'd made such a big deal about it. "Charlotte's making dinner for me. But next time you're in town, let me know."

* * *

From his window, Wade watched Dougal leave the building and head across the street. He was bothered by his friend's request, and not too sure why he'd agreed to dig up the old report. Suddenly Charlotte came into view, carrying several sacks of groceries—probably the fixings for tonight's dinner.

When she spotted Dougal, she hesitated. Then stiffened.

Something about the encounter seemed off.

Feeling voyeuristic, but unable to stop himself, Wade kept watching. Charlotte pushed her hair behind her ear—

something she did when she was nervous. Then she took several small backward steps away from Dougal.

Dougal appeared uneasy, too...shuffling his feet, giving Charlotte several awkward sidelong glances. When they finally parted, each heading their separate ways, Dougal only took a few steps before turning around so he could watch Charlotte until she had disappeared from sight.

* * *

At six o'clock, Wade had to admit he wasn't going to make it through all his paperwork before the weekend. He piled his papers neatly, locked his office, and on the way out said good night to the evening dispatcher.

This morning he'd had the foresight to put a bottle of wine in the back of his truck, so he drove straight to Charlotte's. She called for him to come in the unlocked door. He'd have to talk to her about that. This was a safe town, but there was no sense tempting fate.

"I'm in the kitchen." Her voice came from the back of the house.

He found her chopping vegetables at the counter. She looked up, briefly, and smiled. She'd changed out of the outfit she'd worn to work and was in jeans and a pink T-shirt, pretty in her usual, understated way. His feelings for her were not the crazy, hot, feelings he'd once had for Jamie, but he did love her.

Her refusal of his proposal had shocked him. The possibility that she would say no had honestly not occurred to him. Not that he thought of himself as so irresistible.

Far from it. He wasn't like Kyle—good looking, charming, athletic; nor was he smart like Dougal. He was the steady one. The plodder. He thought he made a good Sheriff. He loved this town and felt deeply responsible for every citizen who lived here.

He'd been lulled into a sense of security in his relationship with Charlotte based on the belief that they shared the same values. They both loved Twisted Cedars— that was the bedrock. And he knew she liked children. He'd seen her during reading hour at the library. Her face would light up, her voice turned all warm and maternal. And the little ones...they took to her, too. Toddlers would scramble over one another for the privilege of sitting on her lap.

He knew she cared about him. She'd never indicated any unhappiness with their relationship. So why didn't she want to get married? He presumed that was why she'd invited him tonight—to talk about these things. But they would leave the heavy stuff until after dinner.

"Smells great, whatever you're cooking." He sat on a stool across the counter from where she was working.

"Ribs are simmering in the slow cooker. I put them on this morning. I'm just making a salad to go with them."

He glanced around the kitchen. Aside from the salad ingredients on the counter, the place was spotless. "Can I help?"

"Maybe open that wine." She glanced up from the cutting board. "The corkscrew is in—"

But he had already opened the drawer where it was kept. He knew this kitchen almost as well as his own. Not only from the times Charlotte had invited him here, but from the days when he, Wade and Kyle had hung out with Daisy. They'd been at the Hammond house a lot back then. His place, too.

Dougal's comment about being trailer trash came to mind. Had they been too snobby to hang out in the trailer park? He didn't think so, but maybe there had been some of that.

He pulled the cork out of the bottle, then filled two glasses and set one within Charlotte's reach. "Dougal came to see me, today."

"Oh?"

He sensed tension in that one word, reminding him of the scene he'd witnessed on the sidewalk. "You ran into him on his way out. I could see you both outside my window."

"Right."

She swallowed. Looked nervous. When she didn't offer

any more, he decided to ask. "Are you still helping him with his new project?"

"A little."

"Because that was what he wanted to talk to me about." Wade took a sip of the wine. "He had a lot of questions about what happened to your Aunt Shirley."

Charlotte set down her knife. "Did he say why he wanted to know?"

He could sense her tension and he felt guilty about upsetting her. He certainly wasn't going to share the information that Dougal suspected her aunt of some involvement in those old murders. But maybe she already knew that. "Seems like there were other librarians who died around that time."

"Murdered," Charlotte surprised him by saying. "Yes."

She glanced at a framed photo on a shelving unit next to the table. It was a photo of three women, taken decades ago when color photography was a new thing. "Is this your mother?"

"Yes. And that's Aunt Shirley to her left."

Wade frowned as he noted that she wore a red scarf tied around her neck. Hadn't Dougal said those women were murdered with a red scarf?

* * *

The ribs were tender enough to slide off the bones, the barbecue sauce just the right mix of spicy and sweet, but Charlotte could barely choke down any of the dinner and she noticed Wade didn't seem to have much of an appetite, either. It hurt to look at him, to see his unhappiness, and to know she was the cause.

If she had said yes to his proposal how different this meal would have been. They would be talking about wedding dates and honeymoons and happy future plans.

And a part of her—a large part—longed for all of that.

Until recently her life had been predictable and safe...each day following a set routine, no surprises and certainly no unpleasant moral dilemmas.

How quickly that had changed. In the space of a few days, she'd turned down a marriage proposal, had a one-night stand, and cheated on her boyfriend.

If that's what Wade was.

After fifteen minutes of polite chat about work, the food, and the weather, he pushed his plate to the side.

"How about we sit on the porch and talk?"

Not her first choice of location, but she couldn't think of a reasonable objection, not on such a fine evening. Wade refilled their wine glasses. She settled into a cushioned wicker chair, leaving the loveseat with the clear view of the beach for him. He didn't pat the cushion beside him and ask her to move, like he once might have done.

Another subtle indication of the changed status of their relationship.

"I guess we'd better discuss what happened on Saturday night." His tone was serious. He sighed. "My timing was bad. I should never have asked you that way."

"But there was a reason behind your timing, wasn't there?"

"The fact that we were at a wedding, you mean?"

"The fact that we were at *Jamie's* wedding."

He looked at her a few seconds before dropping his gaze. "I care about you very much, Charlotte. I think I would make a good husband. I know you like kids, and so do I. Nothing would make me happier than to have them with you."

"Wade, I saw your face when you were trying to avoid watching Jamie walk down the aisle."

"I promise I would be devoted and faithful to you, Charlotte." His warm brown eyes promised her comfort, love and, most of all, safety.

The urge to say yes was almost overpowering. She could easily imagine them as a couple. They got along so well. And he would be a wonderful father.

But he must realize he didn't love her. At least not in the right way.

"I'm afraid I have to say no, Wade."

"You sound pretty sure about that."

"I am."

"Well...I guess that's it, isn't it? I'm going to miss our evenings together."

"Me, too." But at least she'd be free for Dougal...

As if that was going to happen. She needed to get a grip on her imagination.

He got up slowly. Went to the railing and looked out to the sea. "Too bad I spoiled everything with that stupid proposal, huh?"

"We could have continued to date for a few more months, or maybe longer. But we would have ended up in the same predicament, eventually."

He pushed away from the railing, gave her a weak smile. "Guess I'd better be going."

She walked him to his truck. Kept standing there several minutes after he was gone. Told herself she had no reason to feel guilty that she hadn't come clean about what happened with Dougal. They were both free agents now.

chapter eighteen

dougal dropped his groceries on the kitchen counter—a steak and some corn he'd picked up at Sam's Market. He was looking forward to the simple meal, along with a bottle of Pinot Noir from a case he'd bought during a detour to the Bishop Creek Winery on his drive home from Pendleton.

The idea of moving here permanently seemed more attractive with each passing day. Why not? This was a great place to write. He could easily sublet his apartment. Go back next month to get his stuff. Borden was going to be a challenge. He hoped the move wouldn't be too much for her.

While he waited for the water to boil for his corn, he wandered to his writing table and leafed through the pages he'd written that day. No doubt this place was good for his productivity. He'd poured out fifteen pages today. A story was coming together here, he just didn't think it could ever be published, because he had no idea how it ended.

Unless that was how the chain of emails was going to end...with disclosure of the killer.

But somehow Dougal doubted it was going to be that easy.

The lid on the pot started clattering under the pressure of the boiling water. Dougal hurried back to the kitchen, tossed two cobs of corn in the water, and then took the steak out to the barbecue he'd bought and assembled last week.

After his meal, he went for a walk. He followed animal trails through the forest, traveling about a mile before turning and heading back to the cottage. Fifty yards from

home he found what had once been a fenced off area. The fence posts were still standing but the wire had been trampled to the ground, probably by deer. It was too small for an animal enclosure.

Shirley had that well-worn book on growing vegetables—maybe this was where she'd had her garden. He wandered around the patchy vegetation, pulled out a hunk of grass and noted the soil was dark and loamy. Homegrown carrots and peas would sure taste great. He remembered eating some of Stella's when he'd been a kid. Maybe he could try his hand at growing a few things next year—if he stayed.

* * *

When Dougal stepped back into the house, he heard the phone ringing. He had no reason to hurry to catch it, yet he did.

It was Charlotte.

"Dougal?"

Who else did she expect it to be? "Yes. Is Wade still there?"

"He just left."

"That's early."

"Yes."

"So...how was the dinner?"

"It was sad."

Okay then. She hadn't changed her mind about marrying him.

"The reason I was calling," she continued, sounding now as if she were reading from a script, "is because I'm looking for donations for the library's annual used book sale. Proceeds go toward new books for under-privileged children."

"Good cause," he murmured, amused by her spiel.

She went off script then. "Yes it is. And I started thinking it's a shame that so many of my aunt's books are just sitting there, unused. Perhaps even some valuable first editions."

Dougal suppressed a laugh. "It's eight o'clock on a Friday evening and you're calling me—a man you've recently had sex with—about a used book drive?"

She was silent for a moment. He thought he might have pushed her too hard. Then she said, "Kind of obvious, huh?"

"Perhaps you'd better come over here and help me sort out the books yourself."

chapter nineteen

On Saturday morning, Kyle offered to take the kids to the beach so Jamie could finish moving out of the trailer.

"You decide what you want to keep and what you want to throw away," he said as he topped off her coffee after breakfast. "Then in the afternoon, the kids and I will help you haul the boxes home."

"Thanks, honey." Much as she would have enjoyed a few hours on the beach with her new family, she appreciated the opportunity to go through her belongings on her own, free to wallow in the memories to her heart's content.

Once they'd left, she drove to the trailer and parked in her usual spot, to the right of their double-wide. A "Sold" sticker had been slapped over the "For Sale," sign. She'd brought her camera with her, thinking she might mark the occasion with a few photos, but now that she was here, her heart felt too heavy.

So she left it in the car, and went to open the trunk. For a moment she paused, looking back at the pretty doublewide and recalling the day her mother left to go to the hospice. She'd kept her chin up, a smile on her face. "Thanks for the memories," she'd said, slapping the door on her way out. If she'd ever been scared—about the cancer, about the pain, about dying—she'd never shown it.

In her trunk, Jamie had a pile of cardboard boxes she'd picked up from Sam's Market yesterday. She carried them to the door, then unlocked the trailer.

Already her old home had an unused smell about it. Or was that her imagination?

"Just get the job done, girl. Stop moping." She turned on the radio to the country station. Might as well listen while she could, since Kyle preferred classic rock. She glanced around. The place already looked stripped, though all she'd taken so far were a couple of suitcases worth of clothes and shoes and books.

Her mom had believed in traveling light through life and she'd passed that philosophy down to Jamie. Still, there were a few things she wanted to keep.

The photo album, of course. She'd start with that.

It was impossible to pack the album, though, without taking a peek. She had to smile at the early photos of Dougal. Such a serious baby. Then she'd been born, and pictures of Dougal now included her. It was at this point that there ceased to be any photos of her father. Not that there'd been that many to begin with.

On the radio, the top of the hour news began playing. Wow, time had flown without her realizing. She had to stop looking and do more packing. She put the album into a box, and then packed some of her mother's favorite dishes. The soup tureen she'd inherited from her grandmother. The silver gravy boat they'd never used, but which had been a wedding gift.

Next, Jamie opened the drawer where her mother stored Dougal's mementoes. He'd taken nothing but his clothing with him when he'd moved out, leaving behind school yearbooks and report cards, not to mention his high school football trophies. She boxed all of this and shoved it in a corner. Then she carted the boxes with her things out to her car.

Finally she cleaned out the last of her mother's drawers. Most everything had already been given to Goodwill. Stella Ward had helped her sort the clothing about a month after her mom had died.

But there was still one drawer that had been untouched. In it were scarves and accessories and one small box containing what her mother had called the "good" jewelry. Jamie tried on her mother's old wedding ring. So thin and fragile. She put it back in the box with her mother's pearl earrings and gold chain, then carefully zipped the box into a compartment of her purse.

The rest of the stuff was junk. She dumped it all into a large garbage bag. That was when she saw the letter.

It was still in an envelope, with a return address from the Oregon State Penitentiary.

As soon as she saw that, she knew it was from her father.

Jamie sank onto her mother's stripped mattress to read it.

Two pages, hand-written with a date on the top left corner. It had been written about six months before her mother died.

Katie...I just heard about your cancer diagnosis. You of all people. It's so god damned unfair!

How had he found out? Obviously there was someone in Twisted Cedars he kept in contact with. But who?

You fight this thing, okay Katie? Don't give up. And in case you didn't already know—but I'm pretty sure you figured it out at some point—the reason I left was because I loved you. You were the only one who ever saw any good in me.

Her father wrote a little about his life in prison, then reminisced about the first time he'd met Katie—*Stella and Amos had us over for dinner. I went, expecting to be bored senseless. Instead, for the first and only time in my life, I fell instantly in love.*

Jamie's eyes misted over. She dabbed them with the back of her hand so she could read the last paragraph.

Tell Dougal I'd be glad to hear from him sometime. I've tried writing him letters. He never answers. Tell him his old man wasn't all bad. Would you do that for me, Katie?

And that was it. Not even a mention about *her*.

How could there have been? He didn't know she existed. Still. Jamie felt his disinterest like an aching wound.

* * *

Jamie hummed along to Dwight Yokam on the radio as she

left her old home and headed toward the new one. When she arrived, she opened the trunk and hauled out the first of the boxes she'd packed. She knew Kyle would help her with this later, but the boxes weren't heavy and she decided to get the job over with. One by one she carried them downstairs to the storage room.

Previously she'd never given the room anything but a glance. Kyle kept it very tidy. The walls were lined with wooden shelving units, most containing plastic storage tubs with printed labels: Christmas lights, tree decorations, baby clothes, sports equipment. One duffel bag contained Kyle's old football gear and she had to smile. He hadn't played the game in years.

The shelf above the duffel bag was empty. Maybe she could squeeze her boxes up there. As she pushed the cartons over, she noticed a box in the far, back corner marked "Daisy."

Her heart started beating faster, harder. She'd noticed, like their father, Kyle's children never talked about their mother. If they wondered if she would ever come home, they never voiced those questions out loud. Was that normal? She should talk to Kyle about it, see if his kids had ever received counselling.

Jamie glanced again at the box marked with Daisy's name. She should put her own boxes away and just leave. But would a quick peek hurt anything? She pulled down the carton, set it on the floor and then removed the lid. Inside were personal effects...a jewelry box, make-up, and novels. This was the sort of snooping her mother would never have approved of. Even though they'd lived in cramped quarters, her mom had been strict about respecting privacy.

Nevertheless, Jamie continued to rummage through the box, pulling out Clinique beauty products, White Diamond perfume—she recognized the scent, which Daisy had worn back when she was in high school— some costume jewelry and a velvet bag with pearls. Funny Daisy had left so much behind. But then, if you were leaving your husband and children, you probably wouldn't think about trifles like make-up and jewelry.

Also in the box were a bunch of novels…most of them historical romances where women in lovely gowns and cascading curls were held in the arms of dashing rakes with bare chests. Good old-fashioned, fantasy escape stories.

Sorting through the books, she came to a thick notebook. The cover was faded, the edges tattered. With a jolt of surprise, she realized she was holding Daisy's journal. She turned the pages slowly and carefully, startled at how messy the writing was. Daisy had pasted clippings from magazines, ticket stubs, business cards and photographs throughout, creating crazy collages that seemed to have no sense or reason.

"Why won't anyone help me?" Jamie read. The following sentences were illegible, and some had been covered over by a magazine photo of a female lion eating her kill. Jamie read the caption to the photo, and was appalled to find out the "kill" was actually the lion's cub.

Jamie flipped the page, and eventually found another line she could make out. "I never thought it would be like this. Why doesn't anyone warn you? I wish—"

"Jamie? Are you down here?"

She gasped. Oh no. Kyle. She slammed the journal shut just as her husband entered the storage room. His gaze dropped to the book in her hand, then to the open box. His expression darkened and for the first time in their relationship, she felt a little bit afraid.

"Sorry. Oh, God, I shouldn't be looking through this stuff should I? I'm such a snoop."

The angry look was gone. He shook his head at her. "I told you I would take care of the boxes for you," he said mildly.

"I know. And I should have left them for you." She started to repack Daisy's box, but he stopped her.

"Just leave it, Jamie. I'll put that away later. I'm saving those things for the kids, when they're older. If Daisy never does come back, at least they'll have something to remember her by."

She hesitated for a second before accepting Kyle's hand and allowing him to help her up. Was this a good time to mention the idea of counselling for the children? She glanced at his eyes, and shivered at his stony, cold expression. No, it wasn't.

They climbed the stairs in silence. She could hardly blame him for being annoyed with her. She'd had no right to look through Daisy's belongings and certainly not to read her journal. But now that she had, she couldn't help feeling sympathy for the other woman. If Daisy's mind had been in the same shape as that journal, it must have been quite a mess. But what had Daisy wished she'd been warned about?

* * *

Jamie was still sleeping when she heard a timid voice.

"Are you awake yet?"

It was Cory. Jamie opened her eyes. The little girl was standing on the other side of the open bedroom door.

Jamie patted the empty space beside her. Kyle must be up already. Oh, right. He'd told her he was playing golf this morning.

"I made you breakfast in bed."

Jamie sat up on her elbows, cleared her throat. "How nice. Come on in, Cory."

The little girl nudged the door wide open before she entered with a carefully balanced tray. "I made you oatmeal and juice. Your favorite."

"How did you know oatmeal was my favorite? Mm, that smells good." She sat upright, pulled the covers up to her navel and then took the tray from Cory's hands. "Did you make enough for two?"

"You have oatmeal every day. That's how I know it's your favorite. And I've already eaten. Chester and I had cereal with Daddy before he went to play golf."

"Sorry. I've been lazy." She stirred the lumps out of the oatmeal, then took a big spoonful.

"That's okay. Daddy said we should let you sleep. I've been waiting a long time."

Which explained why the oatmeal was cold. Jamie took another bite, then some juice. "So what would you like to do today?"

Kyle had suggested she and the kids meet him at the club-house for a late lunch after his game. It would have been nice to spend the entire day together, but he was playing with business associates and they'd be discussing a new condo development.

"Cross your fingers for me," he'd said last night. "If this financing comes through, we're almost guaranteed to make a pile of money."

"We could go to the beach again," Cory said. "But I think Chester wants to stay home and play video games."

"Is that what he's doing now?"

Cory nodded. Her hair was in desperate need of a good combing and her T-shirt was stained. Jamie suspected the kitchen would be messy as well.

Jamie quickly spooned down the rest of her cereal. "That was very nice, Cory. How about I get dressed so we can get started on the day?"

"I'll put the dishes in the dishwasher."

"You don't need to do that, honey."

Cory beamed at her, then left with the tray. Jamie wondered how long this super-pleasing phase was going to last. She hoped that soon Cory would be comfortable enough to just be herself.

Jamie spent ten minutes in the bathroom, then dressed in shorts and a T-shirt and went looking for the kids. She found them in the living room, where Cory was perched on her brother's chair watching him play Xbox.

"Hey Chester. What game is that?"

"Madden NFL." His eyes never left the screen.

"So you like football, do you?"

"My Dad was offered scholarships to play college football. He turned them down to work in the family business. When I'm older, I'm going to play football, too."

"That sounds like a good plan." She glanced out the window into the big back yard. "It's a nice day. What do you say we go outside and toss a real football around for a while?"

"Do you know how?" Chester sounded skeptical.

"Sure. I have a perfect spiral. My brother taught me. Dougal used to play on the same high school team as your father."

"I've got a football," Chester said. "Can we play now?"

"Sure. Cory, are you in? It's more fun with three."

She looked thrilled to be included and nodded emphatically.

They slipped on sneakers then went out the back door. Jamie hadn't thrown a football in years, but the technique came back naturally and her first spiral only wobbled a little.

"How do you do that?" Cory asked.

Though they were still small, both kids had good arms and a lot of stamina. An hour passed quickly with the three of them scrimmaging while Chester provided a running commentary of the action. Jamie had never heard him speak so much or with such animation.

Until, finally, Cory went for a catch and ended up nicking the ball with the end of her fingers. She yelped as the fingers were pushed back the wrong way. "Ow! I broke my finger!"

Jamie took a look. "Maybe just sprained. We should put some ice on it, though."

"Can't we keep playing without her?" Chester had run to capture the ball and now he held it in one hand using the grip Jamie had taught him.

"Later," Jamie suggested. "It's time we stopped for a snack, anyway. Should I make popcorn?"

"I'll do it!" Cory forgot about her injury as she raced her brother inside.

Jamie lingered on the lawn. All morning her thoughts had been ping-ponging from Daisy's diary, to the letter from her father she'd found in the trailer. Figuring the kids wouldn't miss her for a few minutes, she dug her cell phone out of her pocket and called Wade.

"Jamie?" he said, as if he couldn't believe it was her.

"I have a favor to ask. Do you think you could find out if my father is still in the State Penitentiary?"

"I don't need to check, Jamie, I know. He's out."

Oh my God. Dougal probably knew and he hadn't told her. "Any chance you could find out his address, or a phone number?"

"He would be on parole. So maybe. But are you sure contacting him would be a good idea?"

She wasn't. And she was pretty sure both her brother and her husband would have major reservations, too. But she also knew she would always regret it if she didn't at least try to reach out to him.

"I found a letter he wrote to Mom before she died. It was a nice letter, Wade. He didn't sound that bad..."

She could hear Wade sigh. "I guess I could put out a few feelers. But don't get your hopes up."

chapter twenty

as far as Dougal was concerned nothing could be sexier than this: a librarian wearing only her eyeglasses, her hair tousled from recently having sex, totally engrossed in one of his books. *A Murder in the Family*, to be precise.

The print-out had arrived in the mail while he'd been in Pendleton. His last chance to check over the manuscript before it went in for publication. He'd been glad to delegate the job to Charlotte.

He tried to hand her a cup of coffee—he'd just brewed a new pot—but she waved for him to put it on the bedside table.

"Is the book any good?"

"Hmmm." She didn't even look up for a second this time.

"I'll take that as a yes. You have great tits by the way."

Still no response.

He went back to the living room where they'd already packed two boxes of books and were working on the third. At least, they had been working until Charlotte spied the final line edit copy of his upcoming book sitting on his desk.

"May I read this?"

He'd been flattered by her interest. "On one condition."

His condition had been that she let him take her back to bed. Sex with the librarian was remarkably good. *Everything* with the librarian was remarkably good. Talking, going for walks, sharing meals, even sleeping seemed nicer with her in his bed.

He pruned through the books on the last two shelves,

finding another dozen titles to put in for the sale. He finished his coffee, cleaned up after their late breakfast of toast and eggs, then went back to the bedroom.

Charlotte was on her stomach now, still naked, legs bent at the knees so her feet dangled in the air. He felt a strange, light-headed emotion. Happiness?

He kissed her toes. "Finished, yet?"

"Oh, no...."

"I'm getting bored."

"Go for a walk. It's a nice day."

"How would you know? You haven't looked up once since you started reading."

"You should take that as a compliment."

"I'm beginning to think you only like me for my writing ability."

Finally she put down the manuscript pages. She studied his face solemnly. "You must be kidding."

"Well, yeah, I was." He settled on the bed beside her, taking her into his arms. She smelled like coffee and sex and vanilla. "Why didn't you want to marry Wade?"

He expected her to say she hadn't loved him. Instead she said, "I'll tell you if you tell me something first."

"What?"

"Why didn't you go to your sister's wedding?"

"Because I warned her not to marry that creep."

"Yes, but why? What do you have against Kyle? You were friends when you were younger."

"Yeah, well maybe I wasn't such a great judge of character back then. Kyle was always a cheat. He cheated at school and he cheated on his girlfriends...including your sister Daisy."

Charlotte tensed, but didn't interrupt.

"He was also a mean bastard. Loved to pull pranks. And I always played along. He knew he could count on me to back him up. I'm ashamed, for the way I used to look up to him. Wade never did, you know. That guy always had his head screwed on straight."

Dougal didn't want to talk about this shit anymore. He hated thinking back on all the dumb stunts he and Kyle had pulled. At the very least, he should have told Daisy about the cheating. Daisy had been his friend, too.

"So now it's your turn. Answer my question."

Charlotte took off her glasses, looked him straight in the eyes. "I turned down Wade's proposal because I know he's in love with your sister."

He hadn't expected that. "Really?"

"When he moved back to Twisted Cedars after his father retired, he tried to ask her out. But either he was too subtle, or Jamie deliberately misinterpreted his motives. At any rate, although they spent a lot of time together, he still hadn't managed to ask her on a formal date when Kyle suddenly started showing her interest."

Dougal thought back to the comment he'd made the first time he'd seen Wade. He never would have said it if he'd known Wade had feelings for Jamie. Too bad the fool hadn't acted on them before it was too late.

"What if Wade hadn't been in love with my sister. Would you have said yes to his proposal then?"

She put a finger on her lips. "Only one question, remember?"

* * *

The phone call from Jamie had caught Wade off guard. He knew he should have refused her request. But saying no to Jamie wasn't easy. Besides, he'd already agreed to do a similar favor for her brother, so what the hell.

He set aside the Sunday paper. Nice day for a stroll, he might as well head to the office since he needed the exercise and fresh air. Last night he'd put in a few too many hours, and more than a few too many beers, at the Linger Longer. He figured he was entitled. In the space of one week, he'd lost two women. Not that Jamie had ever been his.

Still.

Sitting at his desk, he felt useful, at least. *Look at the bright side, Wade,* he could imagine his mother saying. *You have a job, a home, a community of friends and neighbors.* This was all true, and he knew he should be grateful.

Wade fired up his computer to check the records. Then felt the back of his neck tingle when he saw an outstanding warrant for Edward Lachlan's arrest. He'd skipped out on his parole shortly after his release, whereabouts currently unknown. Wade fired off a quick email to Jamie, advising her to let the matter drop here.

Next he searched the data base to find out when Shirley Hammond had died: April 7, 1976.

A damned long time ago. Hell, the records could have been destroyed by now. Shaking his head at himself, Wade descended to the storage room in the basement. The ACL in his knee—an old football injury—ached a little with each step. The rows of file cabinets in the record room seemed daunting at first glance. He didn't come down here often. All he had to do was ask Marnie for a file and it was on his desk five minutes later.

She could be a nag, but she was efficient.

The records were organized by date. And, amazingly, they went back as far the seventies. Within ten minutes, he'd found the report his father had filed after finding Shirley Hammond's body.

Wade had expected certain routine comments and an irrefutable conclusion, but the report turned out to be more interesting than that. He pulled out his notepad, jotted down the salient points before returning the file to the cabinets. Marnie would freak out if he didn't.

He looked over his notes one more time, and then called his father.

"How's it going, son?"

They chatted for a few minutes before Wade brought up the purpose of his call. "Dougal Lachlan's back in town. He's doing some research for a new book and he wants to know about Shirley Hammond's death."

The line went silent for a moment. "One of the saddest cases I ever worked on."

"I know. What I was wondering Dad, is whether there was anything about the case that didn't make it into your report?"

"Funny you ask that."

He waited.

"A few weeks after Shirley's death, the board realized that the library improvement fund—ten thousand dollars—had gone missing."

"Really? That was a lot of money back then."

"Sure was." His father sighed. "Folks trusted her. They'd bring their donations straight to the library and she'd put the money in a cash box she kept locked in the bottom drawer of her desk. But after she died, we couldn't find it."

"Any theories on what happened to the money?"

"Well, most of us figured she must have spent it or lost it, somehow. We tried to keep it quiet for the sake of her reputation, and to spare the family."

"Do you think that's why she killed herself?"

"Must have been. A real shame, though. I know her brother would have gladly replaced the money if she'd only asked. He did it anyway after she was gone."

* * *

As he made the turn to the Hammonds' cabin off the Forestry Road, Wade was surprised to see Charlotte's BMW parked behind Dougal's car.

He recalled the awkward encounter he'd witnessed between the two of them yesterday. Was it possible they were disagreeing on rental terms? Maybe now that he'd moved in, Dougal wasn't as happy with the cottage as he'd expected.

Wade slid out of his truck, feet landing firmly on a thick carpet of pine needles. Sure was quiet out here. He inhaled the woodsy scent. The aroma of coffee was in the air, too. Fried eggs and toast. His stomach growled.

Wade drove out this way now and then, to check on the place and make sure it hadn't been vandalized. Luckily it seemed the local kids had never ventured this far for any of their parties. They mostly preferred the beach, just as he and his buddies had in their day.

The weathered A-frame had to be almost fifty years old, but it still looked solid. Before he could knock, the door opened. Dougal looked preoccupied. He brushed a hand through his hair, settling it down somewhat.

"Hey, Wade."

Maybe he should have called first. Never occurred to him he might be interrupting something. "Mind if I come in?"

After a brief pause, Dougal stepped aside.

The scent of breakfast was stronger in here. Wade could feel his mouth watering...but then he saw Charlotte and his mouth went dry.

She was in jeans and a T-shirt, with the same disheveled look as Dougal. Now it was all too clear what he'd interrupted. It wasn't breakfast nor was it writing and research.

"Hi, Wade," she said, her voice quiet. She tucked her hair behind her ears, then looked uncertainly toward Dougal.

Wade didn't anger easily, but Jesus Christ. So soon?

He thought back on the accidental meeting he'd witnessed between these two yesterday and realized this wasn't the beginning. Something had already happened between them. He remembered how excited she'd been about Dougal showing up at the library. Naively, he'd assumed it was the challenging research that had her so pumped up.

"On second thought, this can wait for another time." As he turned to leave, Charlotte rushed to the door.

"Don't do that, Wade. I was just leaving myself. Thanks for helping me sort my aunt's books, Dougal." She slipped shoes on her feet, grabbed one of several cardboard boxes stacked by the door and went out. Dougal picked up the remaining boxes and followed. It all happened so quickly Wade was left speechless.

Suddenly alone, he scanned the room with investigative

thoroughness. The dish rack held enough plates for several meals...so she'd probably spent the night. A frying pan...still on the stove, the coffee pot...half full.

The bedroom seemed to be upstairs. But the cushions on the sofa were tousled, and a quilt and several pillows were strewn on the floor.

He kept tracking the evidence, couldn't stop himself. An empty bottle of wine on the coffee table. He caught a glimpse of pink and ducked his head. Yup, just as he'd thought—a lacy thong mingled with a pair of men's black cotton briefs under the couch.

"She's gone. Sorry about that." Dougal was back, sounding a little breathless.

Sorry about what, Wade wanted to ask. Screwing my girlfriend?

Some men might have slugged Dougal at that point. But Wade kept quiet as Dougal went to the fridge, pulled out a beer and tossed it to him.

"Want to go for a walk?"

Wade pulled the tab. Nodded. They fell into step easily once they'd left the cottage behind. The woods had a calming effect, as did the warmth of the afternoon.

"Look, I'm sorry if you're upset about Charlotte—"

"Let's not talk about that right now." Wade kept his eyes on the trail. He'd been pretty taken aback. He needed time to process what he'd discovered before he discussed it with anyone. Let alone the guy who was sleeping with his ex-girlfriend.

Ex.

Funny to think of Charlotte that way. He felt a pang of sorrow. Knew there were things he was going to miss and that taking that relationship beyond friendship might have been a huge mistake.

"I checked into those records you were asking about."

A jay squawked from somewhere in the towering treetops. Both men glanced up, then at each other.

For some reason Wade was reminded of the school-

aged Dougal. He'd been quiet, dependable, a hell of a student and a pretty mean half-back. But no matter how many hours of the day they spent together, there'd always been something inscrutable in those dark brown eyes of his.

"You found the report that was filed when Shirley Hammond died?"

"Yeah, I did. And there were some peculiar things in there. Like for instance, she hung herself with two silk scarves that she'd knotted together."

"Were the scarves red?"

Wade didn't need to pull out his notebook. "Yeah. Pretty weird, huh? If I was going to hang myself, I'd use rope. It's strong and available everywhere."

"Was there anything to suggest that someone else might have done it?"

"Not at all. In fact, a reference book was open on the floor nearby. It had directions on how to hang yourself. Trust a librarian to even think of looking in a book for something like that."

They came across a big tree that had fallen over the path. Rather than walk around it, they both sat on the broad trunk, and took pulls from their cans of beer. An odd congeniality settled over them. It was like they were kids, again, talking over an assignment at school, or a new football play.

"Did the report say who found the body in the library?"

"It was Amos Ward. He'd been installing some new shelving units on the main floor. Forgot his toolbox and came back to the library around closing time. The front door was unlocked, but no one was there. He finally checked the basement and that's when he found her."

"Did Amos cut her down?"

"No. He checked her pulse, and then called the Sheriff's office. Like I told you before, my dad was first responder. I called him this morning, to see if he remembered anything that wasn't in the report."

"And did he?"

Wade nodded. "After her death, the Board discovered ten thousand dollars of library funds were missing—funds that Shirley had been responsible for."

Wade swallowed the last of his beer. He glanced at Dougal, who was watching him thoughtfully.

"I suppose, back then, the missing money might have looked like a motive for the suicide?"

"No one could say for sure, since there was no note. But there was speculation. For the sake of Shirley and her family's reputation, her brother replaced the money and it was kept quiet."

"I appreciate your checking into this for me," Dougal said.

"No problem. So, what do you make of it?"

"Something doesn't smell right. Seems to be a regular problem in this town."

"Maybe this town doesn't have a problem. Could be it's you. Too much imagination."

"That's possible, too," Dougal agreed.

chapter twenty-one

Sitting at the computer in the kitchen, Jamie checked her email and found a message from Wade. "Can't find any trace of your dad. He doesn't have a current Oregon driver's license. Sorry, Jamie. But maybe it's for the best."

Not surprised, but saddened, she turned to Cory and Chester. "Time to hit the shower, kids. We have to meet your dad for lunch in about one hour."

"Me, first," Cory said. Chester didn't argue. He asked Jamie if he could play his video game while he waited for his turn.

"Sure." When she was alone, she responded to Wade, thanking him for making an effort.

After that, she changed into a blue sundress, noticing as she glanced at the mirror that she was getting a good tan. As she smoothed lotion over the rough spots on her elbows and knees, she thought about the man who had supplied her with her olive complexion, last name, half her DNA, and not much else.

In the letter he'd sent to her mother, he'd sounded keen to talk to his son. Would he be as happy to meet up with a daughter? One he presumably hadn't known existed?

He hadn't been spoken of much when she was growing up. Her mother seemed to shrink a little any time the subject of Edward Lachlan was raised. She knew Dougal had been embarrassed for their mom, that she never found a man who seemed to want a long term relationship.

But Jamie thought it was the other way around. It was their mother who wasn't interested in falling in love again. She went to the Linger Longer to relax and have fun. But she'd given her heart to Edward Lachlan. And that had never changed.

Despite the fact that he'd gone to jail, her dad couldn't have been all bad. Or why would her mom have continued to love him? The fact that she'd saved his letter proved that she had.

And the fact that she hadn't thrown it away, even though she knew she was dying, meant she'd wanted Jamie to find it. She hadn't had the strength to tell her daughter about her father when she was alive. But she'd kept the door open to the possibility that Jamie would find him after she was gone.

"We're ready." Chester was at her bedroom door.

She forced a smile. "Let's get going, then."

The Rogue River Golf and Country Club had been built on a bluff overlooking the ocean. The drive was only fifteen miles, but they were all uphill on narrow, winding roads. Jamie gave the road her full attention. It had taken more than a few lives over the years, not just Patricia and Jonathan Hammond's.

When they arrived she was able to park her convertible next to Kyle's SUV. As they walked toward the clubhouse, she spotted Kyle on the green for the eighteenth hole. His hair seemed even more golden than usual in the afternoon sun, and he looked tall and lean in his powder blue golf shirt and tan slacks.

When he'd sunk his ball, she called out to him. He glanced their way, then smiled and headed toward them, calling something back to his buddies.

"Hey guys. Good timing." He put a hand on his son's head, then his daughter's, before giving Jamie a warm kiss. He smelled like sunshine and grass and she wished they were alone because right now she wanted to be with him in the worst way.

But then his father approached. "Hey kids. Got a hug for your grandpa?"

The kids practically tackled him, but Jim didn't seem to

mind.

Soon they were seated on an outdoor terrace. A server appeared within seconds to take their drink orders. Jamie glanced around the table, feeling a little bemused. These people were all her family now. It felt nice, but also surreal. She couldn't help but miss her Mom and wish that Dougal were here, too.

They were on dessert, when a group of men in their fifties headed for a table nearby. One of them was Ben Mason, founding partner at the accounting firm where Jamie worked. When he spotted Jamie, he smiled and headed her way.

"Nice to see you here. Have you finally taken my advice and started playing golf?"

According to Ben, it was a necessary skill if she wanted to get ahead in her profession. The business community in Twisted was small and inter-connected. Almost all of them were members here. "Not yet, Ben. I'm having lunch with my family."

It was so lovely saying that. *Family.* Ben said hello to Jim and Kyle, then Jamie introduced the children. They were amazingly well behaved, not even squirming in their chairs as most children would in such an adult setting.

When the niceties were over, Ben said, "Let me know if you change your mind, Jamie. I'd be glad to teach you."

"Jamie is too busy for golf right now." Kyle placed his hand over hers. "When the kids are older I'll make sure she learns the basics."

Jamie flushed at his overbearing comment, but said nothing.

Later that night when they were alone in their bedroom, she raised the subject.

"I wish you wouldn't have spoken to Ben that way. Isn't it up to me to decide whether or not I play golf?" She sat on the side of the bed, still in her dress, needing help with the zipper but too annoyed to ask.

Kyle pulled his shirt over his head. "You told me you

found the game boring." He took off his watch next and set it on the bureau beside his wallet.

"I do! That's not the point."

"Sorry, honey. I don't get it." He was just in his briefs now. And though she was still angry, a part of her had to admire how hot he looked.

Maybe he hadn't realized how his comment to Ben had come across.

"When you speak on my behalf, you make me feel like a child instead of your wife."

"Are you sorry you married me? Are the children more work than you bargained for?"

"Of course not," she said, though in actual fact their life together was a lot different than she'd imagined. "I just wish we had more time together."

He pulled her up from the bed, put his arms around her. "We will. When the kids are older. And at least we have our nights..."

Slowly he worked the zipper down to the small of her back. He slid his hands under the fabric and cupped her ass, pulling her into him...kissing her until her concerns were forgotten.

* * *

Dougal took a few hours to digest the news Wade had provided, sitting at the kitchen table, making notes and integrating the facts with those he already knew. Charlotte's perfume still lingered in the air of the cabin, but he did his best to ignore it.

She'd obviously been upset that Wade had seen them together. Best let her work out for herself what that meant.

After dinner, Dougal called Stella. "Is Amos home?"

She hesitated. "He's at the workshop."

"Is there a phone in there?"

Again there was a pause. Dougal realized she wasn't happy about this call. Was it because she didn't want him to speak to her husband? But finally she responded by giving him Amos's cell phone number.

"Thanks, Stella." He disconnected then redialed.

"Hello?" Amos sounded wary.

"Hey, Amos. It's Dougal."

"I know. Your name came up on the display."

"I was wondering if I could buy you a beer at the Linger Longer tonight."

"That depends. If you want to shoot the breeze—sure. If you're looking to hire me for a project, I'm booked up until November. But if it's Shirley Hammond you want to ask about, I'm not interested."

Dougal had to laugh. "How'd you know I had some questions about Shirley?"

Amos cleared his throat. "I've heard you're hanging out at the library these days, working on a new book, asking lots of questions about the past. You ought to leave all that alone, boy."

Dougal was no longer amused. "You found her body, didn't you, Amos? The day she committed suicide."

"I did and it's nothing I ever want to talk about again. Pretty much the most awful thing I've ever seen."

"I'm sure it was. But did you—"

"Forget it, Dougal. I'm fond of you, and I'd gladly meet for a drink and maybe a game of pool sometime. But as far as I'm concerned, questions about Shirley Hammond are just plain off limits."

* * *

For most of that night Dougal pondered his conversation with Amos. Why was the subject of Shirley Hammond off limits? He could understand that finding her body must have been upsetting. But after all these years the shock should have worn off.

He wished he could talk the situation over with Charlotte. But she'd taken off pretty quickly after Wade arrived. He wasn't sure calling her tonight was a good idea.

The next morning, Dougal still wanted to talk to Charlotte. What was he—obsessed? He tried to focus on his writing, but it was difficult when he didn't even know if this book would ever get finished. He was pretty much dependent on Librarianmomma to feed him more information about the other women who'd been killed. And he hadn't had a message from her in a long while.

He could always try contacting her. But for some reason he felt reluctant to do that.

He wished he had Charlotte here to distract him. It was kind of puzzling how it seemed the more he saw her, the more he wanted her.

It was almost like he was mooning over the librarian.

He didn't do mooning, for God's sake. Wasn't his style.

Still, she was a puzzle, and puzzles *were* his style. According to Charlotte, she hadn't said yes to Wade's proposal because he was in love with Jamie.

That didn't rule out the possibility that she had loved Wade.

But why should he care? She was sleeping with him. Wasn't that enough?

The obvious answer—that it wasn't enough or why was he even thinking about this—made him testy.

He got up for some coffee. The stuff left in the pot smelled rank. Suddenly he felt stifled. He needed to go for a drive.

Shoving his laptop and notebook into the passenger seat of his car, he took off—in the opposite direction of Twisted Cedars this time. The next nearest town to the north was forty minutes away and when he arrived in Port Orford, he drove around for a bit until he'd found a café with wireless.

Inside he ordered a large coffee and a bagel, placed his laptop on a corner table and turned it on. He didn't normally check email when he was writing—too distracting. But today that was exactly what he needed. His thoughts were driving him crazy.

And like a special bonanza, there it was. Another message from Librarianmomma.

You'll want to check into Bernice Gilberg from Corvallis and Isabel Fraser from Medford next. That's the complete list. I'll leave it your hands now. You already know about Shirley so you should be able to figure out the rest. If you can't, I'll be waiting to hear from you.

Dougal stared at the message, heart working so hard he could feel the force of the blood moving through his veins.

He couldn't deny the feeling. Excitement.

Two more victims. Two more chances for him to figure out what was going on here. And that reference to Shirley. How did Librarianmomma know he'd been asking questions about her? Was she someone in Twisted Cedars? Maybe someone who had heard about his questions?

God, he had so many questions. Most of all, about himself.

Who got hyped about shit like this? He was such a screw up. Now he was glad he hadn't given in to the urge to call Charlotte after she left on Sunday. He didn't do relationships, because it wasn't safe.

As simple as that.

He read the message again, feeling the unwanted thrill.

Face it. He'd *wanted* to hear from Librarianmomma again.

And now he had. He had no doubt what he would find when he went to the library tomorrow to conduct his research. Bernice Gilberg—dead. Isabel Fraser—dead. Both would have been strangled with a red silk scarf. Just like the scarves that Shirley Hammond had tied together in order to kill herself out of remorse for what she'd done.

That was what he knew. But there was so much missing. What linked these four women, beyond the fact that they were librarians? Why had the murders been spaced one year apart? And the million dollar question—what was Shirley's connection to the crimes?

He thought about the picture of her wearing her red scarf. Somehow she'd been involved, right from the beginning. But it was hard to imagine a woman committing such vicious crimes. Strangulation required a certain amount of strength.

Dougal reread at the message. *I'll be waiting to hear from you.* He wondered if he should hit reply. Ask Librarianmomma all the questions that were driving him crazy.

His fingers hovered over the keys.

But he couldn't do it.

These messages could be coming from a witness. But they might be from the killer, too. And if that was the case, he did not want to engage with her unless absolutely necessary. Better to keep whatever distance he could.

* * *

As he drove back to his cottage, Dougal puzzled over the identity of Librarianmomma. Who was this person? Did the timing of these emails have something to do with the death of Charlotte's parents, two years ago? They would have been Shirley's closest relatives. Maybe the person who knew about the murders had wanted to protect them and had kept quiet until now.

Of course, this was assuming that Librarianmomma was a witness. But if she was the murderer, why come forward now? Perhaps she'd received a bad medical diagnosis and wanted to come clean to clear her conscience before death?

Weak. But so was every other explanation he came up with.

Once home, Dougal went for a walk to think things through. The murders happened so long ago. Why choose to reveal it all now?

And why spill the beans to him?

But maybe that question wasn't so difficult. He'd been selected because of his profession and because of his hometown. The information was printed in the bio on the inside cover of all his books, as well as his website.

Dougal trudged on for over an hour. In the short time he'd lived here, already he could see where his footsteps had beaten a path through the old forest. Having a path was good. Since there were few landmarks, it would be all too easy to get lost, especially on a cloudy day or if he got caught out after nightfall.

He stopped for a moment, to take his bearings.

Around him the woods were silent. Eerily so. He had the strange sensation of being watched, and though he knew it had to be his imagination, decided to head back to the cottage.

Twenty minutes later, he passed Shirley's old garden. Wouldn't hurt him to get some exercise out here. Maybe he should pick up a spade next time he was in town and turn over these weeds.

Just five minutes from home now. He paused for a moment, feeling it again, the presence of someone...or something...watching and waiting.

God, this isolation was getting to him. Maybe he should break down and call Charlotte. No. Bad idea. He'd go to the bar.

chapter twenty-two

Cory's small hand felt warm and precious in Jamie's grip. The little girl had been holding on tight ever since Jamie showed up in the classroom. She was thrilled Jamie had volunteered for the field trip to the Sheriff's Office.

Not so Chester. He had barely nodded at her when she walked in the door. Now he seemed to be pretending that she and Cory were total strangers.

Their teacher, Mrs. Wood, was a tall, unflappable woman, who never needed to raise her voice in order for the children to listen to her. She'd been warm and welcoming to Jamie and it was clear she had a soft spot for the motherless twins.

Five other parents had volunteered to accompany the twenty children in this class to first the Fire Station and now the Sheriff's Office, where they were being given a tour and lectured at intervals on the importance of being a law-abiding citizen. Or else.

"And here is our temporary lock-up." Deputy Michaels opened the door on a small, cement-floored room with a privy in one corner and a cot in the other.

"Ewww."

"Yuck."

"Gross."

Questions followed, a lot of them from Chester who seemed to be a natural leader in the class. She noticed several of the boys looked to him first, before reacting to comments from the deputy or Mrs. Wood.

When the day was finally over, and the children had been car-pooled back to the school, Jamie felt exhausted and in awe of Mrs. Woods who spent every working day dealing with twenty, nine-year-old children. In the school parking lot, roll call was taken, students accounted for, and then dismissed. Jamie turned to Cory and Chester.

"Anyone interested in going out for ice cream?" She wanted to end the day on a festive note, and definitely felt she had earned a double chocolate scoop herself.

Chester looked tempted, but he'd been invited to play at a friend's house, and when she gave her permission, opted to do that instead.

Cory squeezed her hand even tighter. "Can we still go—just the two of us?"

"Sure. Maybe we'll do some shopping, too."

"Chester hates shopping."

"A lot of guys do."

They ordered cones from the Sweets Shop on Driftwood Lane, window-shopping as they strolled toward home.

"Look at this." Jamie stopped at a display of wicker patio furniture in the hardware store window. "Wouldn't this be wonderful on our front porch?"

"But we already have chairs on our porch."

Yes. Ugly green plastic ones. "These are prettier, don't you think?"

"Would Daddy like them?"

"I'm sure he would. Let's go inside and see if they're comfortable." They finished their cones and Jamie used a tissue to clean Cory's mouth and hands. Then they went inside to see if the cushions were as comfortable as they looked.

"Soft, huh?" Jamie smiled at Cory who was on the chair next to hers.

Cory nodded.

Jamie needed no more encouragement. "Let's get them."

"But Daddy—"

"Let's surprise him. It'll be fun."

Jamie lowered the roof on her convertible and with the store manager's help, crammed the chairs into the back seat, the cushions in the trunk. Jamie drove home, anxious to set up the new furniture. When she arrived, Stella emerged from the house, followed by Liz who was wearing denim overalls and carrying two buckets of cleaning supplies. She'd forgotten it was cleaning day, today. It was a new luxury in her life—one she wasn't sure she could get used to.

"Buy something new?" Liz checked out the chairs overflowing from the back seat. "Sweet."

"Yeah, for the porch." Jamie held out a hand for one of Liz's buckets. "Let me help you with that."

"I'm fine," Liz insisted.

Jamie watched as she stowed the cleaning supplies into her rusting Jeep. "This is so strange. I've never paid anyone to clean my home for me before."

"Well, enjoy it," Stella said, without rancor, as far as Jamie could tell.

She wasn't sure she could. "I'm used to doing my own vacuuming and dusting."

"Don't you dare do us out of this job, Jamie." Liz wiped her hands on the front of the overalls. "I need the money for my mortgage payments."

When she'd signed the final papers for the sale, Jamie had been surprised to see Liz Brook's name. Apparently Kyle hadn't even realized she was one of the women who cleaned his home two times a month. In a way Jamie was glad the trailer had been purchased by someone she knew. Hopefully Liz would take good care of it.

Jamie turned to Cory. "Let's see how the new chairs look on the porch."

Liz helped them unload the chairs and cushions and set the furniture on the porch, moving aside the old plastic chairs to make room for the new ones.

"That looks real nice," Stella commented. "I always thought those plastic chairs were a travesty on such a gorgeous porch."

"They'd be nice on the cement block by my new trailer, though." Liz grinned. "Hint, hint. And you thought I was just being nice, helping you like this."

"Take them—they're yours." While Liz was putting the chairs in the back of her car, Jamie took Stella aside and told her about the letter from her father she'd found.

"What do you think I should do?"

Stella shook her head. "Honey, Amos and I have never forgiven ourselves for being the ones who introduced your mother to that man. I know you're a softie, like your Mom. But please don't try to find him. Trust me when I say that would be a very bad idea."

* * *

When Kyle arrived home an hour later, Jamie and the kids were in the front yard playing football. As soon as he stepped out of the car, Chester tossed him the ball.

"Think fast, Dad."

He caught it easily, tucked it under his arm and frowned. "What's that on the porch?"

He'd noticed the new furniture. "It's a surprise," Jamie said brightly. "Cory and I went shopping today after the school field trip—which was quite a success by the way. I don't think any of those grade four kids is going to risk a night spent in that lock-up."

But Kyle wasn't looking at her. He strode up the stairs, examining the chairs, then glancing back at her.

"What was the matter with the old stuff? Not good enough for you?"

"What?" She felt as if he'd slapped her. Why would he say something like that—especially in front of the children? "I used my own money if that's what's worrying you. I thought it would be a nice surprise."

"What would have been nice would have been to be consulted. I want you to feel at home here, Jamie. But these are the sorts of decisions we should make together, don't you think?"

She sucked in a breath, hurt by his displeasure. Her

voice wobbled slightly as she said, "We can always take it back for a full refund if you don't like it."

"That's good. You should do that." He checked his watch. "Almost dinner time, isn't it? Let's go inside."

* * *

Kyle went straight to his office once they were inside. Jamie bit back an urge to yell something nasty after him. She didn't appreciate the way he just assumed she would cook while he retreated to his office. Especially after that ridiculous scene about her purchase.

She decided she might as well throw together a stir fry while she cooled down. It wasn't until the meal was ready and she'd set the table, that Kyle emerged, heading, as usual, to the fridge for a beer.

"God, I'm hungry," he said, not seeming to notice she was quieter than usual.

After they'd eaten, Kyle supervised the twins with their homework, then their baths, leaving her to clean the kitchen and prepare lunches for the next day.

Working alone in the kitchen Jamie told herself these were the sorts of growing pains all newlyweds went through.

But it didn't wash.

She hadn't changed a thing in this house, hadn't so much as rearranged the contents of one of the kitchen cabinets. Sure she'd added her clothes to the empty bureau drawers upstairs and to half of the closet, but other than that—and the two boxes of belongings she'd stored in the basement—she'd demanded precious little accommodation from Kyle or his children.

Did he have to get so riled up about the patio chairs?

She said good-night to the kids while they were brushing their teeth. Kyle paced the hallway, ear to his Blackberry—checking his messages, she supposed—while he waited for them to finish so he could tuck them in.

She slunk to the bathroom off the master bedroom, where she locked the door and then filled the tub for a long soak. Being able to have a bath in a full length tub was one major advantage to living in a house instead of a trailer.

As she settled into the hot water, she wondered if Dougal might have had a point about Kyle. Marriage was about compromising—but shouldn't it come from both sides?

* * *

An hour later, Jamie was in bed reading when Kyle came to apologize. She'd been trying to concentrate on her book, but it was difficult.

"I'm sorry, honey." Kyle sat on the mattress next to her and stroked her hand tentatively. "I was way out of line. Of course you can keep the patio chairs."

She was glad to hear him say that. She didn't want discord in their marriage. Certainly not over such a trivial matter.

"I don't understand why you were upset in the first place."

"I guess I'm not used to change. My parents weren't ones for updating or following trends. We waited until something broke down before we replaced it. Old-fashioned, I know."

He made it sound like her purchase had been frivolous.

"With two incomes we can certainly afford the odd luxury."

"You're right. And it's only natural that you'd want to have some things here that reflect your taste rather than my mother's." He touched her chin, lifting her face so her eyes would meet his. "Are we okay?"

She didn't feel okay. Not really. But she nodded.

"Good." He kissed her lightly on the mouth. "That was a client on the phone, by the way. We're working on the sale of an old farm outside of town, and the purchaser wants to discuss the contract. I'm going to have to go out for a few hours."

"Oh."

"I'm sorry, honey. I'll try to be as speedy as possible."

What had he done before they were married, she

wondered, when he received these late night calls? But she didn't voice the question. One fight a night was enough for her.

He paused in the doorway. "What do you say to getting a sitter on Friday and going out to the Linger Longer?"

"That sounds like fun."

After he'd left, she tried to go back to reading her book, but she was intensely aware of his footsteps going down the stairs, then the front door closing. A few minutes later, she abandoned her book and went to the kitchen. A glance out the window confirmed that his vehicle was no longer in the drive.

She'd been thinking she might make herself some tea. Instead, she went down another level to the basement and turned on the light in the storage room. The boxes she'd packed on the weekend were right where Kyle had placed them. She looked beyond them, seeking out the carton marked "Daisy," but it was no longer there.

chapter twenty-three

eight o'clock on Friday night at the Linger Longer, Dougal spotted Wade sitting at the bar and went to join him. He'd been here a few times this week already and this was the first time he'd seen Wade. His old friend looked at him warily. He'd removed his hat but was still wearing his uniform.

"You're not meeting Charlotte here, are you?"

"Nope." Dougal ordered a whiskey. "You?"

Wade shook his head. "That's over."

"Despite what you saw the other day at my place...there's nothing between us. Nothing serious, anyway." He hadn't talked to her since Sunday. He'd avoided the library, driving to Port Orford, instead, to check his email messages and grab supplies.

"Are you sure? Don't mess with her, Dougal. She's too nice a person. And I mean that."

"I know. That's why she's better off with me out of the picture."

"You've told her that?"

"God, you're acting like her older brother. Give it a rest, okay?" He knocked back some whiskey, and it burned like guilt going down his gut. Sure he could call Charlotte and make a clean break of it. But that was what a nice, thoughtful guy would do. And if he was that guy, then he wouldn't need to make the call in the first place.

"How's the research going?" Wade asked.

"Interesting. I've got the names of all four of the murdered women now."

"All strangled with a red scarf?"

"Yup. The pattern is one killing per year, the first in Roseburg in 1972, then Pendleton in 1973, Corvallis in 1974 and Medford in 1975."

"Where the hell are you getting your information?"

"Confidential source." He nodded at the bartender as he passed him his drink.

"And you still think Shirley was somehow involved?"

"Her death in 1975 was just three months after the last murder. Plus, I find it curious that she was wearing a red scarf in the most recent photograph we found of her."

"I've got to admit—you're starting to intrigue me."

"You know something else that bugs me? I've spoken to one of the original investigating officers in Medford. He tells me that only after the 1975 killing did they realize they might be dealing with a serial killer. Can you believe that?"

Wade rubbed the side of his face, thinking. "We're talking about the seventies. Serial killers didn't have the profile back then that they do now. Not even in the police department. Each of those deaths would have been investigated in the jurisdiction where the body was found. And since each death was a year apart and took place in a different county..."

The murderer had been smart enough to space out his killings and to move around, yet he'd never strayed beyond Oregon. There had to be a reason. The deaths had followed a pattern—Dougal just couldn't see it.

Damn it. He ordered a second whiskey. "Buck a game? Loser pays?"

"Rack 'em up."

As they carried their drinks to the back of the room, Wade said, "Given all the years that have passed, the killer you're looking for may already be dead."

"Maybe. But if he was in his twenties—and the majority of serial killers start then—he could still be alive." Dougal was reaching for a cue, when his sister and Kyle walked in.

He watched them for a few moments—long enough to

get the impression that his sister wasn't as deliriously happy as she'd been the last time he'd seen her in the bar with Kyle. Was the gold coating coming off the marriage so quickly?

Wade was eyeing them, too. "Has your sister forgiven you for skipping her wedding, yet?"

"I doubt it." He set down his cue. "Excuse me a minute." He wove through the crowd, brushing against shoulders and backs as he made his way to the table where his sister had just parked. He passed Kyle who was on his way to the bar. Kyle nodded, then paused to say hello.

"Hear you've rented the Librarian Cottage for a while."

"I did."

"Would drive me crazy. Living in that shack out there in the woods by myself. You should drop by our office sometime. I guarantee I could find you someplace a lot nicer. How does an ocean view sound?"

"I like the forest. But thanks." Dougal moved on, touched his sister on the shoulder when he reached her table. "Hey there, Jamie. How are you?"

She fixed her eyes—round and warm, just like their mothers'—on his and waited.

"I'm sorry I couldn't go to the wedding." He forced out the apology because he knew she expected it, even though if he had the day to live over again, he'd make the same decision. He just couldn't give even tacit approval to this marriage.

Of course, she'd tell him to jump in the Rogue River if he told her that.

"How long are you staying in Twisted Cedars?"

She hadn't exactly accepted his apology. But she was moving on, and that was good with him.

"Not sure, yet. Maybe permanently." He noticed Kyle coming toward them now, two drinks in hand. "If you want to go for lunch some time, give me a call, okay? I don't have internet or cable, yet, but the phone was hooked up this week and the number is listed."

"Actually," Jamie said quickly, her gaze on her husband who was making his way back to their table. "How is Monday? Could you meet me at the trailer? I have a box of stuff to give you."

"Sure. Monday. Lunch time. I'll bring sandwiches."

Wade didn't say a word when Dougal rejoined him, just lined up his shot and scattered the balls. They played out the game silently, grunting when the other guy made a good shot—which was rare. They both seemed to be more aware of the couple on the dance floor than the positions of the balls on the pool table. When the game finally ended, Wade leaned in to him.

"When we were kids, I thought the world of that guy."

Dougal knew he was speaking of Kyle.

"Pretty deluded, weren't we?" He wondered if Wade knew how often he had been part of Kyle's deceptions and pranks. He hoped not. "Were you living in Twisted Cedars when he and Daisy got married?"

Wade shook his head. "I went to college at Blue Mountain in Pendleton. Came home for the wedding— Daisy was four months pregnant by then."

"What did you do after college?"

"Worked as a deputy in Umatilla County. Stayed there until my folks told me they were retiring to Palm Springs. Dad thought I might be interested in running for Sheriff. Obviously, I was."

"So by the time you moved back here Daisy had already run off?"

"Long gone."

"Where do you think she went?"

"Somewhere in Sacramento. Charlotte has a joint bank account with her sister. Every month or so Daisy takes out some cash, but always from a different ATM so we can't pin down the neighborhood. I suspect she's changed her name and that's why she's so hard to find."

"Why would she do that? Do you think she's afraid of Kyle?"

"Maybe."

"Physically?"

"I can't say. But Kyle was never one to fight with his fists."

Dougal hesitated. He wanted to throw the guy under the bus. But he had to agree with Wade. There were other types of hurting, which they both knew about too well. But before they could discuss it further, Charlotte entered the bar. Damn. The whole gang was here.

* * *

Charlotte had never been one to go to the bar alone. But since it seemed she was going to be single for the rest of her life, she was either going to start doing things on her own or divide the rest of her days between the library and home.

The first people she noticed when she stepped in the door of the Linger Longer were Kyle and Jamie swaying to a slow song with drinks in their hands. "Get a room," someone called out, but only in jest. Kyle smiled and pulled his wife even closer to his chest.

Charlotte sighed. That was when she spotted Wade and Dougal over by the pool table. What were *they* doing together? At that moment Wade noticed her, too, and her gaze skittered guiltily away. She made her way to the bar, ordered a beer and settled on a stool in a quiet section. Having lived in Twisted Cedars all her life and working as she did at the library, she recognized a lot of faces. People smiled and said hello, but they were engrossed in their own conversations, their own lives.

She realized then that it had been a mistake to come, that she actually felt more alone here than she had at home. She drank her beer like it was a glass of water, then dug in her purse for her wallet.

"My treat."

Dougal was standing beside her, placing a ten on the bar beside her empty glass.

He had been in her thoughts almost constantly since she'd run out of his cottage last weekend, but she hadn't heard a word from him.

"Would you like another?"

She studied his face, trying to read his intentions. Was he being polite? Did he feel obligated? Or maybe he just wanted to spend the night in her bed.

"I'm finished. Thank you for the drink, but goodnight." Part of her wanted to take his money and throw it back at him. But though she knew she ought to be angry at him, she wasn't. He hadn't promised her a single thing, and she'd had no right to expect so much as a phone call.

She slid off the stool and headed for the door. Dougal followed. Once they were outside, she turned to him. "What are you doing?"

"I'm going to walk you home."

"What if I don't want you to?"

He sighed. "You're angry at me. I don't blame you. I'm not the right kind of guy for you, Charlotte. I should leave you the hell alone."

He turned to go inside. Good grief, he really meant it. She grabbed his arm. "What if I don't want you to leave me alone?"

His muscles tensed under her fingers, lines of indecision formed around his eyes and mouth.

"Let's just go for a walk, okay?" She held out her hand, and after several seconds, he took it. They headed down the street, to the path that led to the ocean, following the same route she'd travelled just minutes before. They walked past the Visitor Information Center, then beyond the Ocean View Motel, with its blinking green "Vacancy" light, to the spot in the dunes where they'd made love the first time.

"You want a husband and children one day, right?"

"Why do you assume that?" It was true, she had vaguely thought her life would lead in that direction. But right now, she felt too stubborn to admit it.

"Cause that's what women like you always want. And you need to know right now, I can't give you those things."

He tried to pull away, but she held on tighter than ever.

"Has anyone ever told you that you think too much?"

He stared into her eyes for a long time. The ocean was a quiet murmur tonight, the air still. She could feel the heat from the sand reaching up to the sky.

When he finally kissed her it felt natural, right, inevitable. As they sank to the sand, she realized the oddest thing.

She had so many fears and anxieties. But she always felt safe in Dougal's arms.

* * *

"Would you like to come in?" Charlotte asked, thirty minutes later.

They were on her porch, at the back door. Her hair was full of sand, her clothing wrinkled, her lips swollen from his kisses. Dougal wanted to take her into the shower, then back to bed.

But he'd just done what he'd expressly intended not to do. He couldn't compound the mistake and spend the night here, in her home.

"Not a good idea."

She raised her eyebrows.

"Go to sleep, Char. Tomorrow you'll thank me for leaving. I'm not good enough for you. It's as simple as that." He gave her a gentle push, forcing her over the threshold, then closed the door.

For a moment he stood there, feeling like hell. Then he made his way back to the bar, to the car he'd left parked there, and forced himself to drive home slowly, recognizing that he was finding it difficult to concentrate on the narrow, twisting road.

He wished he could blame the rye. But he knew his insanity went deeper than that. He just couldn't seem to stay away from Charlotte. He'd already hurt her some, he was pretty sure about that. And he would hurt her worse if he kept this up. And then there was his sister. He wouldn't accomplish anything by having lunch with her. Yet, he'd found himself making the suggestion anyway.

God, he felt like he was going crazy. It was this damn book—no, he couldn't call it that. Research project more like. He still didn't know where it was all heading, whether he would find the answers that would let him piece together the entire story. Next week he would travel to Corvallis, then to Medford, to follow up on the phone interviews he'd made earlier. But he already suspected the ultimate answer lay right here in Twisted Cedars, if he could just uncover it.

Because Twisted Cedars was his town. And he must have been chosen for a reason.

But what if he never did figure out what had happened all those years ago? Then he'd have wasted all this time. It wasn't like him. His agent was waiting for the next book proposal. He'd never let so much time slide between projects before.

Maybe his writing career was over?

Was that why he'd returned to Twisted Cedars? Because he'd realized he was just a trailer-park kid after all?

As soon as he reached the cottage, Dougal's anxieties slipped away. This was his place. At least he'd figured out that much. If he never published another novel, he would be okay. He turned off the ignition and stepped out into the quiet of the woods. The librarian's cottage waited patiently for him. He unlocked the door, switched on a light, and glanced around. All was as he'd left it.

He headed to the bathroom where he turned on the water, dropped his clothes, and then stepped into the shower. Sand streamed from his body, stopping when it reached the floor of the tub, stubbornly refusing to swirl down the drain. Less visible, but as efficiently eliminated as the sand, was Charlotte's scent. He erased it with the soap and the water, and tried not to think about how much he wished she was with him right now.

chapter twenty-four

Sorry the place is such a mess." Jamie sat at the table in the trailer. Stripped of the stuff that was meaningful to her, the rest in boxes, disassembled, ready to be picked up by Goodwill tomorrow, the place was not only a mess, it was bleak.

Dougal had already loaded his box into his car. He hadn't even bothered checking to see what was inside.

She was worried about him. He looked sad and tired, his dark hair a crazy mess, his face unshaven.

"To be expected, I guess. Moving is always a hassle." He set a paper bag on the table then pulled out sandwiches and colas. "Tuna," he said, picking up a half and taking a bite.

Had he chosen tuna sandwiches on purpose? Their mother must have packed a thousand of them for their lunches over the years. So much so that Jamie had grown to hate them. Still, she dutifully picked up a half.

"I took the family photos over to Kyle's. I'll be happy to divide them up with you, if you want."

"No. You keep them."

She took a bite, found it tastier than she'd expected. Dougal was still chomping at his, looking around as if he couldn't even remember a time when he'd lived here.

Yet he had. For eighteen years. Fourteen of those years had been with her, yet she couldn't say she knew the man sitting opposite her very well. Dougal had always kept so much of himself hidden, unlike her and their mother. For Jamie it was natural to talk about problems when she was upset, and to share her joy when she was happy. She remembered Dougal calling her a chatterbox, complaining to their mother that she never shut up.

He hadn't been a mean brother, though. He'd helped her with her homework, and taken care of her when she was sick and their mother had to work.

He'd done a lot of ignoring her, too, especially as he grew older.

"I'm glad you've decided to stay in Twisted Cedars for a while. Maybe you can come over for dinner sometime."

His dark eyes, like always, seemed to be holding something back when he looked at her. "It's better if we just get together for lunch every now and then."

"You don't need to be jealous of him, anymore. You're a successful author. You have no need to feel inferior to anyone."

"You think I'm jealous?"

Jamie shrugged. Of course he wasn't going to admit it. "What I meant to say is that he's my husband now. That makes him part of your family. I think it would be nice if you could try to get along."

Dougal said nothing to that. He finished his sandwich, then took a long drink of the cola. "So who bought the place? Do I know them?"

"You do. You hired her to clean out the Hammonds' cottage before you moved in."

"Liz Brooks?" He looked around the double wide as if trying to imagine her living here.

"Yeah. Apparently she likes our town and plans to stay. She'll take over the cleaning business when Stella retires...and that day can't come too soon for Stella. The arthritis in her knees is really killing her. Plus...losing Mom really took something out of her."

Dougal nodded. He finished the last of his sandwich and stood. "I should be going."

Jamie cleared her throat and looked away. "Um...when I was cleaning out Mom's jewelry drawer, I found something interesting."

"Yeah?"

He was out the door already. She had to run to catch up to him. "A letter. From our dad."

Dougal stopped in his tracks.

"Would you like to read it?" She'd brought it along with her and now she passed it to her brother. He hesitated, but reluctantly took the pages. His jaw tightened as he read. When he was done, he pushed the pages at her.

"This changes nothing. He was a monster."

"But—"

Dougal looked at her hard. "You aren't thinking of tracking him down are you?"

"M-maybe..."

"Don't. Trust me, you're lucky you never met him. He killed my pet kitten. Did I ever tell you about that?"

"No." She couldn't take her eyes off her brother. He so rarely offered her stories from the past, she was afraid to even breathe in case he got distracted.

"He and Mom had an argument. The poor kitten got in his way, so he just picked her up and hurled her out the window."

Jamie covered her mouth with her hand, stifling the cry that came instinctively.

"I found her in the hedge." Dougal's gaze went to the line of old junipers that still defined the boundaries of their lot. "But she was already dead. He'd twisted her neck before he tossed her."

* * *

Dougal drove from the trailer park, through town, to the highway, hands shaking, stomach in knots. He knew his sister meant well, but at that moment he was furious with his mother. Why had she kept that letter? She must have known Jamie would read it. And that she'd fall for all that sap their father had written. As if he'd ever really loved his wife. And as if he truly cared about his son.

Thinking about his family was bloody painful. So he switched his thoughts to Charlotte.

Making love to her on Saturday night. That had been great.

Not so great had been the way he'd felt when she'd looked at him so trustingly after it was over. He'd left, which had been the smart thing.

Since then he'd been tempted many times to call her, but hadn't. It seemed every time he resolved to keep his distance, he did the very opposite.

Thank God he was getting out of town for a while. Maybe distance would clear his head.

But this project of his was making him crazy, too. He was all too aware that he was being manipulated by whoever was sending those emails. But to what end? He had no idea, yet something compelled him to find out as much as he could. So he kept driving north on the one-oh-one, straight to Corvallis. He arrived about four hours after he'd left Twisted Cedars, with an empty tank and an equally empty stomach.

He filled both with one pit stop at a gas station connected to a Jack and Jill. After his burger and fries, he settled with a cup of coffee and the file he'd started on Bernice Gilberg.

Bernice had been fifty when she was murdered, a grandmother. She'd been working as a volunteer at the library the day she was lured down to the basement and summarily strangled with a red silk scarf.

He'd managed to track down some information on one of her grandchildren, a Derek Gilberg. After gulping down the last of his coffee, he pulled out his phone and called the guy at his work number.

"This is Derek Gilberg," said a soft, effeminate, yet decidedly male voice. "How may I help you?"

Dougal introduced himself, but got no further.

"*The* Dougal Lachlan? The author?"

"Yes."

"I've read all your books."

"Well, thank you. That leads nicely into the reason for

this call. I'm working on something new, a crime that occurred back in the seventies. And I was hoping I could speak to you about it."

There was a silence. Then, "This must have something to do with my Gran."

"It does."

"The police never found the guy who killed her."

"I know. I was hoping we could meet and talk about it."

"I'm at work right now, at the Valley Library at Oregon State in Corvallis."

"I realize that. I've just arrived in town. I'm at the Jack and Jill off Highway 33. I could meet you on campus whenever it's convenient."

"I have meetings all afternoon. And I'm afraid I have commitments tonight, too. Would tomorrow morning work? Around ten?"

Dougal sighed at the delay. That's what he got for not phoning ahead. "Sure, I can make ten."

"Good. Let's meet in the quad out front of the library."

"Thanks." Dougal called the Corvallis police department next, and asked to speak to the Detective he'd called earlier in the week. They made plans to go out for a beer, but the meeting yielded nothing new for Dougal's case notes.

He found a motel for the night and spent his evening downloading old programs of *Dexter* and watching them on his laptop.

The next morning he went back to the Jack and Jill for breakfast, then used his GPS to navigate his way to the university, got directions at a campus information booth, and then drove to the library quad.

Though it was a moderately warm day, the clouds were thick and low, and Dougal felt the weight of them as he strolled through the pleasant-looking campus. He'd never gone to college and he eyed the passing students with more than a little envy. He'd spent his early twenties working nights in a bar, crashing for a few hours in an apartment he shared with two other guys, then getting up to write until it was time to work again.

Ahead of him he saw the Valley Library, a big, curved building with an impressive grand entrance. He sat on a low concrete ledge to wait. Eventually a man in his forties exited the library. He was short and plump, neatly dressed with a goatee and dark-framed eye-glasses.

"You must be Dougal Lachlan." He held out his hand as he approached. "I recognize you from your cover jacket photo."

Dougal hated that picture, considered it pretentious, too artsy. "Thanks for taking the time to meet with me."

"Not a problem. You're talking about an important part of our family history. We were devastated by that tragedy."

Dougal nodded. There was nothing he could say to that. Thirty-eight years might sound like a lot. But murder left scars that ran deep.

"Want to grab a coffee while we talk?" Derek asked.

"I've just finished a cup, but I can always do with more."

Derek led him inside the university library, to the Java II coffee shop...a large, open circular area with wooden tables and chairs. They ordered their beverages then sat in a quiet section.

"Interesting that you chose to work in a library. Does that have anything to do with your grandmother?"

Derek stroked his goatee and nodded. "She used to read to me when I was very young. And every week she'd take me to story circle.

"At the public library where she volunteered, on Monroe Avenue?"

"Yes." He swallowed. "I was nine-years-old when she was murdered. I wasn't told much by my parents, but I could read very well and I got all the details from the newspapers, which made a big deal of the fact that she was killed in the basement. As a result I developed a childish fear of basements, which I'm ashamed to say I haven't totally overcome, even as an adult."

"She was lured down there by the murderer, wasn't that the theory?"

"That's what they surmised since there was no evidence she'd struggled. Who knows what excuse he gave her to get her down there. Her duties normally wouldn't have taken her anywhere but the children's section, which is on the main floor."

Derek used the male pronoun when talking about the killer. This was to be expected, as the majority of serial killers were male. But it made Dougal realize that he, himself, had begun thinking of their killer as female. "How was your grandmother's body discovered? It would help if you could go through the events in chronological order, if possible."

Derek touched his goatee again, it seemed to be a compulsion with him. "I'll try. It happened on a Thursday. Gran's shift was supposed to end at three in the afternoon. But when it came time for her to check out, no one could find her. Her coat and purse were still in the staff room. One of the employees began looking for her, and after checking all the obvious places, went into one of the meeting rooms in the basement, where the archives are stored. She'd been killed right there, left on the floor, with the door closed, but not locked. The medical examiner told us later that she had died less than an hour before she was found."

By the end of his recitation, Derek's voice was trembling.

"I'm sorry to make you re-live this."

"It's okay. Believe me, I've gone over the details countless times on my own."

"I can imagine." If something like this had happened to his mother or sister, he knew he'd have done the same. "I assume the police questioned all the staff members to see if they'd noticed anyone unusual in the library that afternoon?"

"Yes. Unfortunately all sorts of people wander in and out of a library and this was before the days of video surveillance. The librarians and staff members did their best to remember, but came up with no real leads for the police to follow. Most of them admitted to being distracted at work that day anyway. There was a big library convention in town that weekend. The closing dinner was scheduled for that evening."

"So no suspects were identified. And I take it no physical evidence was found at the scene, either?"

"No. Other than the red scarf. But it was a brand sold commonly in stores like JC Penny." He shrugged, then looked at Dougal hopefully. "You haven't told me anything about your project. Do you think you may have found the monster responsible for this?"

"I haven't found him or her yet, but what I do know is that your grandmother wasn't the only victim. Three other women who worked in libraries were killed the same way. Each death was spaced about a year apart. And a red scarf was used at each death scene."

Derek looked astounded. "This is the first I've heard about a serial murderer."

"I can't prove the murders were connected. It's a theory I'm working on."

"The lack of a motive for the murder was the thing that drove us most crazy. Especially Gramps. We couldn't understand why anyone would harm a kind, helpless woman like Gran."

"It could be that there was no reason. She was just in the wrong place, at the wrong time, and a very sick man did a very sick thing."

"You know, if that were the case, it would almost be a relief. My gramps got it in his head that she must have been living a double life. He became a very bitter man."

"Is he still alive?"

Derek nodded. "He has mobility issues, so he's in a

care home. But his mind is as sharp as ever. It would be such a blessing if he could know that Gran truly was an innocent victim."

"Well, tell him what I've told you. That may help settle his mind." But Dougal knew that what this family really needed for closure was for him to find the person responsible.

Unfortunately he was no closer to that answer than he'd been a day ago.

* * *

Dougal thought about visiting Bernice Gilberg's husband at the nursing home, but decided against it. He didn't want to open old wounds unnecessarily and he doubted the ninety-year-old could add anything to what Derek had already told him.

He did make a trip to the public library on Monroe Avenue, however. He toured the relevant areas, taking notes and photographs, before leaving to drive to Medford.

One should never be in a hurry when on a research trip—that's how important details were overlooked. But as he drove he couldn't seem to stop craving the sanctuary of his cottage. And Charlotte.

He wanted to go back.

Instead, he headed to the Interstate and drove south to Medford. He took the time to tour a vineyard on the way and when he finally arrived at the city limits it was getting dark.

Resigned to another night in a nondescript motel room, he pulled over to a lodge where he planned to spend the night writing about Bernice Gilberg while Derek's story was fresh in his mind.

He had spewed out twenty-three pages before he realized he was starving. Too tired to go in search of food, he checked the time and considered calling Charlotte.

Bad idea. He went to bed instead.

chapter twenty-five

You okay in there?"

Absorbed in the job of sorting through old books for the upcoming sale, Charlotte started.

"Sorry to scare you. Didn't realize you were alone." Luis, the school janitor, had a push broom in hand, probably wanted to give the gym a good sweep before the night was over. Graying, with stooped shoulders, he ought to be old enough to be retired by now. He'd been the janitor back when she'd gone to Twisted Cedars Intermediate School.

"Just give me ten minutes to finish with this box and then I'll be out of here." The other volunteers had left over an hour ago. But then they had families waiting for them. All she had was an empty house and a phone that might contain some messages, but not from the right person.

She was such an idiot. Until Dougal came back to town, she'd had no idea she had such a self-destructive streak.

What would Ann Landers say? She'd turned down a marriage proposal from one of the finest men in town, a good friend, solid, loyal and dependable—and taken up with someone who was the exact opposite.

Dougal never called. He didn't take her out for dinner, give her compliments, send flowers. All he seemed to want from her was research information for his book and, occasionally, sex.

And she willingly complied on both counts.

Without complaining.

On Friday night she might as well have said to him: "Sure, drag me out in the sand for some sex, then leave town without a word. I don't mind."

"Okay," Luis said. "I'll finish up with the bathrooms down the hall and then I'll come back."

"Thanks, Luis."

He let the door swing shut behind him and the room fell silent again. Charlotte glanced around at the tables of books, most of them full, with more boxes of books tucked under the tables ready to be pulled out for display once the others were sold.

Tables were organized by genre. Just like at a book store, fiction was separated from non-fiction, then sub-categorized into mystery, fantasy, horror, literary fiction, bestsellers, beach reads...and so on. Based on the quantity and quality of the donations, she foresaw that they would make more than they had last year.

She turned her attention back to the box in front of her, which contained the books she and Dougal had salvaged from her aunt's cottage. She set them out on the table for mysteries, placing them wherever she could find room. Though volunteers were asked to make their best effort to categorize books by genre and sub-genre, they did not organize within those categories. They simply didn't have time. Besides, rummaging through a random bunch of mysteries, looking for unexpected treasures, was part of the fun.

As she pulled out the last book, Charlotte realized it was in the wrong genre. *The Scarlett Letter* ought to be included in classics. Looking closer at the old book, she noticed something had been tucked between the pages. It was a letter, in an opened envelope.

The envelope—postmarked from Portland and addressed to Shirley Hammond at her Twisted Cedars address—had been torn open on the side. Charlotte pulled out two sheets of paper. The letter, dated in the spring of 1972, was typed. The return address was from a private adoption agency.

"We are very sorry to inform you that our premises

were recently broken into and the files containing information about our adoptions for the period of September to November 1950 were stolen. We assume they were taken by an adopted child attempting to circumvent the confidential terms of adoption in order to find his or her mother.

"Our agency conducted nine adoptions during this period, including yours, and so we felt it only correct to contact you and warn you that you may be approached in the near future by someone claiming to be your birth child.

"In this event..."

The letter went on with some vague advice and an apology which Charlotte skimmed over. The important information, to her mind, was in those first three paragraphs.

She had never heard her parents mention anything about Aunt Shirley having had a child and given it up for adoption. But why would they? The baby had been born decades before either she or Daisy. And it would hardly have been fodder for conversation in any case. In the 1950s pregnant teenagers—because Shirley would have been only sixteen in 1950—were considered a source of shame and disgrace.

"Still working?"

Charlotte jumped, then slipped the letter into her purse. Turning, she smiled at the janitor. "Sorry, Luis. I guess I've done enough for one night. I'll get out of your way now so you can finish cleaning."

* * *

Dougal left his motel room in Medford at noon on Wednesday. The cleaning woman was outside the door, waiting impatiently. She gave him a terse nod, then pushed her way inside to collect the dirty linen.

Outside it was already hot, with no ocean breeze to offer any relief. Hard to believe that Twisted Cedars—so much cooler and windier—was only seventy-five miles away, on the other side of the Coast Range.

Medford was a bigger city than Corvallis, but it was no New York. As he drove toward the Pear Blossom Assisted Living Home, Dougal reflected that the citizens of Medford probably lived under the delusion that they were safer here than if they lived in a big metropolis like Manhattan.

But if there was one thing he'd learned in his years of research, it was this. No town was too small to have a dirty underbelly. Ugly crimes like rape and murder happened everywhere, and that included pretty little cities in Oregon.

He'd phoned ahead, so the staff at the Pear Blossom would be expecting him. He was directed to a Nurse Stevens, a seemingly sensible and kind woman in her early fifties.

"Ruth has been with us for a long time. She's highly functioning and suffered with macular degeneration for several decades on her own. When she lost her sight completely, she made the difficult choice to leave her home of fifty years and move in with us. It's sad, really, because if she had any family at all she would still be fine living at home."

Nurse Stevens led him out to a courtyard. They found Ruth Fraser—Isabel Fraser's mother—sitting in a shady patch next to the fruit tree for which the home was named.

For a ninety-year-old, Ruth's posture was remarkably erect. Her hair was still thick, cut to a fashionable length at her chin and she had covered her blind eyes with a pair of designer sunglasses that made her appear rather chic. Her white cane was propped on her lap, where her hands—which truly showed the ravages of nine decades of living—were also resting.

She tilted her head as they approached. "Is this my visitor?"

"Yes it is, Ruth. Dougal Lachlan, the author. Did you bring your book for him to sign?"

Ruth nodded, and only then did Dougal notice the paperback on the bench next to her. He picked it up and sat in the space. "It's nice to meet you, Ruth. Thanks for agreeing to talk to me."

"A visitor is a rare treat for me these days. Not to mention a famous author."

"I'll leave you two to chat then. Mr. Lachlan, when you're finished, please sign out at the front desk?"

When he nodded his agreement, she left them alone.

"I was told you're writing a book about my Isabel."

He thought about all the things he could tell her. How he'd never felt so unsure about a project in his life. That he knew there was a story to be told, just wasn't sure he'd ever discover enough to tell it. Instead, he said, "Talk to me about your daughter."

Her face brightened—even with half of it hidden by sunglasses, he could tell that much.

"She was a wonderful girl, the pride of my life. She was only fourteen when we lost her father. In the line of duty, they called it—he was a police officer. But it was flat-out murder. A man he'd put in jail got out on bail and came after him. We went through a terrible time. I was afraid the loss of her father would turn Isabel bitter. But she was stronger than I gave her credit for. She finished high school, went on to college. I was so proud. And when she decided to come back to Medford after graduation, I admit I was relieved."

"She was living with you when she died, wasn't she?"

Ruth nodded. "I know what you're thinking. She must have been a dull, quiet girl. A forty-five-year-old librarian who still lived with her mother. But she wasn't. Isabel had so many friends. She was outgoing and fun. Oh, did that girl love to talk! She was often giving speeches at the library— and she was good at it."

Dougal leaned back in his seat. Thanks to this woman, and Medford's balmy climate, he was warm, inside and out. He listened through several stories, most of them made him laugh.

"Thank you for letting me share my happy memories about my girl. But I know it's the bad stuff you came here to talk about."

What an indictment, Dougal thought. "I know her homicide was never solved by the police. Did you have any private theories about what happened?"

"It was just one of those things, Dougal. Like when lightening kills one person standing on a golf course, but leaves the three men standing next to him unscathed. I've lost my husband, my daughter and now my eyesight. But I don't feel as if a black cloud hangs over my head. I've had a lot of good luck too, you see. I like to think so, anyway."

Dougal let her words settle in for a while. He felt in no hurry to move. He opened the book he was still holding in his hands, removed a pen from his pocket, and signed.

When he was done, Ruth asked him to read what he had written.

"It was an honor and a pleasure to meet you." He closed the book and pressed it into her hands. "May I visit again, sometime?"

"I will pencil you into my schedule, Dougal." She smiled slightly. "And I do look forward to reading your story. I hope it comes out as an audio book."

chapter twenty-six

The elementary school celebrated the last day of the school year with a family barbecue, starting at three-thirty in the afternoon. Jamie left work early to attend. She'd baked brownies for the affair the previous evening—something that had really made her feel like a mother, as she remembered her own mom doing the exact same for her on more than one occasion.

Three days had passed since her meeting with Dougal. She hadn't taken any further steps to find her father—but she hadn't written off trying, either.

At twenty-to-four she met Cory in the parking lot behind the school. A row of barbecues were already in full commission, grilling burgers and hot dogs. She let Cory add the brownies to the other dessert contributions set out on a table beside a tub of ice containing juice boxes.

"Is your father here, yet?"

"He's playing football." Cory pointed out a group of fathers and sons scrimmaging together. Jamie sensed Cory felt left out.

"Let's go."

Cory glanced hopefully toward the game. "Girls aren't playing."

"Why not?" Jamie took Cory's hand and walked to the edge of the field. She waited until one of the fathers noticed them.

"May we join in?"

The father seemed surprised by the request, but at that moment Kyle spotted them. Her heart lifted as he smiled, waving them onto the field. "You can both play for our side.

We were one player short, anyway."

It was simple, disorganized, spontaneous fun. No one played set positions. At one point Jamie snagged the ball only to be tackled by her own team-mate.

She was cushioned on the way down, when Kyle pulled her on top of him.

"Hey—" she sputtered. "We're supposed to be on the same side."

"I couldn't resist. You look so damn cute. Where'd you learn to catch a ball like that?"

She just grinned, and he helped her up, and the next minute Cory made an amazing interception, much to the astonishment of all the boys.

"Run, Cory, run!" They were all cheering for her, even the fathers playing on the other side. As soon as she scored the touchdown, she threw the ball triumphantly to the ground, then searched the crowd of players for her father's face.

At his proud smile, Cory just shone. The happy glow stayed with her all evening, throughout the dinner, then later on the walk home.

"Time to hit the shower, kids," Kyle announced when they stepped in the front door shortly after eight. "Cory first, then Chester."

As the kids ran off, he snagged Jamie around the waist. "As soon as they're in bed, I have plans for you, sweetheart."

She loved it when he was in this playful mood. "Let me guess...do your plans involve tackling, turnovers and double coverage?"

"Add a tight end and a wide receiver, and I think you've got the idea."

"Hm. I think I'll go have a bath, then slip into something more...appropriate...for the game."

"You do that. I'll handle the kids. Just give me half an hour."

Before they were married, Kyle's fathering skills had

been one of his most endearing qualities. Having been raised by a kind mother, herself, she appreciated that quality above all others in a parent. And that was what she had seen in Kyle. Patience, good humor and kindness.

He could be firm, too, when the situation warranted, and that was something she admired, as well.

What she hadn't realized was how unyielding he could be in his firmness. How quickly he could shift from the kind, understanding parent, to the uncompromising, demanding one.

Now, after almost a month under the same roof, Jamie realized that the twins watched their father closely for signs that he was switching from one mood to another. Tonight he had been the fun dad, and as she soaked in the tub—very much anticipating the future pleasure Kyle was promising—she could tell his good mood hadn't dimmed.

The master bathroom was separated from the children's by one thin wall and Jamie could hear the conversation between Kyle and his kids.

"Did you remember to brush your teeth?"

...a pause, and then Chester,

"Can you play football tomorrow night, too?"

Kyle's answer was evasive, then five minutes later it was Cory's turn to brush her teeth.

"Dad, do we have to go away to summer camp this year?"

Jamie's heart dropped. Much as she loved Cory and Chester, she'd been looking forward to having Kyle to herself for a while. He'd promised her a trip to San Francisco for their honeymoon—something she was planning on asking him about later tonight.

"Remember when we looked at the website you thought it would be fun," Kyle replied.

"But that was before we had Jamie."

"Jamie has a full-time job and you guys are too young to stay home alone while the two of us are at work."

The sound of running water washed away Cory's

answer to that. A minute later, the bathroom door closed and Jamie could hear footsteps padding toward the bedrooms.

She pulled the plug and stepped out of her warm bath water, feeling slightly guilty. She hadn't realized the kids didn't want to go to summer camp.

Kyle hadn't said anything more to her about quitting her job. But she could see how much easier his life and the kids would be if she stayed home full time. She just wasn't sure how she would feel about it. She'd always worked, or gone to school. Wouldn't she be bored? Yet she had friends who were stay-at-home parents and they were among the busiest people she knew.

Fifteen minutes later, Kyle entered their bedroom with an open bottle of wine and two glasses. She had some sensual music by Diana Krall playing in the background and a row of candles burning on the bureau.

"Nice." He gave her that smile. The one that made her instantly hot. They managed one sip of the wine before they set down their glasses.

The sex was heated and intense. After, Jamie curled up to Kyle's chest and sighed. "What a great night."

It had all started with that football game, she thought. Kyle had been proud of his children, how well they'd played. And he'd been impressed with her, too. "I'm so glad you were able to get off work early."

She felt a slight tensing of his body. She lifted her head. "Is something wrong?"

"No."

But Jamie could feel the difference in his muscles, which still hadn't relaxed. "Are you sure?"

"If you must know, our accountant quit today. Olivia gave me her letter of resignation about a half hour before the barbecue."

"Why?" Olivia was in her fifties and had solid bookkeeping skills, though she always came to Howard & Mason for help with income taxes, and for advice with transactions she'd never handled before. Jamie had worked with her a few times and was under the impression that she enjoyed her job—especially spending the money she earned on holidays with her husband.

"Just said she wanted to take an early retirement. God knows why she picked now. Maybe it's a health issue she didn't want to talk about."

"I hope not."

During their discussion, Kyle had shifted. Now several inches separated them in the bed. Jamie waited for him to mention how difficult it was going to be to find a replacement for Olivia. Surely he had to be thinking that she would be the perfect solution.

But he said nothing more on the subject, just stared up at the ceiling with a worried frown.

Maybe he was waiting for her to jump in and offer to help?

"If I was to quit my job at Howard & Mason, and go to work for you and your dad...what would that be like?"

"Are you seriously considering it?"

"Yes."

He hugged her close. "That would be so great. Olivia used to work three days a week...I'm sure you could get the job done in less time than that. You could make your own hours. Work from home when it suited you."

The flexibility did sound wonderful. But she'd be making a lot less money. "Did you pay Olivia by the hour?"

"Yes." He mentioned a sum that was even lower than she'd expected. "But I've told you before—you don't need to worry about money. Come with me to the bank and I'll set you up with a joint credit and debit card. What's mine is yours, remember?"

"I appreciate that, honey." He had been after her to combine their finances even before their wedding date. But she knew she would never feel comfortable spending his money unless it was for food or something for the house or the children. Plus, she liked having her own nest egg tucked away in her brokerage account.

If they had started out as a young couple together, that would be one thing. But everything he had he'd been given by his parents, or built up during his marriage to Daisy.

On the other hand, if she quit her job and showed Kyle that she was truly committed to him and his family, surely that would bring them closer? And maybe put a stop to this niggling feeling she had that something just wasn't right.

"I'll give Howard and Mason my notice tomorrow."

chapter twenty-seven

home. Dougal tossed his duffel bag on the front area rug and set his briefcase beside it. The place smelled citrusy and fresh. Liz Brooks, he realized. He'd forgotten she was scheduled to clean last week.

In New York he'd done his own housework...such as it was. He'd grown up with a mother who cleaned homes professionally and she'd made sure both her son and her daughter knew how to do things properly.

Though she was a lot younger than his mother, Liz seemed to come from the same school of thought where cleaning was concerned. As he moved through the living room to the kitchen, then up the stairs to his bedroom, he couldn't see any spots she'd missed with either the dusting rag or the mop.

On the quilt he found a pile of folded laundry. On the very top was a pair of Charlotte's pink underwear.

Now what had Liz made of those?

He went back downstairs to the table where he did his writing. He'd left out some papers, the time-line he'd drawn up with the names of the victims, the map of Oregon with the murder locations circled in red.

Probably meant nothing to Liz, but he made a mental note to be more careful with his notes in future.

Dougal grabbed a beer from the fridge and cracked it open. He sat on the sofa to drink it, but felt the same restless energy that had been building inside him during the long drive from Medford. He felt the need to do something, physical. Might be a good time to work up the soil for his garden. The small shed out back had gloves and garden tools, so he polished off his drink, then made his way to the sunny patch in the back.

The weeds he'd sprayed earlier were all dead now. One by one he yanked the limp, brown plants from the ground, leaving them in a pile to be disposed of later. Then he struck his spade into the ground and began the hard work of turning over the soil.

Most of the plot was pretty hard going, though one section was softer than the rest, which made for a nice change.

By the time he finished, he was starving. He had a quick shower then contemplated the contents of his fridge and then his freezer. Nothing here to work with.

He called Charlotte's number.

"Hello?" She sounded cautious.

"Hey, Charlotte."

"I—Dougal?"

He shouldn't have called her. He knew it. But now he had her on the line, he had to brazen through. "Fancy a steak dinner? I was just about to fire up the barbecue."

The pause at the other end of the line was not comfortable.

"Charlotte?"

"Snapping your fingers again, are you?"

He thought this over carefully. "I'm sorry. I'm being presumptuous. You probably already have dinner plans."

Another unnerving silence. Then, "Actually, I don't. Can I bring anything?"

"Uh...steaks would be nice. And do you have any salad fixings?"

* * *

As Charlotte added two New York strips to her basket, she couldn't believe she was doing this. Once she'd added French bread, lettuce, tomatoes and avocado, she headed for the till.

At least Dougal had apologized for asking her to do the shopping.

"I'm sorry. I spent most of the week on the road. I just got home and the proverbial cupboard is bare."

He might at least have offered to take her out for a meal.

Rather than tell him to call her back another time when he had a better offer, she'd sighed and volunteered to stop at the market on her way out to his place.

And here she was. She handed over her credit card once the groceries had been rung through, then took her two bags and left. It was late, now, almost dark. Normally she would have eaten dinner hours ago, but thanks to stopping at the school gym to do a final sorting of the books for the sale this weekend, she hadn't had time.

The letter she'd found in her aunt's book was in her purse to show Dougal. But her aunt's secret baby was the last thing on her mind as she turned onto the deserted forestry road.

Instead, she was thinking about how isolated this place was. What a great place for mysteries...and secret affairs. Not that her relationship with Dougal was a secret. But it wasn't exactly out-in-the-open, either. Maybe she should be the one to suggest they go out for dinner sometime.

Though some conventional and old-fashioned part of her balked at that idea.

When she arrived at the cottage, she parked next to Dougal's SUV. Dougal must have heard her drive up, because he had the door open before she reached the stairs.

"You're an angel." He took the bags from her hands, then waited for her to precede him into the cottage.

"Nice to see you have some manners, at least."

He was in jeans, bare feet and a black T-shirt. Unusual for him was the fact that he was also freshly shaven. "Okay. That's the second dig tonight."

"And it may not be the last."

She watched him empty the bags. When he pulled out the French loaf, he inhaled with appreciation. "Did I say angel? I meant goddess."

At least he was supplying the wine. An open bottle and two full glasses were on the counter. She helped herself to one and took a sip.

"So how was your trip?" she asked.

"As expected." He took a sip from his glass, then gave her a light kiss on the lips.

She pulled away before he could take the kiss further. "So maybe now you can tell me what the hell is going on. The last time I saw you, I thought you'd decided that you were no good for me."

"That's still true. But unfortunately I'm a selfish bastard. I missed you while I was gone. And when I got back—I had to see you."

That was all it took. God, she was so easy. He slipped the wine glass out of her hand and then he was kissing her for real, stripping off her clothes, leading her to the bedroom.

When they were done, the propane tank was empty, so no barbecued steaks. Charlotte didn't care.

* * *

When Charlotte awakened on Saturday morning, it was to the sound of songbirds. The sky was pink outside the open window, and Dougal was sleeping on his stomach, his face turned in her direction. She resisted the urge to kiss him. A thought was nagging at her. She'd forgotten something important.

Dougal opened his eyes.

She wondered if he'd expected her to sneak out during the night. But he seemed pleased to see her. He shifted to his side and put his arm around her waist.

"How are you feeling?" he asked.

"Good."

He nuzzled closer. Kissed her neck.

"Very good." She could see where this was going, but just then she remembered her aunt's letter. "Oh my God."

"You're getting your lines wrong," Dougal murmured, as his hands roamed down her back. "That usually comes at the end."

She wiggled out of his arms. "I just remembered something important. I meant to show you last night...before you distracted me."

Dougal propped himself up in the bed, frowning. "Can't it wait another hour?"

"I might forget again." She pulled on the T-shirt Dougal had discarded last night, then went downstairs to retrieve her purse. Before she could climb back to the bedroom, Dougal had joined her, dressed only in his jeans.

Charlotte pulled out the letter. "I found this in one of Aunt Shirley's books we donated for the fundraiser."

Dougal glanced at the return address on the envelope. "What's this about?"

"Read it."

When he was done, he let out a low whistle. "So your aunt Shirley had a baby out of wedlock, as they used to say in the day, and gave it up for adoption. This was scandalous stuff in the fifties."

"Yes, based on those dates, she must have been only sixteen when she had the baby. And, if it was her records that were the target of that theft, she was contacted by that same child twenty-two years later."

Dougal checked the date of the letter again. "Just four months before the first murder. This could be pivotal."

"I know." Charlotte waited for Dougal to say more, to somehow make sense out of the tangle of murders and clues they'd uncovered so far. But he surprised her by going to the kitchen and starting a pot of coffee. "You want to make breakfast?"

"I don't think well without food and caffeine. And we skipped dinner last night, remember?"

Charlotte made toast from the French loaf she'd bought yesterday, while Dougal fried up the steak with some eggs. They ate at the table, not talking, each lost in their own thoughts. Halfway through his meal, Dougal's eyes brightened and he set down his fork.

"It has to be Librarianmomma."

"Pardon?"

"The person sending me those emails was the baby your Aunt Shirley gave up for adoption. I had in mind that the email sender was a "momma." But maybe he or she used that moniker because they *had a librarian for a mother*."

Charlotte took a moment to think about it. "That actually makes a lot of sense. So, if the baby was born in 1950 and it's 2010 now, then he or she would be sixty."

"Yes." Dougal brought out the three emails so they could read them again.

You don't know me. But you should. I've got a story that will be the best of your career. Back in the seventies four women were killed. Librarians. No one ever solved the cases. But I know what happened. Ever hear of Elva Mae Ayer? She was the first. Check it out then let me know if you want the names of the others. I am here and willing to help.

The next year Mari Beamish was murdered. There was a pattern, but don't feel bad if you don't see it yet. The cops never did make the connection. Those were different times, before computers and all the advances in forensics. Now you get to be the hero who pieces it all together. You can thank me later.

You'll want to check into Bernice Gilberg from Corvallis and Isabel Fraser from Medford next. That's the complete list. I'll leave it your hands now. You already know about Shirley so you should be able to figure out the rest. If you can't, I'll be waiting to hear from you.

Charlotte read them twice, then focused on the third one. "Look at this. Librarianmomma says you already know about Shirley. How could that be?"

Dougal glanced out in the distance, rubbed his chin. "My guess is that Librarianmomma is someone close to hand. Someone who is keeping track of our progress with this case."

Charlotte was inclined to agree. It felt like a major breakthrough until she realized the list of sixty-year-olds in

Twisted Cedars would be quite a lot of people to check out. Plus, they still didn't know if this Shirley's child had been a witness to the homicides—or the killer.

chapter twenty-eight

Jamie spent her weekend washing clothes, buying last minute items, and checking off the detailed packing list provided by Wolf Creek Summer Camp. Cory and Chester would be spending the next two weeks riding horses, swimming, canoeing, singing around campfires and playing games. They would sleep in bunkhouses and eat their meals at the camp kitchen.

Jamie had read the brochure, studied the website, and thought Wolf Creek Camp sounded terrific. She'd never had an opportunity like this when she was growing up.

But nine was rather young to be leaving home and family for two weeks. And she could tell both Cory and Chester were nervous.

On Saturday night they both asked to talk to her.

"You'll still be living here when we get back?" Cory had asked.

"Of course. You can't get rid of your evil stepmother that easily."

Cory giggled.

"You're going to have a lot of fun. And we'll be in touch. Phone calls aren't allowed, but, I'll write letters. And you'll always have Chester to talk to if you're feeling homesick."

In Chester's room, she found the young boy fussing over his ant farm—something new he'd started a few weeks ago.

"I'll look after them," she promised. "And you keep an eye on your sister, okay?"

"I bet the horses are going to be really big," he said as

he hunkered under his covers.

"Maybe. But they must be pretty gentle if they trust them with children." With Chester it was always best to appeal to his logical side. "A camp like that wouldn't be able to afford liability insurance if children were getting injured on their horses."

"Oh. Good point."

He sounded so grown up. Yet looked so cute and young with his big eyes peeking out from the covers.

"Your dad and I will write you every week," she promised. "Sleep tight, honey."

* * *

Dropping the kids off on Sunday afternoon was more difficult than Jamie expected. Cory was clingy right to the end, and though they walked through the premises with her, met the counselors, introduced her to her bunkmates, nothing seemed to make her comfortable.

All the other parents had left, and games were starting, when she finally agreed that they could go. She had tears in her eyes as they drove away, though.

And so did Jamie.

"You have a soft heart." Kyle patted her hand gently, leaving one hand on the steering wheel as he negotiated the rutted country road.

"They're so young."

"Next year they won't have to go to camp if they don't want to. Because you'll be home."

Yes. That was true. She wished now that she'd made the decision to quit her job earlier so the twins didn't have to go through this. But then, what about the honeymoon? Her and Kyle's relationship was the bedrock for this family. And she and her new husband desperately needed time together.

They'd been married less than a month and already secrets were building up between them. She still hadn't asked him about that box of Daisy's. He must have moved it because he was afraid she'd go snooping again. Which she *had* tried to do. But why hadn't he said something? Of course, she was no better. She still hadn't told Kyle she was contemplating finding her father.

"Have you given any thought to booking our trip to San Francisco?" she asked.

"On Tuesday I need to go to Coos Bay to close a condo deal. Should take two or three days, at most. How about we leave on Friday? We can stay in the city a few nights, then maybe tour Napa Valley."

"Sounds perfect." She would talk to him about her father, and ask about Daisy, too. No more secrets.

* * *

That Monday Jamie worked out a transition schedule with Ben Mason where she would spend alternate days finishing her files for them, and working at Kyle's office. She felt like a traitor, leaving the accounting firm which had been so good to her. Not to mention letting go of her dream of being the first female partner invited to the firm. But she had made a decision and a promise to Kyle and she was going to keep it.

On Tuesday, after saying goodbye to Kyle, Jamie went for her first day of work at Quinpool Realty. She hesitated before pushing through the glass front door. She'd been here on other occasions, to meet Kyle for lunch, and once to sign the contract when she'd first put the trailer up for sale. But this was different.

This was a new phase in her life. Her position here might be a lowly bookkeeper, but Kyle kept encouraging her to think of the arrangement as a partnership. "It's a family business, and you're part of my family now." She prayed that it would work out for the best, and then forced herself to step inside.

The office was quiet. The front desk—once Olivia's and now hers—was empty. Olivia had left the surface bare of all but the phone and the computer. Behind the desk was a bank of file cabinets. At either end were two doors. The one to the right led to Kyle's office.

The one to the left was Jim's, and even as she glanced at it, the door opened and her father-in-law emerged.

"Jamie. I'm so glad you've decided to come work with us. Quinpool Realty has always been a family business, and you're family now."

Her chest muscles tightened. She didn't know why she felt as if she'd just joined the mafia. Jim was a perfectly nice man. Kyle and the twins adored him and he was a well-respected local businessman.

"Thanks Jim. If you don't mind, I'll just putter around today and get a feel for the way Olivia did things. Since I've done your taxes and helped Olivia with the occasional transaction, I'm sure I'll have everything figured out soon."

"Of course you will. Olivia wasn't the brightest bulb, but she was well organized and usually reliable...before she decided out-of-the-blue to retire, that is." Jim handed her a mug, with the company name in blue letters. "Here, now that you're part of the team you should have one of these. Coffee is over there," he nodded to the kitchen in the back. "I just made a fresh pot."

"Thanks Jim." Coffee seemed like the perfect place to start.

* * *

A couple of hours, and three cups of coffee later, Jamie was beginning to have a good handle on things. She'd also fielded several calls, discovering that part of her new duties included being the unofficial receptionist.

She was printing out the latest trial balance when she noticed something had been left in the printer tray—it was a conformation for a hotel booking for Kyle's business trip. She almost threw it into recycling—since he was gone, he obviously didn't need it—when the word "Sacramento" popped out at her.

Hadn't Kyle said he was going to Coos Bay?

She checked more closely—maybe this was for a different trip, something of Jim's?

But no, the dates were for tonight and the next night,

and the hotel was in Sacramento.

Maybe there'd been a change of plans and Kyle had forgotten to tell her. She went back to the computer and opened the Travel Expense Account. The entries here were of no help, as the only back-up provided was reference numbers. Knowing that for income tax purposes the numbers had to lead to a physical file with actual invoices, Jamie scoured the cabinets for a travel expense file. There was nothing. The files were probably in Kyle's office.

At four, Jim left to meet with a client. Jamie got up from her desk. She'd noticed Jim lock his office, then drop the key into a decorative pot on a high shelf next to the front door. She fought with her conscience for a bit, but she knew she'd never sleep tonight if she didn't at least try. Sure enough, there were two keys in the pot and one of them fit Kyle's office door.

She'd been in Kyle's office before, but never alone. The walls were covered with framed certificates, and scenic shots of Twisted Cedars and the Oregon Coastline. On his desk were his kids' school pictures, as well a framed copy of their "Save the Date" cards. Which reminded her, their wedding photos would be ready soon.

The thought was almost her undoing.

She'd been so rosy-eyed and optimistic when she'd married Kyle. But a lot had changed since then. Unexpected shifts, like the way Kyle had slowly ceded his household and childcare responsibilities to her. And bigger issues, like the way he'd hidden Daisy's journal. And lied about his business trip.

It didn't take long to find the file where Kyle kept his travel expense receipts. All the times he'd told her he was going to Coos Bay—every single time—he'd gone to Sacramento, instead.

A wave of hurt swept over her, bringing her to her knees. Tears filled her eyes, but she brushed them away. She had to think. Daisy was in Sacramento, too. Maybe Kyle was secretly looking for her, for the sake of his children?

But if that was the case, why wouldn't he trust her enough to tell her?

* * *

At five in the morning Jamie woke up with the sound of her heart pounding in her ears, her body damp with sweat. She'd dreamed of Daisy. The woman had been standing over her bed, staring down at her. The vision had been so real, so rich in detail. She could have sworn she'd actually smelled Daisy's signature perfume.

Kyle had phoned her last night. She'd let it go to messages.

She wasn't ready to talk to him.

She now knew for sure that what she and Kyle were going through was not just the growing pains of a new marriage. It was something much bigger. There was too much Kyle was keeping secret. He had to be up to something.

Dougal had warned her.

But she hadn't listened, because she didn't want to believe him. She'd desperately longed for the inside Kyle to match the outside one: golden and handsome and good. Not a lying manipulator.

Or was she being too hard on him? Maybe if she gave him a chance to explain...

Jamie tossed from one position to the next. She'd pledged to love and honor this man. Not only that, but she'd made a promise to his children. They were counting on her, too.

But how much could she be expected to give? Not only was she handling most of the childcare now, she'd actually given up the job she'd loved for Kyle.

An ugly suspicion had her bolting upright in her bed. Was it possible Kyle had manipulated her on that front as well? Had his accountant really chosen early retirement—or been forced to take it? In the morning, she would call Olivia and double-check. And if she caught Kyle in another lie, she wouldn't give him any more chances.

* * *

Finding Olivia Argent wasn't easy. She didn't answer her home phone or her cell, and when Jamie drove over to her house a neighbor informed her that Olivia and her husband had taken off in their trailer for a camping trip. Jamie called at least a dozen campgrounds before the manager at the Little Redwood Campground in the Siskiyou National Forest confirmed she had the Argent's booked in her registry.

Jamie loaded up her car with provisions for a long drive—take-out coffee, bottle of water, and snacks. She turned off her cell phone—which she'd neglected to power up the previous night—and slipped a Prairie Oyster CD into the player.

The song was about ancient history and Jamie sang along, wishing it was true, that history didn't matter. But whether it was the events of a day ago, a week, or even years, history did matter. Very much.

And that was why she was driving out to a remote campground to talk to Olivia in person today. She needed to look into Olivia's eyes when she gave her answers. She had to know for sure that she was getting the truth.

Because if just one more of Kyle's stories didn't hold up, then despite her wedding vows, she was finished.

Leaving would not be easy. It would be heart-breaking. She'd banked everything on this marriage and she wanted so badly to be proven wrong, yet she didn't hold out high hopes.

The sick feeling in her gut only got worse as she neared the campground. She couldn't drink her coffee, let alone eat the snacks she'd brought along. When she finally arrived at Little Redwood Campground, she checked with the front office for directions to the Argent's site. The setting was so beautiful and peaceful, yet her stomach churned worse than ever as she followed the directions to where the Argent's truck and camper were tucked into a grove of ancient redwoods.

She got out of her car. "Hello?"

All was silent and still. The wooden picnic table next to the camper had a lantern on top and nothing else. She knocked on the trailer door but there was no response. She tested the door. Locked.

Jamie sat down to wait. After half an hour, she settled on the grass, in the sun, and soon her late night caught up to her.

* * *

Jamie awakened to the sound of voices, approaching footsteps. Instantly alert, she rose and brushed off bits of grass and needles. Olivia and her husband were dressed in shorts and T-shirts and both wore caps. They had fishing rods and tackle, and a bucket that looked like it had some weight to it.

"Hi, Olivia, Bert."

"Jamie? What are you doing here?" Olivia set down her rod, her expression unwelcoming.

"I need to talk to you."

"Some problem with the accounts?"

"No. Nothing like that."

"Then...?"

The woman's hostility was obvious. Jamie felt her suspicions grow stronger and her stomach knotted tighter.

"Olivia, Kyle told me that you took early retirement from the business because you wanted to spend more time with Bert. Is that true?"

Olivia's eyes narrowed. "He really told you that?"

"Yes."

"Well, that's a load of crap. I was let go. He told me I was redundant."

Jamie's heart sank. Another lie. Oh, God. And if she called Kyle on it, he would, no doubt, manufacture an explanation. And it might even make sense. But she didn't want to hear it this time.

chapter twenty-nine

Jamie couldn't face the prospect of going home to Kyle's empty house. She felt like her head was exploding and her heart was breaking, all at the same time. Worst of all she couldn't stop thinking about Cory's question: *Will you still be here when we get home?* Poor thing. Cory had been abandoned by two key people in her life—her mother and her grandmother.

Now it seemed as if Jamie might have no choice but to leave her as well.

What she needed, Jamie decided, was a drink. People. Noise. Distractions.

* * *

The Linger Longer was quiet, but then again it was only Wednesday. Just two tables were occupied, and as luck would have it, one was with her brother and Charlotte Hammond.

"Hey there." Maybe it was a sign, running into her brother this way.

They welcomed her to their table and Dougal ordered her a beer. "Where's Kyle?"

"Away on business. The kids are at summer camp for two weeks."

"So, for one night, you're a single woman again, huh?" Charlotte said, her tone friendly.

There was an interesting vibe between her brother and Charlotte. Jamie wondered if her bachelor brother was finally falling in love. She had a hard time picturing quiet, studious Charlotte with her brother. But they both loved books, so they had that much in common.

"When Dougal was a kid he used to spend a lot of time at the library."

"Part of my misspent youth," Dougal joked.

"I know," Charlotte said. "I used to see him there. Not that he would have noticed me."

"Well, maybe he did," Jamie said.

Charlotte shook her head, smiling. "A plain-looking, skinny girl, four years younger? No way."

"We were both kind of invisible to him back then, weren't we?" Jamie said. "At home Dougal could go an entire week without saying one word to me. Unless it was, 'get out of my way,' or some other sweet thing like that."

"Daisy was the same with me. She'd get angry if I just *looked* through her make-up drawer in the bathroom." Charlotte glanced at Jamie's new wedding band, then grimaced. "Sorry. That was tactless."

"Don't worry. Daisy's your sister, so of course you should talk about her. And she and Kyle have been divorced for so long, it's not an issue for me, at all."

"Thanks for being so sweet about it. It is nice to talk about Daisy sometimes. Even if it is just to complain that she hated sharing a bathroom with me." Charlotte laughed.

"Dougal didn't have much choice about sharing with me and my mom. What we never had much of in our trailer was space."

Charlotte's expression turned wistful. "It must have been kind of cozy though, huh?"

Her response was totally unexpected. It confirmed to Jamie, that even though she and Dougal had been poor, they'd been lucky in lots of other ways. "You're right, it was cozy. And fun most of the time, thanks to my mom."

"I was close to my mother, too. Not so much my sister. Something I've always regretted. Now I just wish I could see Daisy again. That would be enough."

"She's never in touch?"

"Not unless you call making regular cash withdrawals from our joint account staying in touch."

Charlotte's cheeks suddenly looked hollow, her eyes haunted. Jamie thought of Daisy's journal. Kyle had said he was saving Daisy's stuff for the children, but she wondered if he had ever offered to let Charlotte look through it. She would guess not, but as Daisy's sister, surely Charlotte had the right.

Jamie's beer went down fast, and she ordered another, along with a plate of wings and another of nachos to share with the others. She asked Dougal how his research into the librarian killings was going, and he told her they'd had some new developments.

As Dougal and Charlotte filled her in, Jamie stared from one to the other. "But this is freaking unbelievable. How is it no one ever caught this killer?"

"You'd be surprised how many homicide investigations went unsolved in the 70's," Dougal said. "There were few state crime labs and no DNA testing. Email didn't exist yet and individual law agencies had no ability to share database information via the Internet."

"I guess it would be pretty amazing if you could find the killer now, huh? Forty years later?"

"Yeah. It would bring resolution to the survivors, that's for sure. It's awful to live without ever knowing the truth about what happened."

Jamie nodded. She could imagine, all too well. Suddenly, despite the risk of having Dougal say he'd told her so, she had to share her worries about her husband.

"Dougal, I'm afraid you might have been right about Kyle. He's not the man I thought I married. I just found out today that he manipulated me into quitting my job at Howard and Mason so I would work for his company and spend more time looking after his children."

"How did he do that?" Charlotte asked.

Jamie explained about Olivia Argent's so-called "retirement." "But that's not even the worst thing. He told me he was going on a business trip to Coos Bay, to finalize some condo deal. But I found out yesterday he was really travelling to California."

"Does he have business dealings there?" Dougal asked.

"Not that I'm aware of. I'm afraid he might be having an affair."

Dougal swore. But to his credit, he didn't rub in the fact that he'd warned her not to marry Kyle.

"Don't overreact," Charlotte counseled. "Talk to him first. Give him a chance to explain."

Dougal shrugged. "Sure, talk to him. But if I were you, I'd be contacting a good attorney sooner, rather than later."

* * *

Dougal had fought a war with his good intentions where Charlotte was concerned—and lost. That night, after Jamie left, he asked Charlotte to come home with him. For some reason, perhaps because she could tell how worried he was about his sister, she agreed. On the drive home, they compared thoughts on what Jamie should do about Kyle.

"She should leave first, ask questions later. The guy's a goddamned liar."

"Makes me wonder if he's lied about Daisy, too."

Dougal reached over the gearshift to squeeze her shoulder.

Making love turned out to be the perfect antidote for their troubled emotions. But later, when Charlotte was sleeping peacefully in his bed, Dougal still felt restless. One minute he was wondering what Kyle was up to in California. The next he was puzzling over the connection between the librarian murders. He and Charlotte had managed to find some answers lately—but they still had no idea why the killings had been exactly one year apart? And why in those particular locales?

Maybe there was something he'd missed in his notes.

Quietly he slipped out of bed and into his jeans and a sweater. He sat at the dining table, going over his notes for almost an hour, before he found something he'd missed. It was so obvious, now, he felt like an idiot. Gilbert had told him there was a big library convention in town when his grandmother was murdered. Of course, that had to be the big Oregon Library Association Conference. According to Charlotte, the same conference that her aunt and mother always attended.

Dougal went back to the notes he'd taken from the OLA newsletters in 1972 through 1974. And sure enough, the date and place of the conferences coincided with each of the four murders.

He couldn't just sit on this. He had to wake Charlotte and tell her. He was just getting out of the chair, however, when he heard her voice.

"Dougal? Have you found something?"

Her instincts were impeccable, he marveled. Or maybe he'd been making more noise down here than he'd intended. "The connection between the murders. They happened every year at the OLA's annual conference."

"Really?" Charlotte hurried down the stairs, her hair a mess, her body wrapped in the throw blanket he kept on an upstairs chair.

He showed her his notes. She nodded, then her eyes brightened. "Hang on, let me get something." She went to the curio cabinet and pulled out four snow globes. "From the moment I saw these, they struck me as strange. My aunt had some good quality china in here. Why would she also save these tacky snow globes?"

Dougal took them from her and set them down on the table. Sure enough, she had one for each location where a murder had taken place. "It's almost like they're some sort of trophy," he said.

Charlotte looked appalled. "Are you suggesting my aunt really did kill those women?"

"She would have had opportunity," Dougal said. "And these trophies are suspicious. But was she strong enough to strangle another woman? And what would be her motive?"

"Maybe someone gave her the snow globes and she didn't know what they stood for?"

Dougal nodded. "Someone like the child she'd

abandoned all those years ago."

"Yes," Charlotte said. "Librarianmomma."

* * *

They went back to bed an hour later. Dougal had no idea how well Charlotte slept, but he fell into such a deep fog that he didn't wake up until nine the next morning. He knew right away that Charlotte was gone, probably she'd wanted to shower and change at home before heading in to the library.

His plan was to get out of bed, but somehow he fell back asleep, into a twisted dream about the past. Kyle was there. Wade, Daisy, and his sister, too. Jamie was in some sort of danger, but no one would believe him. They laughed. Told him he was crazy. Then, abruptly, he found himself alone, in the woods behind the cabin. And he could hear crying...

Who was crying?

When he woke the second time, it was almost noon. His head was pounding. That dream. His subconscious was trying to tell him something. But what?

As he was brushing his teeth his thoughts skittered back to the conversation with Jamie last night at the bar. She'd told him Kyle had been in California. An idea occurred to him, then. He spat out the toothpaste and grabbed his phone.

Fortunately she answered right away.

"You said Kyle went to California. Do you know where, specifically?"

"Sacramento. Why?"

He swore. "I'll tell you later. Just, get out of the house, Jamie. Don't be there when he comes home."

Soft hearted Charlotte had kept her joint account with her sister open all these years, because she was certain her sister needed that money to survive. But what if someone else was using her banking card? Someone who was privy to her access code. Someone like her ex-husband? He could have used a disguise to trick the video cameras at the ATMs.

Or paid a woman who looked a bit like Daisy to make the withdrawals.

There was only one reason Dougal could think of, for Kyle to make such an effort to create the illusion that Daisy was still alive. But if Kyle had been responsible for her death—what had he done with her body?

Dougal went to the kitchen to put on the coffee. What would he do in Kyle's shoes? Dumping a body in the ocean would be easy—but there would be a chance it would wash up or be discovered by fishermen.

The other obvious choice was burial.

Coffee spilled to the counter, as Dougal dropped the scoop. Pieces were coming together so fast now, he knew he was onto something.

The crying in the woods from his dream. The patchy area of the old vegetable garden. No one would look for a body if they didn't think anyone had died.

Dougal pulled on a pair of work gloves, then went to get the spade he'd bought the other day.

The day was already warm and he expected his work to be hard. Maybe he should eat something first. At least go back and finish brewing that pot of coffee.

But he couldn't wait. He had to do it now. He all but sprinted to the garden plot, straight to the area he'd found so much easier to turn over the other day.

He started to dig.

He scooped out dirt, one spade-full at a time, tossing it behind him, then digging in again. He kept at it for over an hour and had a hole about five feet deep, before he found something other than roots or rocks. It looked like a piece of fabric. He tossed off his gloves, then sank to his knees and brushed the dirt away with his bare hands. Not fabric, but plastic. Looked kind of green. Maybe a tarp?

He expanded his digging area, slowly revealing more tarp, and more, until an hour later, he'd excavated an area of about five and a half feet long and three feet wide.

Sending up a prayer to an unknown being, Dougal

tugged on the tarp, pulling it free from the ground. Falling to his knees again, he pushed aside more dirt, the dank smell of it filling his nostrils.

Finally he found the edge of the tarp and was able to start peeling it away. His pulse pounded heavily in his throat. At one point he had to stop to gather his courage. Then he resumed pulling, unraveling layers of plastic until finally he was able to glimpse what lay beneath.

A skeletal arm, from which dangled a watch he'd seen before.

He dropped the tarp and pulled himself out of the hole. No way in hell was he looking further. As the shock wore off, and his ability to process rational thought returned, he realized this was a crime scene. Evidence. He should tamper with it as little as possible.

He planted the spade into a pile of dirt, dusted off his hands, then headed for the cottage to call Wade. But as he walked, he was thinking of how this would affect the women he loved. Poor Charlotte. And Jamie, too.

This was going to hurt both of them.

chapter thirty

at work on Thursday, Jamie left her cell phone off. If Kyle called her, she didn't want to talk to him. He was supposed to be home later tonight. Hell, tomorrow they were supposed to leave on their honeymoon. She could just imagine what her brother would say about that. As far as Dougal was concerned, the next conversation she had with her husband should take place around witnesses.

Though it was supposed to be the day she worked at Quinpool Realty, Jamie spent the entire eight hours of her work day at her accounting firm. She felt so safe here. She hoped when she came begging for her job back, they would give it to her.

Finally, at five o'clock, just before leaving for the day, she switched her phone on. Sure enough, there was a missed call from Kyle. But what alarmed her more were the five missed calls from Dougal. She tried him back, immediately, but he didn't pick up.

She tried Charlotte next, but she didn't answer either.

Instinct warned Jamie something was wrong.

Hurrying to her car, she got in and drove, first to the library, and after that, to Charlotte's house. She found no one at either place.

Jamie headed to the highway, next, driving fast until she reached the Old Forestry Road.

With each mile, her stomach clenched tighter. For Dougal to have tried to contact her that persistently, something had to be very wrong.

The trees on either side of the road seemed to be taller than usual, darker, pressing in toward her car as if begrudging the strip of land that snaked through their midst. She felt as if she were leaving behind, not only civilization, but also time. She was going back in history, to a time when her big brother had had all the answers.

If only it could be so simple now.

When she was less than a quarter-mile away, she could see lights. Too many lights.

She rounded the last bend and pulled up to a driveway choked with emergency response vehicles, including the Sheriff's SUV and an ambulance. Whatever had happened, Dougal was okay. She could see her brother standing with Wade.

They both turned at the sound of her approach.

She parked quickly, jerking the car out of gear and barely remembering to shut off the ignition before running toward them. Both men looked worried and concerned.

But also, oddly, relieved.

"Thank God. I've been worried sick." Dougal actually hugged her. She couldn't remember the last time he'd done that. Wade put a hand on her shoulder.

"You okay?" the Sheriff asked gently.

"I'm fine, but—what's going on here?"

"I kept trying your cell. Where were you?" Dougal said.

"I had it off. But what's going on here?" She glanced around, scrambling to make sense of all the people, the noise, the vehicles. Spotting Charlotte's sports car, she asked where she was.

"Charlotte's lying down in the cottage," Dougal said.

"Did something happen to her?"

"Just a shock. I found something today, Jamie. I'm sorry. This is going to be hard for you to hear."

She stared at him, wondering when any of this was going to make sense.

Dougal gestured toward an area off in the woods where yellow police tape had cordoned off a large plot of land, including what looked like an old gardening shed." The people around the area were suited up. Crime scene techs, she realized.

"What did you find, Dougal?" she asked quietly.

"A body."

She turned away from the woods, studied her brother's face. Then Wade's.

She was going to ask whose. Then, suddenly, she knew. "Is it Daisy?"

Dougal nodded, even as Wade answered more cautiously. "We suspect so. We won't get confirmation on that until after the autopsy. But your brother and I both recognized her watch. It's quite unique. She wore it all through high school."

Jamie clasped her hands to her heart. The worst had been proven true. Daisy hadn't run away from her children. She was dead.

When everyone had thought Daisy had gone mad, mitigating the pain had been the hope that one day she would get better. One day she might come back.

Now even that hope was gone.

As she watched, two paramedics emerged from the woods carrying a stretcher. She stared at the body bag on top of the stretcher. It seemed almost empty.

She turned away from the awful sight. "What happened to her? How did she die?"

Wade answered. "From the state of her skull, I'd guess a blow to the head."

She stared at him, then her brother, in silent horror. Who had done it? Though no one provided an answer, she could tell what they were both thinking.

The same thing she was.

The most obvious person in cases like this was always the ex-husband, wasn't it?

And she couldn't deny that Kyle had been deceitful. "Oh my God. Kyle's trips to Sacramento. Was he going there so he could withdraw money from Daisy's account?"

"We think so," Wade said.

Dougal pulled her close for a second hug. "I'm sorry,

Jamie. When I advised you not to marry him, I never guessed it would be this bad."

"I was so stupid—"

"Shh. Don't say that. You saw the best in Kyle. You always had a big heart. Just like Mom. And that's a good thing. But we've got a situation now, and the most important thing is for you to keep away from Kyle until we've sorted it out."

She nodded.

"Where are the children?" Wade asked.

"They're at Wolf Creek Summer Camp. We dropped them off on Sunday. They're supposed to be there for two weeks."

"Great," Wade said. "At least we know they're safe for now. Now all I'm worried about is you. Obviously it's not a good idea for you to go back to Kyle's place. And you shouldn't be alone, either."

"You can stay here with Charlotte and me," Dougal offered.

She shook her head. "Stella will take me in."

"I have to go back to town in a bit. I'll drive you there," Wade said.

She wanted to argue. But she was afraid she was about to become very sick.

chapter thirty-one

Wade glanced at the darkening sky. It was going to rain, soon. Good thing they were almost finished with the crime scene. He nodded at one of his deputies, giving him permission to wrap things up. Then he moved away from the action toward the cottage where Dougal and Jamie were sitting on the porch.

After Jamie had vomited out the contents of her stomach, Dougal had gone into the cottage to get her some water and a blanket. Now she was settled in one of the old wooden chairs on the porch.

"I can drive you back now," Wade said. "Have you had a chance to call Stella?"

Dougal nodded. "She and Amos are both at home. They're more than happy to have Jamie come stay with them a few days."

In the SUV, Wade helped Jamie fasten her seat belt before he executed a three-point turn and drove off.

What a hell of a day this was turning out to be. Wade hadn't been close to Daisy Hammond since high school, still her death was tough to take.

It didn't help to know that she'd been murdered and buried on his home turf. True, the crime had happened before he was elected Sheriff.

Still, it felt like a failure on his part.

He checked out the pressing clouds above, then glanced at Jamie, sitting silently in the passenger seat.

Her shoulders were covered in the blanket Dougal had provided. Her expression looked blank, and her fingers trembled on a Styrofoam cup filled with warm tea that one of the paramedics had given her.

She was in shock and he wished it could last forever, because once the numbness wore off, he knew she was going to hurt like hell.

And it wasn't right.

That goddamned Kyle.

The rain started then. A slow, gentle rain—a cleansing rain his mother used to call it. "Just wait until the morning," she would tell him when he was small, complaining about having to stay inside. "The world will be all fresh and clean and beautiful again."

But the stain Kyle Quinpool had created would not be washed away so easily. The pain and hurt would linger for years.

He thought about Chester and Cory.

For lifetimes.

Before dropping Jamie off at Stella's he asked if she knew when Kyle was getting back from his business trip.

She glanced at the time on his dash. "Should already be there." Then she shuddered.

* * *

Though Wade hated leaving Jamie, he did it. Back in his SUV he headed to the Quinpool house and found Kyle's vehicle in the driveway. Wade drove up behind it, effectively blocking him in.

As he headed for the front door, he thought back to all the times he'd visited here as a kid. Sad how things had changed over the years. Back then he'd figured he, Kyle, Daisy and Dougal would be pals for life. Sure hadn't worked out that way.

Kyle was quick to appear at the door, his face either worried or angry, Wade couldn't tell which.

"Where the hell is Jamie? Is she okay?"

"Jamie is fine. But she won't be coming home tonight."

"What are you talking about?" So many emotions flashed over Kyle's face, it was difficult to read them all. But Wade thought fear was one of them. And possibly guilt.

"Aren't you going to invite me in?"

"Tell me where Jamie is first."

"That's not your main concern right now. We found a body buried out beyond the Hammond cottage on Forestry Road."

Kyle grew still and alert, like a cat sniffing for danger. He stared at Wade cautiously, and when Wade offered nothing more, reluctantly stepped to the side.

"You better come in."

Wade nodded. "Good idea."

Kyle led him to the large kitchen at the back of the house. A couple of empty beer cans were on the counter. Kyle pulled out two fresh Buds, passed one to Wade, then popped open the other.

Wade was tempted. He'd never drunk on duty before. But it had been a hard day and it wouldn't be getting any easier in the foreseeable future.

"So. This body...?"

"We'll need autopsy results to be positive, but I recognized Daisy's watch. You know she wore it all the time."

Kyle swallowed. Wouldn't look at him. "What does this have to do with Jamie?"

"She knows you've been going to Sacramento every month and withdrawing money from Daisy's checking account so it would look like your ex-wife was still alive."

Kyle took another drink of his beer, his hand shaking this time.

During the long drive from the cabin, Wade had been thinking. He had a good head for dates and he thought he could piece together what had happened.

"You and Daisy had just signed the final divorce papers, when she came to see you about something, probably involving custody of the twins. I'm guessing the visit was late at night. You invited her in, the two of you argued, you lost your temper and got rough. Too rough."

He stopped. Kyle still wasn't talking.

"Maybe you didn't mean to kill her, just got rougher than intended. But when you saw what you'd done, you panicked. You pulled your SUV into the garage, wrapped her body in a tarp, then loaded her into the back and drove out to her aunt's old cabin. You and Daisy used to go there to be alone. You knew where to find it. And you knew it would be deserted."

He paused. The look on Kyle's face could best be described as horror.

"And you buried her, didn't you? Then you drove back and started spreading the story she'd run off. You destroyed her purse, keeping the bank card so you could use it to make those withdrawals to create the illusion she was still alive…and corroborate your story."

He stopped talking and waited for Kyle to react. Finally he did.

"You really think I'm capable of that?"

Wade hesitated. The fact was, he didn't. Kyle had always looked to others to clean up his dirty work for him.

And then he realized what must have happened. Kyle's parents had moved back in with him after Daisy left. So they would have been in the house, too. They could not possibly have failed to hear what was going on.

"Your parents were in on the cover-up, weren't they?" Kyle's dad, so proud, so protective of the son who had joined him in the family business, would have been the one to figure out what needed to be done.

Kyle swore. "You can't prove any of this. And even if it happened, no way can you prove my folks were involved in any way."

"I'll be able to prove you used Daisy's bank card to make those withdrawals." He held out his hand. "Your wallet?"

Kyle glanced around, probably weighing his options.

"Don't do anything stupid Kyle. I'm going to be taking you in for questioning. You can either hand over your wallet to me now, or to one of the guys at the station, later."

The muscles in Kyle's jaw tightened. Without another word, he pulled out his wallet.

Wade took a quick look. Daisy's bank card was in a paper sleeve, but it was there, all right.

Kyle's eyes flashed with anger. "I should have known marrying Jamie was a mistake."

Wade couldn't agree with him more on that point. "We're already in the process of gathering evidence. Soon I'll have a warrant to search your home, too. We're going to interview your mother and your father, and we'll find out what happened, Kyle. You could save us all a lot of trouble if you just told us the truth. The whole truth."

Kyle's face convulsed then, from fear or anger, Wade couldn't tell.

There was no point in saying anything else. It would be interesting talking to Kyle's mother. If she'd known about this, the guilt was probably driving her mad. In fact, Daisy's death and subsequent cover up was probably what had cracked Muriel and Jim's forty-year-marriage. Only something this drastic could explain why Muriel—who had loved the twins so much—had moved away.

"You can't prove any of this," Kyle repeated. But he didn't sound so sure of himself anymore. As he sagged down on one of the kitchen stools, his gaze drifted to the fridge, where photos and artwork of his kids were displayed. "Nothing you say or do now is going to bring back Daisy. Do you really have to do this? Have you thought about the damage it'll do to my kids?"

Yeah. He had. He only wished Kyle had done the same.

chapter thirty-two

It was a huge relief for Jamie to be sitting at the kitchen table with Stella and Amos and eating some of Stella's homemade chicken soup. Dougal had filled them in on the situation, so they weren't asking her a bunch of questions. They were just letting her be.

After about thirty minutes, Amos, who never was one for sitting still, said he was going out to the workshop for a bit.

"Want some pie, honey?" Stella asked when it was just two of them. "Tea. Or coffee?"

"Tea would be nice."

Once it was made, Stella asked if she wanted to go lie down. "Maybe you feel like being alone?"

Jamie shook her head firmly. That was definitely the one thing she did not want. At least not yet. "I screwed up, Stella. I should have listened to Dougal. Marrying Kyle was a big mistake."

Stella put her hand over Jamie's. "I'm so sorry. When did things start to go sideways?"

"Little things at first. I thought we were going to be equal partners, but he started working later and later. Soon I was handling most of the stuff at home and with the kids. And then he manipulated me into quitting my job."

"Did you actually leave Howard & Mason?"

Stella knew how much she loved working there, and what her ambitions were for the future. "I did. I'm just praying they'll take me back."

"I'm sure they will."

"I hope so. I just feel like such a fool. The first time

Kyle paid any attention to me at all was when I dropped by a yard sale he was having, not a week after his mother moved to Portland. He asked me out for coffee, and was in full pursuit right from the start. I figured he was finally seeing me as a grown woman, not as his friend's little sister. But I think the truth was he needed someone to take his mother's place. Up until then, his mother had cooked meals, run the house, taken care of the twins."

"He could have hired a nanny for that."

"Well, maybe he was attracted to me, as well. But I don't believe he ever loved me. I don't see how he could have loved Daisy, either. Maybe he just isn't capable of caring about other people." She frowned into her teacup. "Though, I must admit, he does seem to love his children. And his parents."

"You want my advice?" Stella asked. "Don't try to figure him out. Men like that aren't worth the trouble. You're free of him now, and that's what matters."

"What about the kids, though, Stella? Chester, and especially Cory, were just starting to trust me. And now I'm going to walk out on them?"

Stella sighed. "No. I'm not suggesting you do that. If Kyle is arrested and ends up in prison, someone's going to have to look after them, aren't they?"

* * *

Dougal held Charlotte until she fell asleep in his arms. Once he'd finished giving his statement at the Sheriff's Office, Charlotte asked him to bring her home, and then she'd asked him not to leave. So he was staying.

This thing with the librarian had snuck up on him. He wasn't sure how. And he sure as hell didn't expect it to last. But who the hell knew. Maybe it would.

When Charlotte had been asleep for over half an hour, he slipped away from her, got dressed, and went out to her porch. The sound of the ocean was a comfort tonight, but he couldn't help thinking that somewhere in this country— possibly in the very town of Twisted Cedars,

Librarianmomma was plotting her next move.

Was she, right this moment, thinking of Dougal the way Dougal was thinking of her?

Maybe. From the tone of the emails it was clear this weirdo was trying to make a connection with him.

On that thought...in that moment...time seemed to halt.

There was another person in this world who had tried hard to establish a connection with him, only to fail time and time again. His father.

He'd written letters and emails when he was in prison, then again when he was released. Dougal had always refused to respond.

Was there any chance in hell that Librarianmomma and his father could be one and the same? When was his father born? Dougal remembered there had been five years between his mother and father's birth years. Katie had been born in 1955. Which meant his Dad had been born in 1950—the same year as Shirley's baby.

Rage began to boil in Dougal's blood. Damn it, if this hunch of his was correct, he'd been manipulated like a warm ball of putty. But his father couldn't have pulled this off alone. And suddenly Dougal was sure he knew who was helping him.

* * *

The light was on in Amos's workshop when Dougal pulled up in the back alley. It was almost eleven o'clock at night. As he left his vehicle he could hear soft strains of country music—probably the same radio station Amos had listened to eighteen years ago. Through the window, Dougal could see the man he'd viewed as a father-surrogate sanding a wooden table.

He wondered if the reason Amos couldn't sleep, was the same reason he was here right now. Avoiding the rain puddles on the old pavement, Dougal made his way to the side door, which he'd used so often as a child it was automatic to give the extra tug it took to open it.

The smell of the place was familiar, too, a combination

of wood, paint and oil. Amos still kept a tidy shop. The shelves were crammed-full, but organized and the cement floor looked clean under the new layer of sawdust.

Dougal hadn't knocked, and Amos was so startled he dropped his sander. His wide, frightened eyes settled down when he saw who it was.

Amos reached over to turn off the radio. "It's late son. You here to check on your sister?"

He hadn't been. But now he wondered. "Is she okay?"

"Seemed in shock to me. But she'll be okay. I left her and Stella alone to talk but the lights went off about an hour ago. Guess they've gone to bed for the night."

Dougal nodded. The anger he'd felt on the drive over here was dissipating now. It was hard to be mad at people you trusted to look after your little sister. Whatever they'd done, it had probably been with good intentions.

He perched on a stool he'd last used as a teenaged boy. "When I first came to town Stella asked me if I kept in touch with my father."

Amos scratched the back of his head, nervously.

"I told her no. But stupidly, I didn't think to ask the same question of her." Dougal paused. "Or you."

Amos looked away. He picked up the sander and put it carefully on one of the shelves. Then he got out the broom and swept up the sawdust.

All the while Dougal waited quietly. The longer the silence extended, the more certain he was that he'd been correct. How else had his father known his mother had cancer? It had to be the Wards.

And finally Amos admitted it. "It was a deal Stella and I made with Ed, back when you were just a tadpole. He came to us after Katie kicked him out. He didn't know what to do. Said he loved your mother, but was afraid he might hurt her—or you, one day. We told him if he left you and Katie alone, we'd keep him updated on how you were doing."

"Did you know he's been baiting me with information on a series of murders committed in the seventies?"

Dougal could tell from Amos's surprised expression that he hadn't. The older man frowned. "He wanted us to relay anything you were talking about. But he didn't say why. I had no idea he was the one who got you poking and prodding into the past like that."

"Did he ever tell you about his past? About his folks? Where he'd grown up?"

"I knew he was adopted. And that his life was tough. But no details."

So Amos didn't realize Shirley had been Ed's birth mother. Dougal's gut told him he didn't know about the murders, either. As far as they were concerned Ed's only crime had been beating his second wife to death.

But there was one other death Amos had witnessed and refused to talk about. Shirley's suicide. So there was something he was hiding about that, too.

And suddenly Dougal had a theory.

"The day you found Shirley's body in the library basement—did you lift the cash from the library fundraiser?"

Dark red color flushed up from the older man's neck. He stared at the floor like a guilty schoolboy. "I wanted to ask Stella to marry me, but I had nothing. I knew where Shirley kept the money, and the key was in her pocket. After I phoned for help, I took the key and helped myself."

Dougal felt sick listening to the confession, disillusioned that this hardworking and kind man was capable of a crime of simple greed. "Did Stella know?"

"I never told her. Sometimes I wonder if she suspected. Maybe that's why we were never able to have children. Because our marriage started off on stolen money like that."

chapter thirty-three

When Charlotte woke up the next morning, Dougal was sleeping beside her. One moment she was smiling and reaching for him, the next she felt as if she'd been punched in the heart.

Daisy was dead.

While the morning sun teased its way into her bedroom window, Charlotte went over the events of the previous day, recalling Dougal striding into the library and demanding her to close early. Once they were alone, he told her what he'd uncovered in Aunt Shirley's vegetable garden.

She supposed she'd been in shock. She refused to believe him. Then she'd insisted he take her there, to the librarian cottage, so she could see for herself.

By then half the staff from the Sheriff's Office, as well as several paramedics, were on the scene. She'd been allowed a brief look at Daisy's watch—to confirm Dougal's identification, but not the remains. After that, she'd felt frantically upset and the paramedics had given her something to calm her down.

Later, Dougal had brought her here. He'd been so kind and gentle with her. Which made her wonder if there was more hope for this relationship than she'd thought.

She gazed at his face, relaxed and unguarded in sleep. Some would say he was too callous for a hero. Too rough around the edges.

But he had redeeming features. His unrelenting pursuit of the truth being the main one.

His eyes opened. He blinked, then touched her cheek softly, so very gently. "How are you doing?"

"I feel weird. When my parents died, the grief was all encompassing. But this is different. I'm very sad. But also, strangely relieved. Ever since she left, a part of me was always wondering where she was, whether she was okay, or hurting and in need of help." She sighed. "Now I know. And at least her suffering wasn't long."

"I heard them talking. Sounds like she died instantly from a blow to the head."

"Who do they think did it?"

"What do *you* think?"

She hesitated. "I'd say Kyle. But I'm surprised. I never liked him much. But I didn't see him as a murderer."

"The guy is a monster. Making cash withdrawals for all these years. Pretending that Daisy was still alive. Holding out hope to all those who loved her."

"I wish we'd been closer. Maybe then, I would have been able to support her better after the twins were born. But no one in our family had even heard of post-partum psychosis before."

"It's hard not to have regrets. Maybe if I'd told Daisy Kyle was having sex with other women, she wouldn't have made the mistake of marrying him."

"I'm not so sure. We all have a way of seeing what we want to see. Especially when it comes to love."

"Speaking of love..." Dougal paused to kiss her gently. "I was thinking of going back to New York and packing up my stuff. Making a permanent move. What do you think?"

She smiled and put her arms around him. "I'll show you."

* * *

The New York apartment smelled stale when Dougal arrived three days later. He'd taken a taxi straight from the airport and was looking forward to seeing his cat. He'd missed the persnickety feline.

He dropped off his duffel bag in his foyer before heading to 5C to get Borden.

He knew his cat would be annoyed.

Just wait until she found out he was moving her from a city apartment to a cottage in the Oregon forest.

He rapped on the door of 5C several times, but there was no response.

Dougal hadn't called ahead to give the old guy any warning, but he hadn't expected there to be a problem. Monty's social calendar was normally pretty blank.

He tried a fourth knock, waited an extra minute, then went in search of the super.

"I can't let you into another tenant's apartment," the crabby old woman told him.

"But he has my cat, was looking after him while I was away. Besides, Monty almost never goes out. He even has his groceries delivered. For all we know he could be dead in there. What do you want to do—leave him there until he starts to decompose and stink up the hallway?" He'd been trying to scare her, but he ended up frightening himself as an unwanted image of his cat, alone with a dead body, came to mind.

His tactic worked. The super snagged her key ring. "Let's take a look."

She was only about thirty pounds overweight, but it was all in her ass. He did his best not to look as he followed her up the stairs.

The super knocked loudly on 5C. "Mr. Monroe?" She knocked again, and when there was still no response, pulled out her key.

Borden was waiting at the door and scooted out as soon as it had opened three inches. Dougal scooped her up. She felt thinner to him and didn't smell that great.

She gave him a talking to, making it clear what she thought of his absence the past three weeks.

"I know, I know, I'm a jerk." He scratched her neck, then the sides of her face. She jammed her head into his palm, like a love-starved...cat. Still petting her, he followed the super inside, stopping short in the foyer.

The place looked tidy and clean, but lifeless. The

shades were drawn, so Dougal switched on a light.

"Monty Monroe is definitely not in here," the super said. "I've checked the bathroom and bedroom."

Dougal went to the spot where he'd left Borden's litter box. Instead of one, there were now four litter boxes. Only two had a few soiled spots in them.

In the kitchen he found several bowls full of dried cat food. And a large basin of water.

"I have a feeling your tenant has moved out."

"What—and left all his stuff?"

"Do you see anything personal? A computer, or laptop? Mail or personal papers of any kind?"

The super made a second round of the place. He heard her opening a few drawers. After ten minutes she said, "You're right. He's gone, the bastard. Didn't even give notice."

At least he'd left Borden with supplies to last her a week or two. Dougal wondered if Monty would have eventually called him, to let him know he'd taken off.

"He was a strange bird," Dougal said. "Wonder why he decided to take off like this..."

"I could care less, why," the super grumbled. "Now I've got to store this junk in case he comes back, and get the place ready for a new tenant."

"Make that two tenants," Dougal said. "I'm giving my notice today, too."

* * *

Dougal cleaned all the cat paraphernalia from Monty's apartment, throwing most of it into the garbage. Made more sense to buy new supplies in Twisted Cedars, then to try and pack this shit for the airplane.

Borden was thrilled to be back in her own apartment. She spent an hour exploring every nook and cranny before settling down for a nap in a patch of sunlight on the couch.

Meanwhile Dougal was busy, arranging to have some of his belongings trucked to Oregon, the rest donated to charity. He packed up his clothes, books and important papers, glad that he, like his mother, had never been one to accumulate much in the way of material possessions.

He was planning to sleep over tonight, then take the plane back to Portland tomorrow. He wondered how Borden was going to cope with being jailed in her cat carrier for most of the day. He should at least line the thing with a clean towel, the old one at the bottom of the carrier was smelling rank. As he made the switch he noticed a piece of paper tucked into the carrier.

An envelope, with his name on the front.

He stared at it for a long moment, his gut churning with a premonition that this wasn't going to be good. Finally he pulled out the single sheet of paper within.

On it was written:

Well done, son. Now write the book.

THE END

excerpt from forgotten
book 2: twisted cedars mysteries

chapter one

Sheriff Wade MacKay was on his way home from a morning fishing on the Rogue River in Oregon, when he found the crashed truck, the body, the unconscious woman.

It wasn't often Wade spent his Friday mornings off duty, but a mental health day was in order after a solid week spent investigating the suspicious death and illegal burial of Daisy Hammond, a friend of his from his high school days. Seven years ago, when Daisy had left her twin children and ex-husband behind, everyone assumed her well-documented mental illness—which began after the birth of her children—was at fault. Random withdrawals from her bank account had fed the assumption she'd moved to Sacramento, where she was living quietly, under the radar.

Not until her remains were discovered by local true-crime author— and yet another former high school buddy—Dougal Lachlan, buried out back of an old cottage belonging to the Hammond family, had anyone suspected foul play. Making the situation even more terrible, a third high school buddy of Wade's, Daisy's ex-husband Kyle Quinpool, was the prime suspect for the crime.

Law enforcement in Curry County had to deal with their share of domestic violence. But homicides, fortunately, were rare. And Wade hoped not to see another one for a long, long time.

Once the sun rose beyond the tops of the tallest cedars, Wade packed his rod and tackle in the back of his truck, along with a cooler containing three summer steelhead trout on ice, all of them around four pounds. The fishing had been a success but he wasn't looking forward to getting home, or to the weekend ahead. Any day now the results from Daisy's autopsy would be in. Then he'd have to haul Kyle to the office for another interview, probably followed by an arrest, this time.

Wade felt sickest about Kyle and Daisy's two kids. Nine-year-old Chester and Cory were away at summer camp right now and had missed most of the drama so far, thank God. They'd been dealing with their mother's absence for seven years already. Now they would likely lose their father, as well, to the Oregon State Penn.

Not exactly your classic happy childhood.

Back in the days when Wade had been young and summers seemed so blissfully long, he'd fished this same spot with his father. Even then he'd known he wanted a simple life, like his parents. He loved this corner of the Pacific Northwest, where there were more trees than people, roads that might not see a driver for days on end. He'd dreamed of being the Sheriff of Curry County, with a home, a wife and kids, and one day a week to spend in the wilderness that was the essence of this place.

At age thirty-three he'd landed the job. Now, a year older, he still didn't have the wife and family. Frankly, his love life was a mess. On a day like today though, being unencumbered didn't seem so bad.

His fishing spot was off Bear Camp Road, a narrow and crooked traverse over the Klamath Mountains that linked the small Oregon towns of Agness and Galice, carrying on to Twisted Cedars, Wade's home. He patrolled here regularly, knew every curve, viewpoint and pothole. Normally he would have made it home in under an hour.

If it hadn't been for the accident.

He was listening to Chopin's Nocturne in E Flat Major when he spotted the overturned four-axle. He slowed and pulled over. Gripping the steering wheel, he took a deep breath, as he transformed from man enjoying a morning off work, to first responder at the site of a traffic accident.

The music continued, impervious to the tragedy in front of him.

He'd owned the disk forever—it was a gift from his mother and inexorably linked, in his mind, to his morning fishing trips. His mom had taught piano lessons to the children of Twisted Cedars—including Wade and some of his friends. For thirty years, Monday through Friday, from four o'clock until the dinner hour, kids would tromp in and out of the MacKay family home for their thirty minutes of musical torture.

Wade still cringed when he remembered the faltering, sour-toned notes that filled their living room during the hours when most of his friends were watching sit-com reruns and snacking on junk food.

The only time he and his father heard anything resembling actual music coming from the baby grand Yamaha in their living room was on Sunday mornings when his mother assumed they'd already left to go fishing. Only then did she play, letting loose all her pent-up musical energy, never guessing her son and husband were lingering on the back stairs, taking in the first half-hour of her concert.

Wade missed his mother's music, though he still had her piano. They'd retired, his parents, several years ago and were living in Phoenix. He didn't get it, couldn't understand living your entire working life in the wild and wonderful wilderness of the Oregon Coast and then trading in ocean, mountains and ancient forests for sun and sand, malls and manicured golf courses.

Wade eased his vehicle further off the road, making sure to leave room for the paramedics when they arrived. It was obvious they'd need paramedics. The truck, which had crashed through a guardrail, lay, like a beached whale, fifty feet down the embankment, backstopped by a grove of old growth cedar. No other vehicle or human presence could be spotted. Wade put on his flashers and called in the accident. Then he stepped out into the hot, heavy July air.

"Hello! Anyone in there?" He went quiet and listened. All he could hear was the buzzing of insects.

Stamped over the scent of pine and dirt and living things was the acrid odor of burnt rubber. He made a quick study of the black skid marks on the pavement, then pressed his fingers against them. Tacky.

Dragonflies looped around him as he scrambled down the embankment toward the wreck.

"Anyone in there?" he called out, again.

No answer.

He touched a hand to the truck, which had flipped over and lay on its passenger side. The engine was no longer running, but the hood was still warm.

"Hello? Sheriff Wade MacKay here. You okay?" Climbing up on the trunk of a white pine that had been uprooted in the crash, he was able to peer inside the driver side window. A big, balding man, in his late fifties, was slumped over his seat belt, clearly dead. Wade managed to open the door enough to check for breathing and a pulse, but he found neither.

Wade had seen a lot of accidental death in his fifteen-year career. He knew how to deal. You didn't look too long. Or think too much.

Averting his gaze, he walked around the wreckage, trying to see inside the other side of the cab. Most truckers travelled alone. Even hitchhikers were rare these days.

But this guy had company, a woman with long hair, reddish-blonde in color and stained with fresh blood. She was strapped into the passenger seat, her body limp.

Thanks to the width of the load, there was space between the passenger door and the ground, about two and a half feet. Wade lowered his body to the carpet of wild grasses and sage and wiggled into a position where he could get a better look. Her weight was partly resting on the door, so he couldn't open it. But the window had smashed and he was able to reach in, check her neck for a pulse.

She was alive, but still losing blood from her head wound.

He ran back to his truck for a blanket and first aid kit. He didn't dare move her, but he could make sure she was warm, and stench the bleeding. When he brushed aside her hair to locate the wound he saw that she was pretty and a lot younger than the driver, maybe in her late twenties or early thirties.

What would a woman like this be doing with a burly, middle-aged truck driver? Could she be his daughter?

He called dispatch again, warned them what to expect, all the while keeping a gentle pressure on the wound. Eventually the bleeding stopped. He applied a rudimentary bandage then turned his attention to some miscellaneous items that had fallen to the passenger side of the cab and were wedged around the woman. He pulled out a black, leather wallet. Inside was ID for the driver: Chet Walker, aged 52, height five-feet, ten-inches, weight two-ten, hometown Klamath Falls. Emergency contact was listed as his wife.

Poor woman would soon be getting a phone call that would change her life.

Methodically Wade examined the rest of the debris in the truck. He found the driver's cell phone, along with empty disposable coffee cups and crumpled wrappers from McDonalds; a square of pale blue flannel; a Mariner's baseball cap, foil-wrapped caramels and a package of gum. But no purse or cell phone belonging to the female passenger.

Maybe she had something in the pocket of her jeans, but he wouldn't be able to get at it until the paramedics arrived.

Wade placed a gentle hand on the injured woman's arm. "Help is coming. You hang tight." She gave no response to his voice. In his mind, Wade went over the accident scene, trying to figure out why Chet Walker had driven off the road. There were no dead animals, the usual cause of single vehicle accidents in the summer when the roads were good.

Maybe Chet had suffered a heart attack or stroke.

Noticing a trail of blood leading from the woman's forehead to her left eye, Wade used the clean flannel cloth to wipe it away. He wished he could do more. She was awfully pale, terribly still.

"They'll be here soon."

She remained as still as ever. He took note of her tanned left hand, and the white line where a wedding band might have been. Her nails were painted turquoise.

Wade glanced up at the sky, and guessed it was an hour past noon. What a turn the day had taken. So much for his peaceful break from mayhem. Then again, he shouldn't complain. At least he hadn't been in the oncoming lane when this truck went off the road.

"Who are you lady?" He spoke again hoping his voice would reassure her, even though she wasn't conscious. "Seems like you were in the wrong place at the wrong time today."

In the distance, he finally heard the sound he'd been waiting for. But even the sirens didn't wake her up.

Order your copy of *forgotten* today.

Twisted Cedar Mysteries Continues with

exposed

(Twisted Cedar Mysteries book 3)

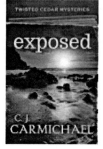

Exposed (Book 3)

* * *

When a young boy goes missing shortly after his father is arrested for murdering the boy's mother, the residents of Twisted Cedars are in a panic. They would be even more fearful if they knew a serial murderer has secretly moved back to town. Local Sheriff Wade MacKay, and true crime writer Dougal Lachlan, finally realize that unless they pool their resources and work together, no one in town is going to be safe.

Order *Exposed*
(Twisted Cedar Mysteries book 3) now

note from the author

I'd like to thank the people who helped me with this novel, my editor Linda Style, formatter Meredith Bond, proofreader Toni Hyatt, and cover designer Frauke Spanuth from CrocoDesigns.

For help with my research, I am indebted to Deputy George Simpson, as well as friends Sue and Greg McCormick who introduced me to the Deputy, as well as shared impressions and memories of their years living in Oregon. Thank you also to District Attorney Everett Dial who patiently answered many questions from me over the phone.

I'm very grateful to the friends and family members who have read preliminary copies of my Twisted Cedars Mysteries and provided much needed feedback: Mike Fitzpatrick, Kathy Eliuk, Voula Cocolakis, Lorelle Binnion, Susan Lee, Brenda Collins, Donna Tunney, Gloria Fournier, Greg McCormack, Sue McCormack...thank you all!

about the author

C.J. Carmichael has published over 40 novels and has twice been nominated for a RITA award from the Romance Writers of America. CJ likes to write stories about mystery, romance, small communities and intrigue. She's inspired by real-life scenarios...the kind you read about in magazines and watch on the nightly news on television. When it's time to take a break from the computer, she heads to the Rocky Mountains near her home in Calgary where she lives with her partner Michael. She's especially proud of her two best masterpieces—Lorelle and Tessa, her daughters. If you'd like to learn more about her books, check out her website: http://cjcarmichael.com and please do sign up for her newsletter.

other novels by C.J. Carmichael

Carrigans of the Circle C (western drama and romance)
Promise Me, Cowboy (story 1)
Good Together (story 2)
Close To Her Heart (story 3)
Snowbound in Montana (story 4)
A Cowgirl's Christmas (story 5)

Family Matters (family drama and romance)
A Daughter's Place (story 1)
Her Best Friend's Baby (story 2)
The Fourth Child (story 3)

Twisted Cedars Mysteries
Buried (book 1)
Forgotten (book 2)
Exposed (book 3)

For C. J. Carmichael's complete backlist, please visit her website: http://cjcarmichael.com